STOLEN *from* GYPSIES

NOBLE SMITH

with illustrations by
CAROL INGRAM

RIVERWOOD BOOKS
ASHLAND, OREGON

First RiverWood Books Paperback Edition: 2003

Cover design: David Rupee, Impact Publications
Cover painting, *The Battle of Issus*, by Albrecht Altdorfer, Copyright Alte Pinakothek, Munich.

First printed in hardcover by Aubrey House, Ashland, Oregon in March 2000

Library of Congress Publisher's Cataloging-in-Publication

Smith, Noble Mason, 1968-
    Stolen from gypsies / Noble Smith ; with illustrations by Carol Ingram. – – 1st RiverWood Books pbk. ed.
        p. cm.
    ISBN: 1-883991-82-X
    1. Napoleonic Wars, 1800-1815 - - Fiction. 2. British - - Italy - -Fiction. 3. Florence (Italy) - - Fiction. 4. Storytelling - - Fiction. 5. Abduction - - Fiction. 6. Nobility - - Fiction. 7. Romanies - - Fiction. I. Title.

PS3569.M537837S76 2003
813'.54- -dc21

                                        2002037111

10 9 8 7 6 5 4 3 2 1   03   04   05   06   07   08   09   10

This book is dedicated with love to my parents,
who taught me how to cachinnate.*

see Glossary

Contents

LIST OF ILLUSTRATIONS

Let it be your aim that, by reading your story,
the melancholy may be moved to laughter and
the cheerful man made merrier still . . .

— CERVANTES, *DON QUIXOTE* —

Enchanted By Gypsies

I

THE GYPSIES

The Gypsy baby was stolen from his little manger moments before his family of jugglers began their remarkable second-act feat in which flaming ax and succulent melon are flung back and forth with such amazing skill that the blades pass through the fleshy globes slicing off rings of fruit (into perfectly sectioned pieces) for the audience to snatch from the air and gobble with giddy glee.

In this case, the gobblers were two dozen impoverished farmers. They stood on the edge of the stone threshing floor that served as a stage (their grubby hovels made do as the backdrop) and ogled at the miraculous feats of dexterity on display in their wee village. They guffawed and screamed and whistled and hooted at the splendid production. For what could be more exciting than sharp ax blades flying and flaming, and succulent fruit flinging and falling? Nothing. At least not for these wretched peasants who spent their entire lives making calluses and getting old faster than was fair. Their bones ached from the moment they got up in the gloom of dawn until the instant they lay their weary bodies down in the gloam of dusk. They did not even have beds, these poor souls! They slept on the dirt floor with the centipedes and the fleas and their other domesticated animals. Maybe, if they were lucky, the sheep would deign to let them snuggle up against their woolly coats to keep the cold away; but sheep are very light sleepers and kick devilish cruel. So often, in the dead of winter, the choice the farmers had to make was between freezing to death or waking up with nasty little bruises all over their bodies.

And the summers! *Horesco referens!* The summers were so hot that sometimes—whilst those poor sods dug in the gritty ground or scythed in the muggy fields—they actually ran out of sweat; and something else (a smelly goat cheese sort of crud) would begin to ooze from their pores, coating their bodies with a pasty, putrefying sheen.

In any event, life for the villagers was not the pastoral glory of the popular painters where bonny shepherd girls— their *nénés* straining against diaphanous gowns—prance through fields of clover, and handsome lads with Roman noses and curling hair gaze philosophically at themselves in mystical ponds. Rather, it was like one of those works by Brueghel where everyone is raw-boned and horrid looking. And what an ugly lot they were, this village of hapless homelies: their bodies were as crooked as trees forced to grow round piles of rocks; their hair was both sparse and greasy and brought to mind a mangy dog that had rolled on his back in a heap of lard; their teeth—'Zounds! I cannot even mention them, for just the thought of those cracked and graying and decaying gnashers makes the roots of my own *dents* shrink and tingle with fear. But their eyes . . . their eyes, as they watched the Gypsy jugglers, were so full of joy and innocence that they would have broken the heart of even that most savage of brutes—Attila—and induced him to hang up his horse-prickers and establish a kindly home for wayward Huns. For a moment, for an ephemeral instant, those ill-favored farmers were as beautiful as elves in a sylvan wood. That was the magical power of the Gypsies: those happy wanderers who travel the countryside in their painted carts and banish bleak reality with glad songs and stories of heroism and feats of breathtaking skill—such as juggling shining, flaming axes and lovely, watery melons!

The Gypsy mother did not hear her little one cry out: she was too busy passing the hat and trying not to breathe through her nose (for it was August and the villagers' sweat had run out in the middle of July); and the crowd was dancing and clapping and calling for "More! More! More!" Her little boy let out a single indignant cry and that was all. He was taken. He was kidnapped. He was stolen from Gypsies.

Miles away . . . miles away the abductress fled through the woods with her little, fat prize hidden in the folds of her cloak. Moving like an agile dog, the old woman leaped the tangled bracken and the snarled branches of the dense scrub oak. She never stopped running. Never looked back. As the sun set, she blended into the night and disappeared like smoke.

2

A Beginning

I must put down my quill for a moment and pause to take my pulse. My doctor—that famous Hungarian who patented a syrup for the relief of constipation—informs me (ad nauseam) that I cannot become too excited else I will do a disservice to my feckless vascular organ. I have just recovered from a month of paralysis. Bedridden for over a month! And so benumbed was I that even taking nourishment became impracticable. My servant, Antonio, had to feed me soup from a bowl as I lay stupefied upon the mattress. The lumpy plaster ceiling (my only vista for those many days) appeared to my delirious eyes as a relief map of some desolate land; for incalculable hours did I plot my escape over that imaginary chart.

Then, the other day after a hard rain, a strange warm wind came down off the Tuscan hills. This zephyr was scented with raspberries and rich wet earth. My soul left my body and hovered in the middle of the room, betwixt floor and ceiling. I knew that the end had come at last.

"Is the end come at last?" I croaked, for I am indeed a thanatophobe and fear death like any sane man should. I felt an angel's wing brush against my nose; it tickled me and I did sneeze. Then a chubby cheek pressed against my own and a little lad whispered in my ear with a stern but cheery voice, "Get up, Ambrogio Smythe. You have a task to complete. The tale of the Gypsy must be told." When I opened my eyes, I was lying back on the bed, covered with a dank sweat. For the first time in a month there was feeling in my limbs. I rose from my bed, my joints cracking like twigs, and shuffled to my writing desk. I keep my secret treasure there: the piece of papyrus bought for many gold florins. It lies between two panes of glass and is covered with thick velvet to protect it from the sun. I lifted the velvet, then the glass, and held the papyrus scrap in my unsteady fingers. Thereupon, I found pen and paper and began to write the stolen Gypsy's tale.

But now I am exhausted again and must rest. Yet, as I sit here, my brain will not be still. My thoughts return to home, and the impetus for my long, bizarre journey. Thus I write in my journal (using the summer-sky-blue ink, for that hue is the color of remembrance) and conjure the past like magician's smoke. The swirling waters of time become frozen—as in one of Leonardo's studies of a churning pool—and I observe many scenes from my youth in perfect clarity, as if they are still-life paintings in a gallery.

From a high view, a bird's-eye-view, I look down upon the courtyard of our manor in Warwickshire. I can see my brother, Aloysius, bane of my life, as an eight-year-old holy terror. He is captured mid-leap. A rapier clutched in his hand catches light on the blade as he shows off his fencing tricks to uncle and mama who are taking tea in the garden. Only I know that the brat is secretly trying to impress the ravishing Sarah, proud daughter of my uncle's deceased business partner and now my uncle's ward. She lurks in the shadow of the doorway—a sleek panther in her lair.

The vision changes. My brother appears forthwith in the courtyard as a lanky, callow manling, straddling his black galloper, dressed in one of his extravagant and gaudy riding getups. Surrounding him are the ladies and gentlemen of one of his innumerous fox-murdering parties. Lord Talks-A-Lot's mouth is shaping an insipid remark. Lady Toplofty's lips are curled in a disdainful sneer. Sarah is there too, astride her chestnut hunter—a haughty glint in her wild eyes. Aloysius has raised a silver goblet of mulled wine to her lips; the vapors from the chalice and the horses' nostrils hang in the air like tuffs of pulled cotton.

At which point the composition turns anew. My frivolous brother is of full age now and is shown to me in the instant of racing through the gate in his chariot-and-four. She is at his side holding the reins! They are stock-still as statues, but there is every color of life to them. Her eyes sparkle with delight and a strand of hair blown from her bonnet caresses her cheek and upper lip. I can almost reach out and touch her . . . move the lock of hair aside with my quivering finger. Then I notice Aloysius' snake-like sidelong glance at her smooth, naked neck. "Lurid, bed-pressing libertine!" I cry, and the chimera vanishes.

All through the years, perched like a gargoyle on a cold cathedral gutter, I sat in my solitary tower room, catching fleeting glimpses of the world outside. Too feeble to leave my sanctuary for fear of hurting my diseased heart, my only solace and pleasure were gathered from books. Mama worried that I would die young like father. He gave up the ghost at the tender age of four and twenty and it was from him that I inherited my weakness. But I have outlived him by five years! Mama did everything in her power to prolong my life: regular bleedings, mercury pills, warm beet enemas; the finest physicians from London, Paris, and even Vienna. None of these treatments or therapies or practitioners, however, were able to strike the spark of life into my frail form; hence, I was virtually imprisoned in my chamber.

I was an imaginative invalid, though. For amusement during this tortuous and tedious childhood, I performed elaborate hand puppet shows. I made the manikins myself, carving heads of wood and sewing intricate costumes from scraps of mama's old clothes. I built vast stages and acted out all the parts, altering my voice to give them character—deep and strong for the chivalrous knight, now soft and dulcet for the virgin damsel. My passion was Crusaders' tales. Once, I recreated the Siege of Acre complete with a miniature mangonel, which flung acorns at the Saracen turrets, and terrible Greek fire (red candle wax poured upon a puppet's head). As I matured, my tastes turned to the Bard, and nearly the entire canon could I perform in repertoire: I murdered Caesar with one hand whilst crying *"Et tu"* with the other; I fashioned a lovely Juliet using a doll's head brought from far-off China; for the witches in the Scottish play, I cut faces into apples, then dried them on strings until they resembled withered, wrinkled crones. To portray the Dane, however, I merely used a bare hand, for Hamlet's thoughts are so very naked, are they not? As I grew into adolescence, my favorite characters became the rascals, rubes and jesters: Pistol, Bottom, the Dromios, Launce, the Fool from *Lear*. I spoke their scenes in lowered voices lest mama hear their bawdy antics! One day, I discovered an edition of *Tom Jones* hidden behind a moldy tome of Seneca in uncle's library. What joy I had dramatizing *his* naughty escapades.

Aloysius never finished a book or play in his life. I would not be amazed if he were illiterate, the nasty brute! But worst of all, as he grew into manhood, he became as handsome as

a Greek god; and like a classical figurine, there was an androg-
yny, a femininity to his beauty that I found noxious. There
was no comparison between the two of us for the favors of a
woman, however. Whenever I glance into a mirror, I see a sal-
low, ill-favored face staring back through cloudy, listless eyes.
The hair, lank and flat (and now thinning if you must know).
The teeth—not so pleasant to look upon. The cheeks sunken,
the nose—droopy. And that is just a description of the skull!
Dear God, the body is like a corpse. All the ribs are countable.
The hips jut out like the handles of a mug. The elbows are so
pointed and sharp they could cut glass. The vertebrae resem-
ble a tiny chain of mountains. The scapula . . . the wings of a
scrawny bird. Death's head upon a mop stick, and all that.
Aloysius used to say I could make a career as an anatomy
skeleton. I would never win the love of a lady. Especially not
one as lovely as Sarah.

But now . . . now that I have actually begun to put this
remarkable tale of the stolen Gypsy onto paper, I feel as
flushed and eager as the proverbial traveler who wandered
into the Pasha's harem on the eunuchs' day off. I look at
myself in the silvered back of my quill case and I actually see
color in my cheeks. My eyes—they scintillate. My arteries
thump like tiny drums. "Antonio!" I cry out. "Antonio! Fetch
the Swiss clock!" Instead, my faithful manservant brings me a
plate of soft mozzarella, basil, and tomatoes covered with
olive oil.

"Is this a clock?" I ask peevishly.

"No. It is your light repast," he says.

"I need to take my pulse."

"The *dottore* says you must not become too excited."

"Antonio, you should have been a parson."

"How come?"

"Because you take great joy in repeating things that wiser
people have already said."

"I'll be right back with the clock."

He worries about me, dear lad. No more wit or talent than a cast iron pellet, mind you, but an amusing attendant. (I cannot bring myself to grace him with the honorific "butler.") And I do have Antonio to thank for bringing the wandering Gypsy to the house that fateful night: a mysterious, massive-shouldered, aristocratic-featured minstrel, telling tales for tokens of brass. This man was unquestionably a descendent of the original Twelve Thousand, those Hindu musicians who, in the fifth century, were sent to the benevolent Persian monarch Bahram Gur by his friend King Shangul of India to play music for his pleasure-starved laborers. Having tasted the nectar of the trek—the liberation of the road—however, these minstrels could not contain their wanderlust, and spread like wildflowers throughout Europe. They were the ancestors of the Gypsies!

The Gypsy storyteller was the one who told me the account of Godfrey, the kidnapped Gypsy, and the telling of it was a mere day before my sudden paralysis occurred. Faith! This is a coincidence that I have just now perceived! The power of his story upon my fragile soul must have been too great! O to think he might have passed by my home without stopping! O to think I might not have learned this extraordinary history! For I must tell you that it was because of the Gypsy people that I departed England. Ever since my youth I have desired to write a history of that luminous race. Scoundrels say that they are degenerate and loathsome, without honor or culture. These statements are dirty lies! The Gypsies are the happiest, most openhearted people on the earth; they sing and dance and praise life under the most dire circumstances; they are as free as the birds! Their language, *Romani* as it is called, does not even contain the word "possession." I, who cannot travel with less than five trunks of personal effects, admire and respect their austerity. Ever since that tribe of players wandered into our village on my tenth birthday, and uncle paid them to perform for me below my window in the courtyard, I have longed to tell their tale.

I can see them now: their little painted cart, the dancers and the jugglers, the sword swallowers and the singers! Never have I heard more soulful music than that day. What, I ask you, have we offered the Gypsy people in return for their gifts of laughter and joy? Nothing, I tell you, but insults and profanation. We have abused them with the same mistreatment given to stray dogs! Nay—to wolves! Shame! Shame on us for the suffering that we have caused them. I vowed long ago to right this wrong.

Therefore, in that eventful third year of the new century, when Aloysius informed us that he had asked for Sarah's hand and that she had joyously accepted, I resolved that I could not stay in our house any longer: I could not suffer to live in the same dwelling where that ethereal gentlewoman was to be defiled daily by my cretinous, mutton-headed sibling. I marched into the study, still dressed in my bedclothes and silk lounging slippers, and informed them all that I was leaving the country. "I will write my history of the Gypsies, come what may!" I boldly declared. Uncle and mama protested: they told me that I would most certainly die; if my poor sickly heart did not give out on the voyage, then Napoleon and his thugs would surely take my life. This last part made my blood run cold, for I often had nightmares that Napoleon himself— wearing nothing but his menacing tricorne hat and high-heeled boots—was crawling into my bed with the intention of strangling me in my sleep! The look of worry on my face made my uncle shake with laughter; the great fatty rolls of his dewlap juked obscenely upon his chest.

Miraculously, auspiciously, a fortnight later, the Peace of Amiens was declared. Soon after, I set out for Portsmouth with my personal physician, that vexatious, sycophantic

quack, the unfortunate Dr. Stoakes. Mama wept. Uncle looked
bemused. But there was nothing they could do. I was the elder
of my father's children and of legal age, and what I did with
my wealth was my decision. Aloysius found it hard to hide his
mirth, for he relished the danger that I was heading into, and
gloated upon the notion that he would soon inherit the title
of "Lord" upon my demise. And Sarah? She kissed my cheek
and wished me bon voyage.

Her kindly intentions had no effect. In truth, I almost
expired from seasickness merely crossing the Channel and
never again will I set foot on a boat, even if it is simply to be
rowed across a duck pond on a windless day. (Praise to the
noble Nelson, one-armed, one-eyed, gaunt, scurvy-toothed
admiral. He flaunted his human frailties whilst flouting the
French fleet!) Indeed, it took me nearly two months in Calais
to recover from the sea-journey. By the time we made it to
Paris, I was so carriage-sick from jostling across the endless
countryside in our road-rattler that I was forced to rent a
charming little *pied-à-terre* behind the Comédie-Française on
the rue de Condé, where I collected pre-Revolutionary wine to
amuse my palette whilst Stoakes tried vainly to find a med-
ication for the rash of gatherings that had appeared upon my
nethers: a demonic plague of carbuncles.

One day, when I had recovered enough to sit down upon
the seat of a carriage again, I actually paid a visit to the
Emperor's monument to pilfering: the Museé de Napoléon. I
viewed the lovely paintings of Venezia that Francesco Guardi
made. (They were stolen from the poor Comte de Pestre-Senef
during the revolution.) I have always longed to see that
famous city, but will not go there until Bonaparte's stink has
been scrubbed clean off its splendid stones. At this gallery I
did also view the puffed up, ludicrous painting by that toady-
ing turd Gros entitled *Bonaparte Visiting the Plague-Stricken at*

Jaffa. In this "vision" the Emperor in all his "glory" struts through the wretched hospital, bestowing his healing touch upon the unhappy victims of the pestilence with a magical gesture of his fat, small hand. This is fallacious history. I know for certain that when *le petit caporal* came to this infirmary he did not linger there; in fact, he scurried through the draggled halls as fast as his terrier legs would carry him. The mendacity of the depiction on the canvas caused my gorge to rise and I was obliged to pump ship then and there. Quite a mess of brie and bread I did make upon the marble floor.

During my entire stay in Paris, not one Gypsy did I descry in that city. They are terrified of the French, you see, and will not go there. I decided that Italy would be more suitable for my research as Gypsies are known to delight in the hotter climes. The Iberian Peninsula was out of the question owing to the terrible, shocking homeliness of the entire Spanish royal family. Therefore, Stoakes and I packed up and hired a coach for the trip to Tuscany, the birthplace of my hero Leonardo da Vinci! Barely two days after we crossed the Alps, the war broke out again in earnest. We escaped imprisonment in the dreaded Bitche prison by mere miles!

It was along this highroad that I found Antonio, an addle-brained Tuscan peasant who had forsaken his service in the Italian army. He had walked barefoot all the way from Prussia, and he stank of piddle and dog. He begged a ride on my carriage, telling me that Napoleon himself was hard on his heels. Despite his obvious defects, I was so taken with his ingenuous smile and honest terror of the "Corsican One" that I let him ride on the roof next to the driver. We ended up in Firenze where Stoakes promptly died of blood poisoning. Fortunately, I soon met the Hungarian doctor and he became my new physician. For a medicine-practicing Magyar he is not as incompetent as one might think, though his accent is

My Florentine Abode

abominable. He is an expert in balneology, the study of bathing in mineral pools as a curative. And he treated my boils with mashed garlic compresses to great success!

Thus, I found myself happily marooned in Italy with no land route back to Calais. My Italian friends suggested I take flight in a fishing boat to Gibraltar, and hence board a man-of-war for the journey home; but as I said before, I refuse to be passenger on another ship and will be happy to have my weary bones buried on Italian soil, rather than suffer weeks of sea-puking hell.

For three years now I have lived in an enchanting house near the Piazza di Santa Croce where they used to joust until the blood flowed and where they now play an equally sanguine game of football. From the vantage point of my bed, I can gaze out the window and see the red brick tower of the handsome Palazzo Vecchio. And if I go to the window and crane my neck, I can see the staggeringly huge egg of Brunelleschi's exquisite Duomo.

In truth, I had meant to travel eastwards in search of the origin of the Gypsies, but my extreme ill health has prevented me from taking to the road. Still, it is pleasant enough here, with Antonio to help me, and the fetching Sophia to cook and clean. Every so often, I am able to walk a few paces by the Arno, except in the summer when the river begins to dry up and stinks like Circe's Pen. Sometimes, if I am feeling up to it, I venture over to the Uffizi and view the extraordinary art; or I visit the Brancacci Chapel and wonder at Masaccio's grand, inspired frescoes.

Now and again, the Gypsies will pass through the city and I put them up for a spell in my home. I have hired an artist to paint their portraits over the years and several dozen of their beaming countenances adorn the walls of my chamber. One fine day, I will show them at a salon in London in an exhibition entitled: *Luminous Depictions of the Gypsies of Tuscany*. My countrymen will flock to see the images of this lovely race and all slanderers who call Gypsies "greasy" and "slovenly" and "ignoble" will be silenced forever.

Even though my life here is pleasant enough, my thoughts of late have lingered upon death; I have already bought a little tomb in the village where Leonardo was born, about twenty miles west of here. In truth, I would not die so soon. There is so much of the world I long to see. Alas, I fear my breaths (and heartbeats) are low-numbered now, and it will be a near-run thing to finish my tale before the dark angel comes a-visiting. The cherubs came to spur me on, they did.

The parchment has been in the air too long! I will return the object to its place under glass—cover it with the velvet. He very nearly would not part with it, the wandering Gypsy storyteller. But I offered him a handsome sum: a prince's ransom. (I do not exaggerate. I am as rich as a Fugger.) The last I heard, the noble spinner of yarns had bought a lovely cart and a team of healthy horses and was heading east into strange lands. Why did I hand out so much gold for this tattered bit of paper? Because it is the proof that verifies the veracity of the story I am about to recount and I treasure it above all my possessions. Thank God I was given the ability to write, one of my only skills save an uncanny nose for superior wines, so that I may have the honor of recording this narrative for the generations to come. When I am finished, I will have it pressed into seven times seven copies and I will donate one each to the finest universities in Europe. (If that hideous gargoyle Napoleon has not destroyed the world by then, as well as burned all of the books with the word "short" in them, and stopped all the presses that have published the phrase "mad, Corsican ogre.")

My book will be bound in the most supple Morocco leather and the letters on the spine will be embossed in gold. In my mind's eye, I open the heavy cover and see the fuzzy words of the title page blurred behind the protective sheet of translucent velum. Like lifting a dancer's veil, I slowly raise the filmy overlay to reveal the sharp, dark outlines of the appellation and monogram.

"Antonio!" I cry. "Where are you?"

He scampers into the room, wiping pastry crumbs from his mouth.

"Here's the clock," he says, as he carelessly slams my valuable Harrison chronometer onto the desk.

"Hold your finger to my carotid artery," I command.

"Hmmm . . . I can't feel anything."

"Perhaps, you great oaf, you should remove your digits from my Adam's apple and place them here on my neck."

"Ah ha! I understand," he cries.

"Now count whilst I look at the clock."

"How is the story coming?" he asks, making a great show of peering at my diary. (It may as well be upside down, for he cannot read, poor fellow.)

"I doubt that you can carry on a conversation and count my pulse at the same time, Antonio," I challenge him.

"Ha! Of course I can," he scoffs.

"All right, then. Have you collected today's letters?"

"*Si, signore.*"

"Has the shopping been done for dinner?"

"*Si, signore.*"

"Are you the illegitimate child of a baboon and a homunculus?"

"*Si, signore.*" An instant later he yells, "*No, signore!*" then smacks himself on the side of the head. He gives me a squinty look and a wry smile that says, *You are very cunning, signore, to make me, Antonio, look like such a fool. Again.*

"Time," I demand.

"Ummm . . . seven?" he guesses.

"Seven is the pulse of a hibernating toad. Now go away. I will do it myself. And Antonio?"

"*Si, signore?*" comes his abashed reply.

"Run to Carlo's and pick up another ream of his best writing paper."

"Will you read to me when I get back?" he asks hopefully. "You know how I love a good story."

"I will think about it."

"It is a *good* story, isn't it?"

"The very best."

"Tomorrow is the day of *clistere di barbabietola**, you know?" There is a menacing tone in Antonio's voice.

"I will read to you if you neglect to buy the bushel of beets, and hide the enema from the good doctor."

"I'll be right back."

* Italian: beet enema day.

3

CARTHUSALEM

"Who was that old woman who stole the Gypsy baby?" cries Antonio, for I have just read him the prologue to my tale wherein the Gypsy baby is taken from his dear little manger.

"You will find out in good time," I reply.

"But I want to know now!" he cries. "Is she a witch? Does she eat him?"

"Antonio, she abducted him."

"Well, where did she take him? To her witch-house? To cook him?"

"You will find out soon enough. That is part of the mystery."

"So she didn't eat him?"

I throw one of my silk lounging-pillows at him and say crossly: "She did not eat him, you dolt! She took him. He is to be the hero of the story. The very one who was stolen from the Gypsies. You cannot have an entire book about a baby that was eaten by a witch. That would be foolish."

"So . . . the baby who was stolen from the Gypsies is the hero of the story?"

"Yes."

"He must be a remarkable baby," scoffs Antonio. "All the babies that *I've* ever seen just sit around, crapping and pissing and making spit."

I take a deep breath. "The story is not about the baby. It is about the man that the baby *becomes*."

"Well, where is he?" asks Antonio.

"I have not read you that part yet!"

"Oh!" Antonio props himself up with the pillow I threw at him and nestles into a comfortable position. Then he smiles. "I liked the parts about those ugly villagers. That was funny."

"Thank you," I reply.

"You really showed what it's like. All that stuff about sleeping with sheep and such. But . . . " he scratches his chin thoughtfully, then says with the sagacious air of a scholar, "you should put something in there about how the villagers have to cut farts all the time. That would make it even a lot more realistic. And very much funnier."

"I appreciate your desire to contribute to the story," I say sarcastically.

"Maybe describe how the butt-crackers sound. And smell too! Oh, that would be funny!"

I calmly ignore Antonio's vulgarities. "Before I continue reading," I go on, "I must set the stage. Our story takes place a hundred and fifty years ago on the coast of Dalmatia."

"Where's that?"

"It is on the eastern shore of the Adriatic Sea."

Antonio scrunches up his nose and stares blankly into space. Then he shrugs. "Where's that?" he replies.

"Look out the window," I command. He does so. "Now turn your head to the left. Your *other* left, silly! Now, go five hundred miles that-a-way," I tell him, pointing southeast.

Antonio turns to me in amazement. "That's a long ways away."

"The city of Carthusalem," I declare, "is where our story takes place. One hundred and fifty years ago it was a very different city than it is today. Presently, it is held in the Ottoman's sway and has the oppressive atmosphere of a little Istanbul. Back then, however, it was under the suzerainty of the Venetians—one of the prizes collected in Dalmatia as a reward from the Emperor for the service of their fleet during the Fourth Crusade."

"So the story takes place a hundred and fifty years ago?" asks Antonio.

"Verily," I reply.

"That's a long time ago, isn't it?" he asks.

"Yes. A long time ago." Antonio tries to count silently to one hundred and fifty with his fingers. I watch him until he gives up at six. "Carthusalem," I continue, "was built upon a high, rocky island that lay barely a stone's throw off the coast. Because of its strategic location and deep-water port, it was forever in the middle of a tug-of-war fought between the two worlds. Centuries ago, when it was but a tiny fishing village, Alexander the Great annexed it and constructed the first wall around the base of the island. After their leader made his unfortunate and fateful return to Asia, the Macedonians who manned this garrison married the local women and lost all of their Greek ways, save a passion for feta and wrestling.

"As the years went by, Carthusalem developed into a thriving city, always balanced precariously between east and west, north and south. The Romans made the first great docks on the island and built a lovely amphitheater in the village that was developing upon the shore. According to the most recent guidebook, this theatre has completely disappeared under a blanket of weeds and lichen. O how I long to excavate those noble ruins!

"The Byzantines were the next people to conquer the city, and they constructed the great keep that still stands high atop the island's tallest promontory. They also built the lovely Cathedral of Saint Melkior, patron of the spice trade. For a short time, less than a decade, the Mussulman captured Carthusalem, and he too fashioned a place of worship. A lovely mosque was constructed in the shore-village and was thought to be so beautiful by the Christians, who retook the city from the Saracens, that they did no harm to it. The Venetians themselves were the ones who added the handsome stone bridge that links the island with the terra firma. They named it 'Dandolo's Bridge' for the ancient, blind *doge* who led the Venetian fleet during the Fourth Crusade.

"Yet it did not matter who conquered the city, be it Roman legionnaire, Byzantine soldier, Christian Crusader, Arab Saracen, or Hungarian adventurer: invariably the invaders became absorbed into the city like water into a mop. When our story begins, Carthusalem—the people, the architecture, even the food—was a pleasant amalgam of Christian and Muslim, Europe and Asia and the Middle East."

"Have you ever been there?" asks Antonio.

"No," I reply. "I have never been there, Antonio. But I have done much research and have read many travel books and these firsthand accounts have given me a vivid picture of the place. Now, imagine that you are a moth. (He protests. He would rather imagine that he is a tiger.) No. You are a happy, fluttery, buttery-colored moth. And you are sipping nectar in a field of red poppies at the edge of a forest of cedars, oblivious to the world around you. Catching you unawares, a breeze whisks you high into the sky, far above the flowers and even the trees, and for the first time you catch a glimpse of the castle of Carthusalem: it sits majestically atop the rocky promontory of the island. The ancient white tower in the center of the castle shines like marble in the sun. For indeed it is marble, and marble doth gleam when it is clean and the sun is shimmering. And it watches over the citadel like a stone shepherd, the other houses and buildings playing the part of the sheep. For they are also bright white, in the manner of sheep, except most of them have quaint blue-tiled roofs, which sheep do not. Like a flock upon the hillside, this herd of buildings rambles toward the sea. But they are prevented from watery doom by the great city walls. As tall as the bastions of Jericho they seem. And rising above them, you—the moth—catch a glimpse of the spires of Saint Melkior and, on the opposite shore, the Mosque's minarets.

"Beyond the city, the sea is as blue as a Swiss Guard's eye, and the hundreds of ships in the harbor rock gently on the waves, a forest of pencil-straight masts. You flap, Antonio, you fly on a gentle breeze that carries you closer and closer to the beautiful city. You pass camel caravans returning from their long trek into the far-off desert cities of Samarkhand and Bhokhara. You observe a mighty troop of the *podestà's* cavalry, riding their proud Arab stallions—gray hair dappled with snowy spots that are as bleached as ocean foam. Over Dandolo's Bridge you fly, through the great city gates and into the cramped bazaar; past the stalls of saffron-sellers and greengrocers and amber-hawkers and sword-sharpeners (the sparks from the grinding stone blaze past your wings like flaming missiles shot from a tiny catapult). You escape onto a dark side street and flit up the edge of a small tower to the third story where there is an open window. You perch on the ledge and rest in the sunlight. There is a man in the room. And you watch him as you clean the dust of Carthusalem from your delicate limbs."

I pick up the notebook in which I have written my story and continue to read.

Carthusalem

4

The Accountant

Godfrey Verrazanno sat at his cramped little desk in
the chamber in the tower above his father's spice
shop on Zim Zam Street and scribbled furiously in
an absurdly large ledger. The book was so huge that Godfrey
had to rest the butt against his groin, and stretch his left arm
until his elbow joint cracked merely to get a grip on the other
end of the tome. He was a hunched and crooked creature, this
young accountant—a careworn, lard-skinned slouch. The
hump on his back was so enormous that whenever he walked
past the camel merchants at the bazaar, they called out bids.
In his somber black suit, sitting at his puny desk, inscribing
feverishly in his giant book, he resembled a demented child
possessed by some evil writing spirit. The quill, as it scratched
against the rough paper, was as loud as a dozen rats scrabbling
against a wall. The movement of dry quill to inkwell and back
again to page, with never a smudge nor drip, was the only
respite from this terrible rasping; yet, it was so practiced and
quick that the pause barely lasted a second and was, in fact,

the exact lull between the beats of Godfrey's heart.

Then the flowing hand suddenly ended its meticulous labor. Godfrey's quill hovered over the page as his eyes squinted to make sure everything was exact and complete. Well pleased, he set the pen into the inkwell and gave a satisfied jerk of the head. For an instant, he thought he heard the quill hiss—like a match extinguished into a puddle—as the tip touched the cool black ink. He closed the ledger with a heavy thump and sat back in his chair and stared into space. It had been a long, weary day, and now he wanted nothing more than to think of nothingness.

His very long fingers absent-mindedly stroked the well-caressed edges of the ledger. These organs of touch—which would have looked quite lovely and even appropriate on a musician or a painter—appeared out of place and somewhat comical protruding from his conservative, businessman's sleeves. These graceful digits, which should have been attached to a Botticelli or a Boccherini, were instead being used to record the mind-numbingly insipid dross of commercial enterprise. Abominable! It would be like using the Holy Grail to drink jug wine. Even the *style* of Godfrey's penmanship was inappropriate for this mundane task, for it was indeed stunning! His numbers were bold and portentous. His dates established a place in time with the force of a capstone dedication carved in marble. And his nouns! Dear God, they leapt off the page as if they were spoken by a master orator. One could smell the exotic jungles of the Spice Islands wafting from his "nutmeg," and hear the creaking rigging and call of the seagulls from his "port duties." This ledger, which Godfrey had labored over for ten years, since he was a teenage boy, this accounting book with its dates and lists and tallies, was a work of *art*. Those Celtic monks, who perfected the art of the manuscript, would have turned emerald green with jealously had they lived to see Godfrey's poetical and inspired hand.

Yet, all of this talent was being wasted like seeds thrown on barren ground or fancies frittered on a determined nun. Not a soul would see the fruit of his dashing hand. More sadly, no one had ever taken the time to gaze into his eyes that were not dull and lifeless, but were quite remarkably the color of polished chestnuts; they were the saddest and most soulful eyes ever to grace the visage of an accountant. Nobody would ever know that trapped inside the ill-shaped husk of this poor creature was beating the heart of a poet.

"This Godfrey reminds me of you," says Antonio, interrupting my narration.

"Whatever are you talking about?" I ask.

"The way that you have described him: 'Ill-shaped husk.' I'm imagining you in my mind."

"Well, he is not me."

"Who is he then?"

"He is the man from the story that the wandering Gypsy told me."

"What wandering Gypsy?"

I let forth a tremendous sigh. "The Gypsy who came to the house. The one from whom I purchased the *artifact*."

"Oh," says Antonio. "*That* wandering Gypsy." He pauses to scratch his arse. "Which one was he?"

I give another a sigh. Antonio's power of recollection is like a very deep well that has lost its bucket.

"There was a Gypsy minstrel who came to the house on a gloomy, ominous eve," I recount. "He knocked upon the door, which you answered. Instead of turning him out into the street, you wisely brought him to my chamber where he told me this story. Now I am writing it down so that it will not be lost to history."

He shrugs. "So where is the baby?"

"Pardon?"

"The baby that was stolen. And the witch. Where is she?"

"All in good time. Now, where was I? Yes. Here we are. The next chapter. It is entitled . . ."

5

THE MERCHANT

A grunting, a straining, an awful heaving of legs and loins and lungs sounded from the spiral stairwell which led to Godfrey's tower. In the duration that it took Godfrey's adopted father, Zalman Verrazanno, to reach the landing, a nimble child might have sprinted up and down the treads and risers a dozen or so times; but Zalman was a great merchant, in both wealth and girth, and the fifty steps that led to Godfrey's sanctuary were more than his chubby lungs could take. Zalman had meant to fling open the door dramatically, but his effort in climbing had so exhausted his strength that the heavy portal merely groaned on its massive hinges and slowly creaked open like a cumbrous lid on a mummy's sarcophagus. Zalman staggered into the room, gasping for breath. The anger that had driven him to make the (dreaded) climb to Godfrey's chamber, coupled with his present physical exhaustion, made it impossible for him to speak the words that he longed to spew. He stared at Godfrey with an expression of absolute frustration: his eyes bulged, his jaw jutted forward, and his jowls vibrated with such force that it looked as though his head were experiencing an earthquake in miniature.

Zalman had not always been so fat; indeed, in his youth he had been a captain of a ship in the famed fleet that defeated the Turk at Lepanto. In those glory days he was as muscular as a galley slave: he could beat any sailor in a race up the rigging and down again; he often claimed that his arm was so powerful that he once dismasted an enemy's ship with one clean stroke of his sword. He had been extremely handsome back then, too. Zalman's father was a half Austrian, half Italian merchant; and from him Zalman had received his great height, Roman nose, and sable hair. Zalman's mother was a Turkish princess, a concubine of the Pasha whom his father had rescued from a shipwreck; it was from her that he had inherited his high cheek bones, powerful body, and azure-colored eyes. In spite of all this wonderful physical birthright, years of prosperity had taken their toll on Zalman's once patrician looks. Now he looked all too highborn; in truth, he resembled a seedy, overfed pope with one foot in gout's door. But Godfrey loved him all the same and respected him like a good son should.

Zalman let forth a strange, hideous screech and grabbed his own hair in his giant fingers, pulling so hard that it brought tears to his eyes. Any other man would have feared for his life in the presence of such wrath, but Godfrey merely sighed and chewed on his pen. He had seen this before. The reason was always the same.

"She is killing me, Godfrey," choked Zalman. He took a deep, rattling breath and stared at the ceiling. "No. Do not try to speak. I know you understand me. Ever since that day you were found in the stables, naked as a mole, crying as if terrorized by demons, desperate to be suckled and held, wanting of mother, *and* of father, alone and cold and miserable, I have loved you like my own son. There has always been a special bond between us. We could exchange more in a glance than most people could in a whole conversation, could we not?" Godfrey smiled and nodded his head. "But her. She. I will not say her name for it burns bitter on my tongue. My daughter, your semi-sister, is causing me great pain. The other day, I ask her, 'Daughter? Where are you going today?'

" 'Out,' she replies. Wait, there is more!

" 'With whom?' I ask.

" 'A friend,' says she.

" 'Where will you go?' I query.

" 'Someplace,' she replies and leaves.

"I employed a man to dog her steps. She lost him. I hired a better man to haunt her ways. She vanished from him. I have threatened. I have begged. She will not listen. She keeps company with scoundrels and says that they are 'Jolly!' If her dear, sainted mother were still alive, she would slap her face for disgracing us so. But I could scarcely scold her as beat her and that is why I'm at the end of my wits. I have decided to cut off her allowance. I know she has friends who would give her money but she is too proud to beg from them.

"So that is why I am here. Good Godfrey. My adopted son. Only you I can trust. My faithful friend and ally. Here you sit, day after day, slaving away at the business. If it were not for you everything would be in a shambles. But as it is, we are doing quite nicely and you are to be commended for it. So! Since you are the only man in this corrupt world whom I can trust, truly, I am putting you in my will as sole heir. No, do not try to speak! As I have said, you are more son to me than any son could have ever been. Even though my blood does not run through your veins, you have my heart. Those adventurers after my daughter's several treasures will now think twice before pursuing her.

"Now that you know what is what, I will tell you something more: I am leaving tomorrow on a voyage to the Spice Islands with our new fleet of ships. I will be gone six months. I travel under the tedious auspices of commercial enterprise, though it will afford great respite from the *business* going on here.

"Here is what I expect of you: do not give your sister any money. Not if she begs on her hands and knees. Not if she whines or weeps or wilts in despair. Not if she threatens or commands. We will dry her up and keep her close to home. This is a great task I put upon you; but I know your stern and cloistered heart will shun all her womanly intricacies. For did I not name you after Godfrey of Bouillon, that famous knight who went to the Holy Land, and so diligently protected pilgrims on their journey to the Holy Sepulcher? Do not try to speak, dear boy. I will leave you now to your work, since I know this prattling interruption has surely disturbed your chain of thought. I will see you at the beginning of the new year. Goodbye."

Zalman lifted his young protégé from his seat, enveloped him in an enormous hug, kissed him on the cheek, then left the chamber without uttering another sound.

"He is the baby," shouts Antonio. "I just smoked it! Just now. In this instant. Godfrey is the baby who was stolen. The witch left him in a manger in this man Verrazanno's house. Ah, this is good, *signore*. This is very good." Antonio cracks his knuckles exuberantly.

"Shall I continue?"

"O, please do. Please continue."

"You will like the next chapter."

"What's it called?"

"I do not know. I have not yet given it a title. But, it should be called 'The Beloved.'"

"An excellent title! Read on!"

6

THE BELOVED

The next day, Godfrey was sitting warped over his accounting book when he heard a familiar nimble footfall dashing up the stairs. The portal door was flung open with a startling crash, and Mamooshka strode resolutely into the room. She had just come from her fencing lesson; her cheeks were still flushed from the thrill of terrorizing her French sword master. Her wild, piercing eyes locked onto Godfrey's countenance with the power of a Gorgon's stare, freezing him into a terribly unflattering pose: he resembled a guilty, furtive ferret dressed in human clothes; he even let forth a terrified squeal—very like the sound a field mouse makes when it recognizes the eagle's shadow and knows it is too late to run for cover.

Mamooshka had always thought that Godfrey looked like a squirrel. A ludicrous, scrunch-faced, grubby little squirrel. "Hello, squirrel," she said with practiced disdain.

Godfrey stared at the gorgeous creature posing regally before him, and tried to swallow the goose-egg-sized lump in his throat. "Aack," was his dismal reply. The skin on his chest seared and burned as an invisible knife traced across his flesh. Mamooshka squinted and smiled predatorily. Godfrey felt the knife dig down to the bone. As she began her slow, haughty, hip-rolling walk toward his desk, his ribs cracked like dry kindling. And when she reached out a slender yet muscular arm, wrapped her long, lovely fingers around his collar, and pulled him out of his chair as if he were a naughty schoolboy who needed a good whack on the nadirs, Godfrey's heart sprung from his chest with the comical sound of a jester's slapstick bladder, and lay throbbing, metaphorically, upon his black sleeve.

"I need money, you little squirrel," she demanded dangerously.

Godfrey smiled meekly and took out his leather coin purse. He counted through the coins, thought better of it, and simply handed her the entire pouch.

She patted him on the head like a good pet, turned on one heel, and strode out of the room, leaving Godfrey to curse his miserable fate.

He walked to the window, leaned on the sill (almost crushing a moth who had been grooming himself on the stone) and gazed upon the minarets and towers and domes of the city of Carthusalem. He could not enjoy the beauty of that sun-dappled Adriatic glory, for he imagined himself a prisoner in some moldy dungeon. These black musings darkened his vision and cast a pall over all that he saw. He was so full of love and despair that he could not restrain his thoughts any longer. The words of passion which he longed to speak to Mamooshka arranged themselves like wingéd creatures, forming a poem of incomparable beauty. If the medieval poet prodigy Petrarch had gazed upon this remarkable poesy, he would have chopped off the fingers of his writing hand in jealousy, and exiled himself to a miserable northern land to serve out the rest of his days weaving rustic baskets of coarse fibers as penance for ever assuming to *think* himself an odist.

Hush! Let us listen in absolute silence as the bard pronounces his masterpiece! Observe him as he holds up a hand toward the full moon, pale and faint in its daylight march across the heavens. Watch in awe as Godfrey's appearance begins to alter. His brow is now keen and proud. His features are sharp and handsome. His chest swells with an intake of breath, and his back becomes as straight as a palace guard's. His emotions, like the crescendo of some lovely melancholy symphony crest and break with the force of waves thundering against a rocky promontory, and his words erupt from his mouth like the golden-tongued troubadour whose—

"Aaaaaack! Burglaaaack! Glug, glug!" squawks Godfrey.

Pardon?

"Aglack! Bur . . . Glack!"

What is this, you ask? Is this some kind of cruel joke?

"Brip! Glack Blap!"

I heard no poetry, you say. No rhyme, no song, no sibilant phrasing of love's cruel torment.

"Glug," said the accountant. "Gurblug Urglug Phhhlak," said the pasty-faced hump-backed beast in an absurd, garbled, unintelligible screech and squeal and croaking of words.

Godfrey turned away from the window, held a trembling hand to his face, and stumbled blindly across the room, groaning with agony. His fingers fumbled on the wall for a familiar rope, and pulled sharply on it three times. Far away, in the main house, a little bell did chime.

"What's wrong with Godfrey?" asks Antonio. "What's wrong with his voice? Did the nasty witch cut out his tongue?"

"Be patient, you will find out," I reply.

"I was in love with a woman like Mamooshka once," he says fondly. "She used to slap me and pull my hair."

"She sounds delightful."

"Ah, *signore*. There's nothing more thrilling than to be manhandled by a strong woman. I can understand why Godfrey is so in love."

"There is one more chapter that has been completed," I tell him.

"Then read on, *signore*, for I long to hear it!"

7

THE LACKEY

Ten minutes later, a clomping, clodding, uncoordinated cacophonous clogging resounded from the stairwell. The maker of this rude noise stumbled through the door and fell flat on his face. This was Godfrey's faithful but ungraceful servant, a rube from top to toe. His name was Short Clog because he was indeed quite short and stumpy, and he always wore wooden shoes. Short Clog was the kind of minion who could invariably be counted on to deliver important messages to the wrong address, make inappropriate ribald puns at the expense of his betters and, most annoyingly, always burn the toast. For guidance, Godfrey had given him a copy of *The Book of the Courtier*; but instead of reading the valuable tome and gleaning from it many beneficial manners that would have made him more helpful to his master, the boobie used it to squash the flies that bred in epidemic proportions in his wicked little chamber under the stairs.

Short Clog never failed to turn the simplest task into the kind of bumbling mayhem that the waggish writers are so fond of displaying in their "comedies." In fact, one theatrical scribe of the day penned a play based on the character of Godfrey's hireling, and it was called: *The Ill-mannered Attendant or How the Minion Got His Come-Uppance.* This broad comedy was a very popular piece and made Short Clog famous throughout the city. Unfortunately, this brush with the performing arts had instilled in Godfrey's servant an annoying habit of speaking his thoughts aloud, as if in wry asides to an unseen audience. Observe.

SHORT CLOG (*sotto voce,* to audience): "My master has been cursed from birth. Which he is unable to make sense or meaning with words, though he understands 'em quite good. I act as his interpreter, among other odious jobs such as clipping his toenails and cleaning his chambers, picking up his socks an' such like that. He has called me up here now so that he can express his lofty thoughts aloud through my modest mouth."

Godfrey, impatient with his servant's monologue, erupted into an angry spate of gibberish.

"Yes, master," replied Short Clog in a wearied voice. "I will help you soliloquy." He cleared his throat and began—quite impertinently and without a cue from his master—to recite Godfrey's favorite lines from the Bard's Danish play, "O, what a piece of work is man, how noble in reason, how—"

Godfrey cut him off with frustrated gobbledygook.

"Aha! I understand," replied Short Clog, nodding his head knowingly. "You wish to do one of your *own* this time. Proceed and I will follow as best I can."

Godfrey paced up and down the floor. Short Clog mirrored his actions apathetically. In truth, the poor brute was fed up with his job as interpreter and had given up even trying to mask his feelings. He loved his master terribly, but poetry, songs *d'amour,* and tender emotions made him queasy: it took all his brainpower simply to decipher Godfrey's jargon, let alone give it the rendition it called for.

Godfrey interrupted his thoughts with impassioned gibberish.

"'O, what I would give to splack! To splack!'" bellowed Short Clog.

Godfrey shot him an irritated glance and babbled directions.

"Och, sorry, master. I understand what you meant to say. 'To speak! To speak!'" Godfrey continued as did Short Clog. "'What accursed crime must I have committed in some other life to deserve this punishment? Like a beast am I. Like a monkey or a goat do I spew and spit.'"

Godfrey paused in thought.

"Like a donkey with the colic too, master," interjected Short Clog, trying his best to be helpful. "And a burbling, brain-sick sheep as well."

Godfrey smiled wryly and splacked some more.

"'Yes, a tortured barnyard resides in my voice, my short friend,'" interpreted Short Clog. "'And I will never be able to confess the love I have for her. She is the air in my lungs, the sun on my face, the earth beneath my feet. I live for Mamooshka. In my heart I betray my adoptive father. For I would give her everything I possess, just to see her puppy.'"

Godfrey rolled his eyes in frustration. He wheeled on his idiot elucidator and corrected him gruffly.

"Aha!" cried Short Clog, understanding what it was that his master had meant to say. "'Happy!' I smoke it, master. 'To see her *happy*.'"

Godfrey slumped onto his chair and cradled his head in his hands. He could not take the agony any longer. The dreadful thought of jumping out the window crossed his forlorn mind. Then he glanced at Short Clog, who was humming an asinine tune and picking both of his nostrils at the same time, and the notion of throwing his servant out *first* appeared, at the moment, to be a much better idea.

Short Clog saw the peculiar smile appear on Godfrey's face, and since he had never seen his master mirthful, misinterpreted his murderous aspect as a grimace of lovesick pain.

"O, don't be sad, sir. I've good news for you today," said Short Clog. "My uncle, the great magician, has just returned to the city. And he is quite anxious to meet you. I've told him all about your little problem and he said, 'O, I can fix that right up.'"

Godfrey asked, "Quack? Quack?"

"No. No. He's no faker. He's a master at these things. Why, once I saw him cure a leaper."

Godfrey emitted a stream of interrogative gibberish.

"No. Not a leper. A *lea*per. A fellow who just couldn't stop prancing about. Then there was the lad with a twitch. My uncle also pulls teeth."

Godfrey expressed himself with hopeful-sounding gibberish.

"That's wonderful, sir. You'll be very satisfied with the results, I'm sure. Come on, then. Let us go to the old forest by the bend in the river."

Short Clog pulled on his master's sleeve and started dragging him to the door.

But Godfrey dug in his heels at the top of the stairs and asked a final question.

"Oh, he can't come into the city, master," replied Short Clog. "My uncle, he's been banned, he has. But he works just as fine out-of-doors as in."

Godfrey, at the bitter end of his meager, frayed rope, allowed Short Clog to lead him to the mysteriously illicit magician, with the hope of a miraculous cure to follow.

8

DREADFUL TIDINGS

Several weeks have passed since I read Antonio the first few chapters of my book. Afterwards, I descended into a fever of tachygraphy and nearly completed the story through my speed writing. A hundred candles have I melted in my mad lucubrations; a whole pound of India ink have I scribbled in my night studies! But this morning I heard some terrible news about the war and I have not been able to work. The Hungarian doctor has come for his weekly visit, so I vent my anger upon him.

"Napoleon is a mad little stinker!" I groan. "A cretinous gnome!"

The doctor squirms uncomfortably and gives me the sign to keep my voice down. "Zare are French *shpion* . . . ze shpies in Firenze," he warns.

"Let them turn me in," I say haughtily. "Let the rats dare!"

"But vhy do you loathe heem so?" asks the doctor. "Napoleon iss uff ze ancient *und* noble Tuscan family."

The Hungarian has offered this base lie on more than one

occasion. He knows how fully it vexes me; I catch a glimpse of the slightest smirk upon his lips as he turns his face away to examine my latest loin-rash.

"This Tuscan connection is merely an invention," I begin with a tremble in my voice, "which has been created by Napoleon's kin to draw prestige from the admirable people of Tuscany." I hyperventilate. I cannot help it. I choke out my words in a hoarse shout: "When I know for a fact that Napoleon's ancestors were Genoese dog buffers who were driven from Italy on account of their depraved and vicious natures."

"You must be shtill," says the doctor, alarmed at my sudden passion. "You vill burst a vessel! Take ziss *medizin* . . . "

He tries to force a spoonful of his vile slibber-sauce into my mouth, but I smack his hand away. (I am in a black humor. I will not be coddled.)

"Do you not see!" I howl. "This is the final straw. This is the end of the world. First he desecrated Venezia, the longest living republic in the history of the world! And now this Austerlitz fiasco. The French are worse than the plague. Pass me the Bible, you twat-faced tweak! I must brush up on my Saint John."

"Antonio vas not to tell you of ziss most recent turn of events in *der krieg*," says my medico, reaching for my wrist to take my pulse.

"Antonio did not tell me about the war," I reply. "I can read the bloody journals, you devilish croaker! Dear God! The flower of Austria and Russia, defeated by this disgusting little Corsican monkey and his band of conscripted maniacs: ex-postal clerk dragoons and hussars who are the bastardy of slipshod tailors. It makes me feel like plunging into the Arno."

"Now, now, *Herr* Smythe."

"Or jumping off the tower of the Palazzo Vecchio!"

"Antonio? *Kommen!*" calls out the doctor for reinforce-
ments.

So I launch my bowl of stool at him.

"I know for a fact that Napoleon's Grand Marshal was
employed as a novice pigeon breeder before the revolution!"

Antonio appears at the door.

"Hiss febrile heart, it iss precariously shtimulated," says
the doctor to Antonio. "He must be grappled vith."

Antonio, as compact and muscular as a tiny bull, lays his
dense, squat body on top of me, pushing me into the bed like
a weary bear who indifferently crushes a rabbit that has
crawled unwittingly into his winter den.

"Shtay like zat for haff ze hour," prescribes the doctor.
And then he rushes off to the kitchen to punish the best of my
wine.

"If I were stronger," I say as I blow Antonio's greasy hair
from my mouth, "If I were stronger of body I would make
straightaway to Paris and assassinate that miscreant."

"Your pillow is so . . . soft," says Antonio languidly, immediately nodding off; the laggard could out-sleep the most
shiftless of cats on any day of the week.

"The self-proclaimed 'Attila of Venice' must die!" I rave.
"The rogue sacked the most beautiful city in the world and
carted off its treasures for himself! He actually scuttled the
doge's gilded barge *Bucintoro* as if it had been a garbage scow,
the foul fiend! This same barbarian is now traipsing across
Europe like one of the Four Horsemen . . . nay . . . like a midget
King Exterminens, spreading ruin and mayhem and evil wher-
ever his little boots tread. I know for a fact that Bonaparte's
horse, Marengo, is barely fourteen-and-a-half hands high. That
makes him a pony, my dear Antonio. The great Napoleon rides
a pony!"

I laugh bitterly, then choke on my wrath and pause to

summon a breath from the depths of my gut. Try taking air
with a lumpish oaf covering you like a fat blanket, if you like.
"Ten days ago," I continue, "Napoleon crushed the Austrians
and Russians at a place called Austerlitz. Fifty thousand of
Europe's finest soldiers—dead! Dead! Dead! And now the
world is doomed."

"Who . . . is the King . . . of Excretion?" asks Antonio with
a leaden voice.

"Ex-terminens! *Abaddon* in the Hebrew tongue. Fallen
angel and king of the locusts. The Revelation of Saint John
prophesied how he will come forth when the fifth angel
sounds his trumpet at doomsday. Exterminens rides a hideous
monster with the head of a man and the body of a horse; and

the king himself is grim to look upon, for his eyes are as red as coals, and his teeth as sharp as a lion's."

"I saw a lion once," says Antonio. He talks out of the side of his maw, like a half-awake child narrating a dream. "In the *piazza*. The lion tamer stuck his head in the animal's mouth, and when he took his head out, it was covered with slabber and drool. Ah how we laughed . . . "

"Exterminens will bring with him all sorts of terrible plagues and cataclysms!" I continue in a dire tone. "And he and his evil minions will torture mankind for five months— their torment is the agony of a scorpion sting. A great eagle will fly above the towns crying: '*Ve, Ve, Ve habitantibus.*' Woe, woe, woe to the ones who live there. And then, as if things were not bad enough, the blasted *sixth* trumpet is sounded. This foul bugle makes the blaring of that other horn seem as innocuous as the playful tooting of a child's tin cornet. For with the blowing of the sixth, a hoard of avenging angels are released at the mouth of the Euphrates river to butcher one third—"

"I love how Sophia puts lavender in your pillowcase," interrupts Antonio dreamily. "It smells nice. And please stop speaking of scorpion stings, red-eyed monsters, angel-trumpets and doomsday. You will give me nightmares."

"I must complete my story of the Gypsy," I state. "Europe does not stand a chance."

"Would you move your elbow?" inquires Antonio. "It's very hard and bony."

"I must finish my narrative before a flood greater than the deluge of 1333 washes over the city, and buries it under a mile of slime and mud. Let me up."

Sophia's head appears at the door. She resembles a Gypsy woman with her dusky eyes, dark olive skin, high cheek bones and raven-hair.

"Good day, *signorina* Sophia," I wheeze.

I must emphasize that I comment on my maid's sultry appearance simply to paint a picture for the reader. On occasion, I have taken salacious delight in the presence of a beautiful woman (my youthful fretting for Sarah was fierce indeed), but since coming to the continent, my ill health has rendered me as ineffective and unappealing as a pale, withered turnip in a winter garden, neglected by hoe and spade. My *arbor vitae* is diffident: I can appreciate Sophia's beauty but only in a wistful way.

"The *dottore* is drinking all the wine!" she hisses angrily. Sophia is a big, strong woman, a regular Penthesilea, Queen of the Amazons; it does not take much more than a gentle scolding from her to send shivers up our spines. When she is fierce and angry like today, Antonio and I become as meek as newborn mice. As she takes in our antics on the bed, me looking wistful, Antonio adjusting into a more comfortable position and grunting obscenely, a disgusted expression overcomes her lovely features. "*Stupidos!*" she says, then storms down the hall to her room and slams the door.

"Keep reading me the tale," demands Antonio. He rolls off of me, grabs the manuscript from my desk, then plops back on the bed. "Tell me the story as I fall asleep, so it will turn into my dream."

9

THE BAZAAR

The camel bazaar: a hot, squalid, crowded sprawl of braying beasts, squabbling dealers, perplexed buyers, and blissful vermin. It resided on a street known as the Crusader's Doom—the main thoroughfare which led from the city gates to the great inner marketplace. The name was in recollection of the two hundred knights of Saint Rufus, vagabond Norman ruffians (kicked out of Sicily by that island's Norman King Robert de Hauteville), who waged a pathetic assault on the city centuries before, only to be wiped out by an attack of slack-bowels at the very ingress of the citadel. Their sullied armor was paraded throughout the streets once a year (to the disgust of many) on the festival of "Norman Day." One could not enter or exit the city without passing through this malodorous emporium.

On this afternoon it was particularly hot. The dingy awnings that protected the stables from the burning sun hung limp in the stifling noonday heat. The camel-sellers, lounging lazily in their hammocks or reclining on pillows and puffing their hookahs, gave the impression of mangy, indolent pashas. For Godfrey, the Crusader's Doom had been an inescapable gauntlet of shame, a painful path which he had been marching since he was a little boy.

"Forty drachmas!" "Twenty guilders!" "A shiny ducat!" cried the camel-dealers as Godfrey walked past their stalls with his diminutive servant scurrying at his side.

"Don't listen to them, sir," said Short Clog protectively. "Some might consider your hump to be a beauty mark," he continued with a jolly smile. "Such as a mole."

But Godfrey was too despondent to even notice the slurs that were slung at him. Instead, he stared with compassionate horror at the piteous camels. Multitudes of giant flies mercilessly sipped the watery wells in the corners of the beasts' sad eyes. He sympathized with the camels' misery. A morose sigh escaped Godfrey's sensitive lips. Short Clog, however, was cursing under his breath. He bristled with indignation every time Godfrey was scorned. Not only did he feel sorry for his unhappy master, but as a long-standing member of the Servant's Guild, he considered it his responsibility to defend the honor of his employer, in accordance with the vows of the sacred *Minion's Oath*.

"Two doubloons!" mocked the callous camel-men. "A choice cut sapphire!"

Why don't they make little lace nets to cover the poor beasts' eyes? thought Godfrey.

Short Clog glared at Achmed, a particularly vapid-looking bursar with massive buck teeth, who had slipped a pillow under his burnoose (creating an instant hump), and was presently imitating Godfrey's garbled speech, much to the merriment of his companions.

"Aaack splack," hoicked Achmed.

"May I have a chinker, sir?" asked Short Clog innocently.

Godfrey fished absentmindedly in his pocket for a copper

coin, then handed it to his servant. Short Clog bowed and scampered off in the direction of the food stalls that lined the opposite side of the street.

One could take used burlap bags and fashion a sort of camel capuche, Godfrey pondered. *Why, the expense would be negligible considering the relief it would give to the wretched . . .*

"Oy! Achmed nasty face?" yelled Short Clog, interrupting Godfrey's camel-bonnet musings.

Achmed turned his idiot's grin toward Short Clog and was nailed in the kisser by an enormous, perfectly aimed ostrich egg valued at one piece of copper. Short Clog, smiling like a little boy, turned to Godfrey and suggested that they should probably run the rest of the way to Dandolo's Bridge.

Godfrey stood dumbly staring at the glistening yellow yolk oozling and goozling down the stunned Achmed's face. The egg guts instantly attracted many dozens of flies, which descended upon the camel-driver's mustache and chin whiskers and gave the appearance he was sporting a living, undulating beard.

The ostrich-egg dealer cracked a smile. The saffron-seller snickered. The greengrocer giggled. And like a thunderclap, the entire market burst into vast amusement. Achmed and the other camel-men, however, were not laughing. Achmed slowly wiped the yoke off his face. His eyes became slits, and his upper lip curled back to reveal his giant incisors. His voice pealed forth in an enraged ululation—a combination of petulant scream and Arab war cry.

Before Godfrey jumped out of his skin with fright, Short Clog grabbed his master's sleeve and ran, pulling him toward the gate.

Achmed grasped a giant *aflachmadramatar*—a wicked-looking tool used to clean a camel's hooves—and set off after them with murderous intent. He was followed closely by his sinister, fork-bearded cousin Faisul and five other brutish camel-dealers, all of them hideously muscled from a lifetime of manhandling dromedaries.

Fortunately, the moment Short Clog and Godfrey rushed through the gate, a troop of the *podestà's* soldiers cantered in on their proud stallions. Achmed and his companions were cut off by this throng, and they lost sight of the egg chucker and his black-frocked master. They cried out in frustration and made a tremendous show of their wrath, stomping and spitting and pulling their hair, until one of the soldiers clonked Achmed on the head with his lance and told him to shut his stupid rabbit-looking mouth, or he'd drag him to the shipyards and sell him to the Ottoman slaver who would then pluck out his miserable, womanish beard hair by pathetic hair until he was as glabrous and emasculated as a eunuch in a Sultan's seraglio!

By the time Short Clog and Godfrey made it to the foot bridge by the river, near the old abandoned Roman relay station called The Broken Tower, they each had painful stitches in their sides. They sat on the grass slope and panted for air. At first, Godfrey was stern with his servant for almost getting them killed. But when Short Clog recounted how ludicrous Achmed had appeared with his beard of flies, both men rolled on the ground until their stomachs ached from laughing. For a twinkling, Godfrey forgot his dreadful, weary existence.

At that moment, however, a cloud passed over the sun, casting the world in a cheerless gray light. A foreboding fear touched Godfrey's heart like the proverbial leprous finger of doom.

"There's a storm coming," observed Short Clog.

"Oho! *Ja! Ja!* A great *shturm!*" rasped a peculiarly accentuated voice.

"What is a *'shturm'*?" asks Antonio who is now wide awake. Godfrey's and Short Clog's escape from the camel-men seems to have captured his attention.

"It is the German word for *tempesta*," I explain, using the Italian for "storm."

"Then why do you not simply have the man say *tempesta*?" queries Antonio.

"Because *'shturm'* sounds funny," I say. "Many German words sound funny to the English ear. For example, take *schnippchen* and *schwachsinnige*."

"Those *are* funny! Ha! What do *they* mean?"

"You will find out soon enough."

"Well, this man in the story sounds exactly like the Hungarian *dottore*. Why is *he* in Godfrey's tale? The Hungarian *dottore* was dead a hundred and fifty years ago."

"The Hungarian doctor is *not* in the story. And he was not *dead* a hundred and fifty years ago, rather he was not yet *born*."

"But when you read that line about the great *shturm*," insists Antonio, ignoring my lesson in chronology, "you imitated the Hungarian *dottore* perfectly. You sounded just like him."

"I am merely using the Hungarian doctor," I spell out, "as a model for this new personage in the story. Even though I am telling the tale of the Gypsy who was stolen, I have some license to expand and . . . augment."

"Well if he is not the Hungarian *dottore*, then who is he?"

"Let us find out!"

I0

The Magician

An old man stepped from the shadows of the forest and smiled at the two with a nefarious leer. He wore a great robe with cabalistic signs and occult symbols sewn onto it with golden thread. On his head was a tall, black felt cap with a brim as wide as his shoulders. His penetrating eyes peered like cold lights from deep-set brows, and when they met Godfrey's, the accountant felt himself overcome by an involuntary shiver.

"Uncle!" cried Short Clog happily.

"*Guten tag. Ich heiße* Azfall," said the wizard to Godfrey. "Now shit down upon *der shtummel und* let me probe you."

Azfall gestured to a stump and Godfrey dutifully sat down upon it. "Open *der mund,*" commanded Azfall curtly and gave Godfrey a little slap on the cheek. Godfrey tilted back his head, opened his mouth, and stuck out his tongue. The old man held a piece of magnifying glass up to Godfrey's mouth and peered intently into that marred maw.

Godfrey held back an involuntary urge to gag, such was

the hideous power of Azfall's terrible breath as it wafted into his nostrils; the stench seemed peculiarly foul coming from one who claimed to be a restorer of wellness. Godfrey also noticed that there was something odd about the old man's face. The wizard's beard seemed almost . . . well . . . crooked. Furthermore, he noticed that his hand—which gripped a gnarled wooden cane—was both slender and unwrinkled . . . more like the hand of a young woman. Besides this, Godfrey wondered why Short Clog's uncle would speak with the accent and manner of a crusty, Austro-Hungarian physician. He shrugged off these incongruities, however, such was his excitement at being in the presence of a healer.

"Ja! Ja! I see it now," murmured the wizard. "O ja! O ja! Ziss iss some-ting terrible. You know vat it iss? It iss some-ting horrible. My accursed man. You vur shtolen from Gypsies!"

Godfrey was dumbfounded. Gypsies? Those gay wanderers who gad about the countryside in their painted carts, banishing bleak reality with happy songs and stories of heroism and feats of . . . He shook his head and asked, "Eh?"

Short Clog spoke slowly to Godfrey, as if talking to an infant. "He said, sir, that, 'You vur shto-len from Gyp-sies!'"

"Ven you vur *der kinder*," continued Azfall, "just ze tiny little baby . . . you vur shnatched from a band of vandering Gypsies *und* taken to live in ze city."

Short Clog slapped his forehead and exclaimed, "That explains everything, don't it?"

"Ja," replied Azfall.

"What exactly does it explain, O wondrous strange uncle of mine?" asked Short Clog. He was beginning to ponder why his own uncle, born and bred in Carthusalem, should now be speaking with such a terribly foreign *voce*. Perchance, whilst his uncle had been studying abroad all these years he had forgotten how to converse properly. He was about to ask him this very question, when the wizard—as if reading Short Clog's mind—turned his terrible gaze upon him and silenced the servant with a flash of his wicked teeth.

"Vat it means," said Azfall, "iss zat he hass been taken from hiss element. He iss cut off from hiss *volk*! His pipples! He iss sundered *und* shplit from zose who are hiss own!"

"Aha!" cried Godfrey with sudden insight. *My folk! My people! The Gypsies!*

"Pipples?" asked Short Clog in bewilderment. "What's a pipple?"

Azfall ignored Short Clog's question and smiled at Godfrey. "Ass you know, Gypsies zay have ze beautiful foishes."

"Beautiful fishes, sir?" asked Short Clog with a snorting laugh. "Ravishing seafood?"

Azfall screamed at Short Clog: "Foishes, you irksome little *schwachsinnige*! Phrasel intercourse! Flowing tongue! Oral communication!"

Short Clog nudged Godfrey and gave a suggestive wink. "We know what he's been thinkin' about on his long, solitary journeys, don't we, sir?" he said and wagged his tongue lewdly.

"You shpeak with your foish!" snapped Azfall.

Godfrey explained to Short Clog that "foish" meant "voice" in the wizard's enigmatic mutation of words.

"Oh, sir, I never would have guessed!" cried the servant. "But what I want to know, my odd-uncle, is why you . . . "

Before Short Clog could finished his sentence, Azfall grabbed him by the arm and dragged him off to the side, out of earshot of Godfrey.

"Listen, stumpy," said the wizard in a hoarse whisper, "quit butting in." Azfall's voice had surprisingly, and curiously, lost its dialect, as if he were a petulant actor breaking character to harangue a pesky stage manager. Azfall held up his fingers threateningly, and made a buzzing insect noise. "Because if you don't," he spat, "I'm going to turn you into a grub!"

Short Clog cringed. Azfall smiled, smacked the little oaf

on the forehead, and strode back to Godfrey.

"Ass I vass saying! Gypsies can make even ze most cynical man veep from zare shtories *und* singing! You should have had ze foish like *der angel!*"

Godfrey erupted into questioning gibberish.

"He wants to know . . . " began Short Clog, but Azfall held up a hand for him to be silent.

"I know vut he vants," said the wizard sagaciously.

"You do?"

"Certainly! He vants to sing. He vants to shpeak. He vants to shout from ze rooftops! He vants to valk into Carthusalem *und* cry out for hiss beloved Mamooshka!"

Man and man servant gasped in unison.

Azfall smiled knowingly and said in a cryptic tone, "I know many things."

"How will you cure my master," asked Short Clog, "O queer and seemingly quite distant relative of mine?"

"I vill un-curse him. Do not ask how it iss done. You vould not undershtand, short man vith annoying questions."

Without notice or warning, the sky bedarkened. Murky, sullen clouds, the color of pitch-black appeared as from nowhere to block the daylight with their haze. Godfrey looked toward the sun. All that he could see was a muted gray disc behind the vapor, and a semicircular notch was now missing from one side.

"Strange! It's becoming night in the middle of the day!" called out Short Clog.

"Quickly, Godfrey!" prodded Azfall. "You must decide! Vill you be made whole again?"

"The moon is passing over the day-globe, sir!" observed Short Clog in stupefaction. "Which it's one of those rare 'eclairs of the sun'!"

Godfrey splacked in confusion.

"It vill cost you no money!" replied Azfall. "I told you so in *der beginn*! Not a happenny from your pocket. Not a note from your vallet! Tell me, quickly! Do you vant to sing like *der angel*?"

"What a fantastic sight, sir," said Short Clog. "It's really quite amazing. The sun is disappearing. Is it the end of the world? The dreaded 'A Pox O' Lips'?" Short Clog covered his mouth with a sweaty palm.

"Do you vant to be un-cursed?" asked the wizard.

Godfrey shouted back in the affirmative.

"Very vell," said Azfall quickly, "you must sign ziss *kontrakt* relieving me of all ze liability." From the folds of his robe he brought forth a long, blank scroll of papyrus. As he dangled it before Godfrey's eyes, the wizard hummed nonchalantly and stared into the distance—as if this were the most trivial of transactions . . . a deal he had made a thousand times before.

Godfrey, no stranger to the law, complained that there was nothing written on the paper. It was without mark of any kind.

"It iss vritten in *die geheimtinte* . . . ze invisible ink," explained Azfall calmly. A sudden gust of wind swirled around them and the scroll came alive between Azfall's fingers, flapping like a captured bat. "Anyvay!" continued the wizard with mounting urgency, "zare iss not time to read it! You must trust me!"

Lightning speared forth from the black clouds, followed by a deafening thunderclap.

"*Schnell*! Zare iss no time!"

Godfrey searched his pockets for a pen, then bellowed frantically.

"My master hasn't got a quill!" said Short Clog.

"Ziss iss unnecessary," said Azfall. "All you need iss a teeny prick!"

Short Clog glanced down at his own minuscule codpiece. A melancholy smile pulled at the corners of his mouth. "I can arrange that, sir."

Azfall revealed a long, golden needle. "Ziss iss ze prick, you silly *zwerg!*" He turned to Godfrey. "Godfrey Verrazanno! Give me *der finger!*"

Godfrey hesitated for a moment . . . a brief, but suspenseful moment. He saw many things at once: the golden needle, Azfall's shining eyes, Short Clog peering despondently at his undersized codpiece. Godfrey felt as if he stood on the edge of a great cliff; a wave of vertigo overcame his body; it was all he could do to hold out his finger. The needle pierced his skin and burned as if it were molten hot.

"Sign your *namen mit der blut,*" commanded Azfall.

Just then, a Gypsy moth landed on Godfrey's wounded finger and buzzed its wings as if trying to dry the blood. Godfrey flicked his finger but the insect would not budge.

Lymantria dispar

Finally, he held it to his mouth, pursed his lips, and sent the moth flying with a puff of air.

Godfrey signed his name just as the moon completely covered the sun. A sudden rush of wind blew in a furious wave as complete darkness descended. Azfall placed a golden tube to Godfrey's lips, and blew into it, swelling Godfrey's lungs with sickly sweet breath.

All is still in that forest, Antonio. The birds have stopped their warbling. The insects have ceased their scrabbling. Even the trees have paused the raspy rustling of their leaves. It is as quiet as the ancient, ruined and abandoned lair of the Minotaur, deep beneath the crust of Crete. This calm is akin to the serenity which enveloped the universe before God's mighty hand stirred the resting atoms of that tranquillity, and set into motion the swirl of motes which in turn assumed the multiplicity of shapes that make up our clamorous globe. And lo! Hey ho! What song through yonder blackness breaks? A man's voice is singing, and the tune is as clear and lovely as a tenor in an angel's choir.

The author must pause at this moment in the story to steady his hand with a glass of wine, for in simply contemplating the following scene, his emotions have usurped control of his body. His heart throbs. His fingers weaken. His eyes well up with tears. His spine dissolves into a warm, gelatinous rope.

"Antonio! Wine!"

Fortunately, this wine is good wine, and its benevolent properties rouse the viscera like a touch from the sun-warmed palm of a friendly, grape-harvesting maiden. This infusion of virtuous heat catches fire in the blood, puts vigor back into the vertebrae, and clears the mist from the eyes like sunshine burning off the morning dew. Another sip . . . yes . . . and his fingers are ready to get back to their work.

The inspirited moon . . . nay . . . the emboldened moon . . . nay . . . (Antonio kindly suggests "That bastard of a moon.") But I settle on, "The presumptuous moon!" Yes! The presumptuous moon, having hidden the glorious rays of his master the sun, thought better of his bold blockade and abandoned the eclipse. The forest was once again filled with light and sound.

11

THE
TRANSMUTATION

Short Clog stood blinking in the brilliant sunshine. It
seemed to him that the world was brand new, for everything, every flower and leaf and rock gleamed with an
uncommon radiance. He searched for his master, but all he
could see was the wizard (who was smoothing his mustache
with a complacent air), and a tall, handsome, sable-tressed
stranger standing on a rock, singing the loveliest song that
Short Clog had ever heard. He could not take his eyes away
from this noble-looking fellow, and he marveled unabashed-
ly at the man's appearance. The stranger was as tall as a Swede.
His flowing hair was blacker than the blackbird's wings. His
chest was broad and his chin was strong. His eyes were bold
and intelligent. Even his eyebrows were keen to look upon, for
as he sang, they capered on his brow with the brazen dexterity of miniature Cossack dancers.

The stranger (obviously a wandering Gypsy king) ceased
his song, put both hands on his sturdy hips, and let loose a
jubilant "Huzzah!"

Short Clog snapped from his reverie and shouted, "Where on earth did my master go?"

Godfrey leapt from the rock and strode manfully to the wizard. "It worked," he exclaimed joyfully. "I am a man. I can speak."

Short Clog pulled on Godfrey's sleeve. "Excuse me, sir. Have you seen a mealy, ill-faced fellow about? Sort of skinny and crooked with a slight hump?"

"It truly worked," exclaimed Godfrey. "Gramercy, good magician! You have transmogrified my mortal coil! Shifted my gross flesh—my earthly frame!"

"O, my not-so-uncle," said Short Clog, addressing the wizard, "what have you done with my master Godfrey?"

"He shtands before you," said Azfall casually.

Godfrey patted Short Clog on the head. "Hello, old friend!" Short Clog's face took on a dull expression as his brain attempted to make sense of the stranger's words. "Have I changed in countenance as well as speech?" Godfrey asked the wizard.

"Ja. Your *geist* . . . your shpirit hass been unfettered! No vun vill recognize you for, indeed, ze old cursed Godfrey hass passed avay, *und* ze new, true Godfrey iss revealed!"

"How can I thank you, sir?" asked Godfrey as he clasped the conjurer's hand and gave it a vigorous shake.

"It vass *nicht*," replied Azfall modestly.

Short Clog stared with stupefaction at Godfrey. "Can it be that my master stands before me? Why, you are quite a handsome fellow."

"I will make straight for my love. Dare I say her name?" Godfrey whispered the word "Mamooshka." Then he smiled and shouted, "Mamooshka!"

"A most excellent yell, master!" complimented Short Clog.

"Come, my friend," said Godfrey with excitement. "Let us not tarry in this place. Though I will always hold this spot dear to my heart (for here I was born anew), I must see Mamooshka at once and speak to her!"

"She vill not be zare," said the wizard softly.

Godfrey reeled as if struck. "What do you mean?"

"She iss gone."

"Run away?"

"Time hass passed vile you metamorfisheyes."

"I do not understand your paradoxical proclamation," replied Godfrey.

"More fish eyes?" asked Short Clog, then let forth a horse-laugh.

"Ze day you left ze city to come to me vass over three years ago," said the wizard.

Godfrey's jaw dropped. "Is this some kind of jest?"

"Ziss iss no *schelmenstreich*!" said the wizard. "Ziss iss no *schnippchen*! I tell ze truth. Three long years. *Und* in zat time, many strange things have happened."

"Three entire years!" said Godfrey. "Verily, if this is the truth you speak, then my adoptive father will have sorely missed us!"

"He vill not miss you," replied Azfall enigmatically.

"Howsoever can that be?"

"He never came back from hiss treep!" said Azfall.

Godfrey's face took on an expression of absolute horror. "His voyage to the Spice Islands? What happened to him? Lord-a-mercy! Tell me, man!"

"Hiss sheep keeled him!" replied the wizard.

"Killer sheep?" asked Godfrey in amazement.

"I've heard of them," piped in Short Clog knowingly. "Quite nasty. They sharpen their hooves on stones!"

"Sheep vrecked!" answered Azfall petulantly. "On *der vass-er*!" He pretended to handle a ship's wheel, and imitated the sound of strong winds and lightning. "Avast der scuppers!" he cried in a distant voice, mimicking a terrified sailor. "Cut loose der flying poopdeck!"

Godfrey slapped a palm to his forehead with sudden understanding. "*Ship* wrecked! Tell me more!"

"I cannot!" stated the wizard flatly.

"What of Mamooshka, my love?" asked Godfrey with apprehension.

"I cannot tell you," replied Azfall; and he turned his face away and grimaced as if to say, *I know what happened to her, and it is not good.*

Godfrey became frantic. "Is she hurt? Is she in some kind of trouble?"

"Zat iss for me to know *und* you to find out."

Godfrey let forth an anguished wail and cried, "O, God! What have I done?" The mellifluous power of his own utterance took him aback. He smiled, a little embarrassed, then played with his new voice, making it even deeper and more resonant. "O, dear God in Heaven! Whatever mischief have I brought about unwittingly?" came his virile moan.

"It iss not vat you haff done," said the wizard portentously. "It iss vat you vill do!"

"You speak in riddles, magician," said Godfrey sharply. "Talk plainly."

Azfall calmly stroked his beard, and his eyes turned grave and thoughtful. "Most of men's lives are shpent doing nothing," he said with disgust. "Just shitting around, eating *und* shleeping. Zat iss vat your life hass been up until now." He stared directly into Godfrey's eyes. "Now, everything zat you do vill haff great consequences for both you, *und* everybody else who comes onto your path."

"What sort of trap have I wandered into?" muttered Godfrey, for the wizard's gaze sent another one of those foreboding shivers up his spine, all the way from bung to neck-nape.

"Say, I've been thinking," mused Short Clog. "If we've been gone for three long years, how come our whiskers haven't grown?" He cleared his throat. "You know. Whiskers?"

"Vat you say, *dumm kleinen mann?*" asked the wizard.

Short Clog stroked an imaginary beard. "Beards! Which I should have a great flowing bugle of a beard. And I should reek too!" He buried his face into his armpit and took a deep snort through his nostrils. This was a grave mistake; in the instant, his flesh turned a pale shade of green. He smiled at Godfrey and Azfall with a peculiar grin, then his eyes rolled into the back of his head, and he collapsed on the ground in a little, smelly heap.

"A thousand *und* ninety five days have passed for ze rest of ze vorld," continued Azfall to Godfrey. "For you, it hass been but three *herzschlags.*" Here he beat his chest dramatically, three times in the rhythm of a heartbeat. "*Ein, zwei, drei!*"

"Whatever am I to do?" pleaded Godfrey.

"You must do vat you must do."

Godfrey nodded his head, finding inner strength with the help of the old man's words. "So be it. Indeed I feel my Gypsy blood coursing through me. I am not afraid. My voice shall be my sword. Thank you for your gift but now I must be off."

"Vait!" screeched Azfall. "Zare iss more! Zare are shtipulations."

"What do you mean? What are these 'shtipulations'?"

"Vith ziss gift of shpeech, zare are certain rules you must follow. First! If any man inzults you, you must inzult him back!"

"I do not need to prove anything to anyone who insults me," replied Godfrey good-naturedly. "Would it not be easier to simply smile and forgive—"

Azfall cut him off with a sneer. "I did not say zat you haff any choice vith zeese shtipulations! Zay vill make you shpeak vithout your vish or vill."

"I do not—"

"Second! If any man veeps, you must veep vith him!"

"What is 'veeping'?" asked Short Clog groggily. He had recovered somewhat from inhaling his own noxious odor and was propped up on an elbow, staring bleary-eyed at Godfrey and Azfall.

"Cry! Ze tears of sorrow!"

"Oh! *Veeping!*" exclaimed Short Clog.

"Finally! Ven you see your true love, Mamooshka . . . " He paused dramatically, then smiled. "You vill be shtricken vith ze old curse."

"'Zounds, man!" cried Godfrey, unable to contain his emotions. "This last shtipulation is insufferable!"

Azfall turned and started to walk away. "Zat iss all, now I must be on my vay. *Guten tag.*"

Godfrey's manly chest trembled in agony. "The old curse! With the one I love! But that ruins everything!"

Azfall whirled on him angrily. "It iss in *der kontrakt* vich you signed!" His voice took on a cruel, wheedling tone. "Vould you like me to reep it oop? I could just reep it oop *und* everything goes to nermal again."

"Nay," said Godfrey. "I cannot bear to go back to nermal. But how cruel. How can it work thus so cruelly? To be so close to telling her of my love. Agads! 'Tis demoniacal!"

"You vill find a vay."

As Azfall passed Short Clog, the dazed servant sat up and waved at him.

"Good-bye un-uncle," he said.

Azfall sneered and waved back sarcastically; then he stalked into the forest and vanished like smoke.

Godfrey sat on the rock and struck a thoughtful pose. "Well. Now I feel I have entered the world of the living. No longer will my life be spent in thought alone. I perceive I am on the cusp of strange things. I'faith! Your uncle is a remarkable man, Short Clog."

Short Clog smiled in agreement. Then his brow furrowed,

and he chewed on his lip. "Except . . . errr . . . that wasn't my uncle."

Godfrey frowned. "Whatever can you mean?"

"Yes. Now that I come to think of it, my uncle was hanged by an angry mob several years ago. Strange that I forgot. I've never seen *that* man before in my life."

"How come this Short Clog is such an idiot?" cries Antonio. "How come he thought this magician was his own uncle?"

"Because the magician cast a spell on Short Clog and made him think that he was his uncle so as to lure Godfrey to the forest."

"When did *this* happen?" he asks in astonishment.

I explain that it happened before Chapter Seven, in the scene where Short Clog comes to his master and tells him about the magician for the very first time.

Antonio scrunches up his face.

"It happened off-stage," I continue. "Everything does not have to take place in front of our eyes. It is a literary technique."

Antonio raises his eyebrows and says with condescension, "Ah, a 'technique,' *signore*. Very educational. But I think I would have enjoyed it more if I had actually seen the magician casting the spell. You know? Sprinkling moon dust in Short Clog's eyes or whatever. It would make Short Clog seem like less of a *cazzo*-head."

"He is a *cazzo*-head," I exclaim. "He is a completely unconscionable nincompoop."

Antonio rolls his eyes. "Now, *signore*, all servants aren't bumbling idiots like this here Short Clog. I may have my own faults, frequent toast burning being one that is uncannily similar to this fictional character. But it just feels like Shorty here should be a little wiser. A little funnier. Maybe even a little taller. Otherwise, it sort of turns him into a . . ." he studies the ceiling, searching for his thoughts. "Ah, what's that *Inglese* phrase you taught me?" He claps his hands. "That's right. A 'hock-kneed clitchy.'"

"A hackneyed cliché," I say, correcting him.

"Yes! That's it!"

"Shall we continue with the story?" I query, for I am tired of humoring Antonio's budding career as a story editor. He secretly desires Short Clog to be the dashing hero but I will have none of that!

Antonio scratches his chin. "There's one more thing. At the end of the last chapter, you said that the magician 'vanished like smoke.'"

"Yes?"

"Well, at the end of the first chapter, after the nasty witch stole Godfrey from the Gypsy jugglers, you said that she too, 'disappeared like smoke.'"

"So?"

Antonio pretends to be modest. "I'm no writer, signore, but this 'smoke' metaphor, used twice so close together in the story, seemed a little, well . . . lazy."

I can't help but sigh. He really has been listening to me these many years as I have expounded upon writing and the elements of style. Unwittingly, I have created that most wretched, odious, and vile of all creatures; worse than any muck-dwelling maggot or louse-ridden rat: a critic. "So what would you have me write instead?" I ask, trying not to show my annoyance.

"In the second instance of the magician disappearing, I would say that he vanished like oats in a horse's manger."

"That is a terrible metaphor," I cry. "Can you not see? It must be instantaneous—like the snap of your fingers. He is there and then *Poof*! he is gone. A horse tediously munching his way through a bag of oats does not convey celerity of dispatch."

Antonio stares at the wall, lost in thought. "He vanished like pastry in a fat man's house," he mumbles. "He vanished like . . . "

"Let us get on with the story," I say and begin to read the next chapter.

The Way Back

12

THE ROYAL SCAMP

After leaving the strange healer who in no way resembled anyone from Short Clog's family, master and servant walked through the forest in the direction of the city. Godfrey's misgivings about the odd magician were quickly dispelled by the delight that he experienced in exercising his newfound ability; he named each thing he saw, simply to have the pleasure of the word rolling off his tongue.

"'Tree,' Short Clog!" he shouted happily. "'Rabbit,' my friend!"

Short Clog smiled with joy, for it warmed his heart to see his master so jolly. "I can't wait to get back to the city," he beamed. "I think we should head straight to the bazaar so that you can purchase a camel."

"One dromedary, please," said Godfrey, rolling the two *r*'s in "dromedary" with the pleasant burr of a Caledonian. He stopped and held up one hand dramatically. "Good Short Clog, my eldest, dearest friend . . . how gladsome and coltish I feel at present. I am overjoyed to be alive—a sensation that I have never had before. My past life was a famine . . . and now it is suddenly a feast. An apple tree laden with fruit. A pail of milk thick with cream, ready for the skimming."

"Mmmm . . ." hummed Short Clog while rubbing his belly. "Apples an' cream!"

"To you I owe all thanks," said Godfrey.

"Oh, you're welcome, sir," replied Short Clog with cheer. "It's a tickle in the old bag and basket to hear you make such lovely chin music. But," he continued blithely, "I'm not really your friend. Not *literally*, that is."

"Whatever do you mean?"

"Well, I was purchased at a very tender age by your adoptive father to serve as your companion. Naturally, as people of my rank generally do, as you got older I moved into the role of your servant, which is what I am now."

"Have I been a ruthless master? Do you hate me?" Godfrey smiled at the sound of his own voice. "Do you loathe me terribly?" he said, putting particular emphasis on the words "loathe" and "terribly."

"On the contrary," said Short Clog as he picked his nostril. "I pretty much do nothin' at all except sit around eatin' as you can see by my voluptuously protruding belly. I merely wanted you to know that in social spheres, you and I would not be considered friends, you being the adopted son of a great merchant and me, the real and true son of a tongue scraper."

"A what?"

"My father has a stall in the market. He scrapes men's tongues."

"What on earth for?"

"It's just something one does when one is of a lower class. He also picks ears."

"And people pay him for this service?"

"They most certainly do. He's an expert. You wouldn't

want a novice scraping your tongue or picking your ear with a shiny metal device, now would you?"

"No, not at all. But . . . " Godfrey smiled and laughed. "'Shiny metal device.'"

"What, sir?"

"I merely love the way that sentence sounds," reflected Godfrey. "Oh! That's good too. 'Sentence sounds.'"

"Here's one, sir," said Short Clog, helping Godfrey along with his word-fun. "Porridge and gruel."

"'Porridge and gruel,'" repeated Godfrey with delight.

"Or, how about . . . turds and turnips and tantalizing titties."

"'Turds and turnips and tantalizing titties,'" said Godfrey with glee.

"Buttocks, sir."

"'Buttocks!'" cried Godfrey with enthusiasm.

Godfrey and Short Clog were so thoroughly occupied with their amusing word game, they did not notice that someone had stepped stealthily from the undergrowth and was now standing in the road directly in front of them, blocking their path. This masked and hooded form assumed a dangerous stance—hand sinister on hip, sword arm hanging loosely at the side—and regarded the vociferators with a dark, threatening glare.

"Nest of spicery," squealed Short Clog.

"'Nest of spicery!'" aped Godfrey.

"Mutual entertainment."

"'Mutual . . . ho ho! Entertainment!'"

"Weeelaaaahhhhh," screamed Short Clog as he caught sight of the dangerous-looking stranger.

"I do not know about that one," said Godfrey. "I have never tried to imitate the sound of a copulating gibbon, but I will give it a go." He cleared his throat and started vocal exercises.

"Nay, sir," explained Short Clog with a laugh. "It was a cry of fear—a startled exclamation of terror."

"I thought it was an animal impression," said Godfrey.

"Hardly," snorted Short Clog.

"What are you afraid of then?" asked Godfrey.

"That lowering, sabre-wielding, murderous-looking fellow blocking the path," replied Short Clog.

Godfrey's eyes followed Short Clog's trembling finger. At the sight of the interloper, Godfrey gave a start, but he did not scream. Rather, he spoke boldly: "Who are you, good sir, to astonish two unarmed men in this dusky light?"

Faster than a lightning crack, the stranger drew his sword and pointed the tip at Godfrey's nose.

"Hello, sir. Nice evening," said Short Clog, trying his best to sound pleasant.

"Your money," rasped the highwayman.

"Excuse me?" asked Godfrey.

"Give me all your money," repeated the brigand.

"Money?" asked Short Clog.

"Do not speak! Money! I want your money!"

"I do not have any," answered Godfrey. "Neither does my servant."

"Don't play games with me!" spat the thief. "I'd slit your throat and leave you dead for no more than looking at me the wrong way."

"That is not very benevolent," replied Godfrey, incensed at the robber's rough tone.

"Benevolent?" roared the outraged crook. "Don't you know who I am?"

"No," replied Godfrey, shaking his head.

"No, sir," piped in Short Clog.

"You are strangers, then?" asked the thief, a hint of relief in his voice.

"Not exactly. We have lived here all our lives."

"All our lives, sir," added Short Clog.

The bandit was thunderstruck. "You've lived here all of your lives and . . . and you've never heard of 'the Dim Avenger'?"

"No. Not really," said Godfrey, stifling a yawn.

"Who's that, sir?" asked Short Clog.

"Why me, of course!" spat the Dim Avenger.

"Are you stupid?" asked Godfrey.

"Are you insulting me?!" The Dim Avenger's blade shook with rage.

"No, not at all," said Godfrey. "It is merely your unfortunate name: 'The Dim Avenger.' It implies someone who is unwise."

"Sap-headed," added Short Clog. "Thick of skull."

"Inept," confirmed Godfrey.

The Dim Avenger stared in amazement at the two men and his mouth opened and closed in anger. He stomped the ground and attacked an innocent fern, hacking it to pieces, crying: "I am anything but inept! I have been at this job for three years and I have never been caught. There is a price on my head worth a fortune. I'm notorious. I'm called 'the Dim Avenger' because I only attack at dusk." The Dim Avenger turned his attention back to Godfrey and Short Clog, peering anxiously at their faces, searching desperately for fear in their eyes; but they were both irritatingly serene.

"Why only at dusk?" asked Godfrey.

"Yes. Why, sir?" asked Short Clog.

"Because if you go out attacking in broad daylight, you'll be recognized. And if you go in the pitch-dark, you can't see anything. This is the perfect time of night."

"Oh, I *see*," said Godfrey thoughtfully. He stared into space and massaged his throat. After a long pause he asked, "Did you make this name up, or was it just *thrust* upon you?"

Short Clog had been thinking along the same lines, and

he queried, "Why not call yourself 'the *Dusky* Avenger'?"

"The what?" blurted the Dim Avenger.

"The *Dusky* Avenger!" repeated Short Clog.

Godfrey smiled. "I like the sound of that." He cleared his throat, then said the name with gusto. "'The *Dusky* Avenger!'"

"Be silent!" cried the Dim Avenger.

"Which you could carry a lanthorn," remarked Short Clog as he scratched the under crease of his codpiece.

"What are you talking about?" roared the Dim Avenger in frustration.

"So you can see at night," clarified Short Clog.

"If I'm carrying a lighted lanthorn, my victims will be able to see *me* coming, you simpleton!"

Short Clog let forth a patronizing chuckle. "That's why, my lad, you blacken the glass with paint so none of the light escapes from the lanthorn." The Dim Avenger and Godfrey stared at Short Clog, astonished at his stupidity. Short Clog smiled knowingly and continued: "My second cousin, Corkin Clog-Snively, was a notorious Lincolnshire bandit. They called his band of thieves 'the Blackened Lanthorn Gang.' Unfortunately, he fell in a ravine one dark night and landed on top of his lanthorn. He burst into flames and was never heard from again."

Godfrey caught the Dim Avenger's eye and made an apologetic face. The Dim Avenger scowled and commanded them to hand over their money.

"I told you before," said Godfrey in a pious tone, "we have nothing but the clothes on our backs and the souls in our bodies and you cannot steal them now, can you?"

Short Clog gave Godfrey a friendly nudge with his elbow as if to say, "Nice retort."

"I think I'll just kill you then." The Dim Avenger held his sword to Godfrey's throat. "Scared?"

"By no manner of means."

"Rubbish! I heard you gulp!"

"I am wanting of drink," replied Godfrey imperturbably.

"You're terrified of me." The Dim Avenger smiled triumphantly.

"Not by a damn sight. I feel sorry for you."

"Aha! Ha ha! Sorry for me?! I feel sorry for you!" The Dim Avenger paused briefly, then asked in an insecure tone why Godfrey felt sorry for him.

"Because no one should live off the fruits of another."

"I am a Royal Scamp," stated the bandit with pride.

"That means he only steals from flush coves," explained Short Clog to Godfrey.

Godfrey chewed his lip thoughtfully, then said, "Even though you only steal from the rich, you are still committing a vile act."

"Do you want me to kill you?" queried the Dim Avenger.

"Why would I want you to kill me? That is a witless request for someone to make of a stranger, 'Pleased to meet you. Would you mind killing me?' You, my friend, need a lesson in xenodochiality."

Short Clog nudged Godfrey again. "What's zero . . . duck . . . ability?"

"Benevolence towards strangers," answered Godfrey. "From two Greek words, *xeno* meaning 'strangers' and the verb root *do*—"

"You've just about said almost your very last word," interrupted the Dim Avenger.

Godfrey felt a puzzling sense of calm. At first he had been startled by the sight of this dangerous criminal. But now, as he looked The Dim Avenger up and down, he felt a sense of . . . well . . . disdain. He was not afraid of this man at all; in fact, he was anxious to put this ruffian in his place.

"You are undeniably brave, threatening an unarmed, defenseless man," he said with disgust. "You are akin to a child tossing pebbles at a caged and truculent lion."

The Dim Avenger scoffed, "And you are a ferocious lion? Ha!"

"I have Gypsy blood in my veins, thou frightener of baby snails, and that is hot enough blood for several men." And he assumed a defiant stance with arms akimbo.

"Here, fool," sneered the Dim Avenger, tossing him his sword.

Short Clog marveled at his master's reaction, for instead of fumbling and dropping the glinting blade, he plucked the haft deftly from the air and whisked it about with the grace of a master swordsman.

The Dim Avenger drew another sword from inside his cloak and circled Godfrey like a mongoose.

"You'd better be careful, sir," cautioned Short Clog. "You don't know what he might have left under that cloak."

"Do not worry yourself, friend, for I will not fight this stranger," stated Godfrey magnanimously. "I refuse to harm another living thing." He stabbed the sword into the ground and let go of it; the weight of the haft made the blade sway back and forth like a living thing, anxious for the fight. "There is more than enough pernicious death-dealing and bloodletting in this world," continued Godfrey in a saintly tone. "Neither his jibes nor his railing nor his intended blows will sway me to violence or hurtfulness of any kind. Rather I will chastise him so roughly and with such conviction that he will see the errors of his ways, weep copious tears, and swear to give up this execrable career."

"Bachelor's son," sneered the Dim Avenger.

"Back-door usher!" cursed Godfrey like a man possessed. He covered his lips with his hand and stared in amazement at Short Clog. *What had just happened?* The crude and discourteous insult had erupted from his mouth as if it had been spoken by another entity. "'Spinkies! What did I say?" he implored in a gentle voice.

"I seem to have touched a nerve," taunted the Dim Avenger. "Thou cow-hearted bung-nipper!"

Godfrey jerked like a mad puppet and yelled violently, "Cloak-twitcher!" He took a step, stumbled, put both hands on his chest as if to contain himself. His voice softened again. "By the holy loaf, what is happening to me?"

"Call me cloak-twitcher, will ye?" seethed the Dim Avenger. "I'll give ye a basting ye shan't forget till Saint Rufus' Day." He cracked the knuckles of his sword hand.

Short Clog slapped himself on the forehead and exclaimed, "It's the magician, sir! Remember the first *shtipulation*?"

"Yes!" Godfrey quoted the old man: "'If you are inzulted you vill inzult back.'"

"Let us do battle," goaded the Dim Avenger. "Or does your funk-arse chafe from the multitude of fartleberries clinging there?"

"Lully prigger!" cried Godfrey.

The Dim Avenger let forth a shocked gasp and squinted at Godfrey, his eyes all a-swivel.

"O, sir," explained Short Clog to his master in a cautioning tone, "accusing a Royal Scamp of stealing wet linen is the worst insult you can offer him!"

Godfrey turned to Short Clog and stated in an amazed, yet controlled manner: "I know this, friend. But I cannot eschew his scorn. Not only do I verbally abuse the thief against my will, but an overpowering desire to engage in angry battle with him burns inside of me like the flame in a glass furnace. *Iracundia inflammatum esse*: 'To be fired with rage.' I cannot control myself!"

The Dim Avenger smiled ruthlessly and said with derision, "Shut your maw and fight, you spindle-shanked-Latin-spewing-hen-spleened-louse-ridden-shirt-lifter!"

Godfrey could not hold himself back any longer. He pulled the sword from the ground, yelled, "Kiss my arse!" and attacked the Dim Avenger with vicious blows.

"You fight well, for a monkey," needled the thief.

"Your strokes are executed brightly for one so dim," countered the accountant.

Short Clog watched in amazement at the speed of the battle. The swords clanged and scraped and clashed. The affronts came at a stichomythic pace.

"Chucklehead!"

"Lackwit!"

"Dung flicker!"

"Gormless turd minion!"

"Your mother was a left-handed trollop!"

"Your father was a club-footed pimp!"

"Is that your codpiece or your dear auntie's thimble?"

"Is that your breath or did a dead ape just fart?"

"Never in my life—"

"Never in *my* life—"

"Have I seen—"

"Have I smelled—"

"Anything—"

"So—"

"Startlingly—"

"Extraordinarily—"

"Ridiculous—"

"Repugnant—"

"As—"

"Thou!"

And then, when least expected, it was over: the Dim Avenger trapped Godfrey's sword hilt on his own handle's hilt catcher and wrenched the sword from Godfrey's magically adroit, yet unstudied hand. The highwayman pressed the blade of his sword against the side of Godfrey's neck. The two panted for breath and eyed one another with newfound respect.

"You fought well for a muttonhead."

"*Cacafuego.*"

"And brave too. I could kill you with a flick of my wrist and yet you are still insulting."

"I can't help it," stated Godfrey truthfully.

"Because of your hot blood?" asked the Dim Avenger.

"Something like that."

"I like you. You've got *sprezzatura.* I shall spare your life." The highwayman sheathed his sword and held out his right hand to Godfrey. "How shall the Dim Avenger know you if ever we meet again in an obscurely lit place?"

Godfrey took the Dim Avenger's hand tentatively in his own. "I am known only as . . . " he stared into the darkness and thought for a moment, "as 'the Gypsy.'"

"Well, Gypsy. Until we meet again. Adieu." The Dim Avenger turned on one heel, strode away into the darkness, and disappeared like smo . . . Errr . . . disappeared like . . . a thing that vanishes before one's eyes unexpectedly.

"Wait, you left your sword," called out Godfrey, but the mysterious stranger was gone.

"What a spectacle sir!" said Short Clog. "I was on the edge of my seat. I thought my heart would burst, it was beating so. Where did you learn to fight like that?"

"I don't know! I've never picked up a sword in my life."

Godfrey absentmindedly held his right hand to his mouth. There was a faint smell there. An odor that must have come from the Dim Avenger's gloved hand when he shook it. A fragrance. Yes. An appealing scent. He couldn't quite place it. The aroma was familiar, and his heart felt oddly unsettled.

"You should have had Godfrey kill the Dim Avenger," states Antonio. "Then he would have become a hero when he got back to town and Mamooshka would have fallen in love with him. That's the kind of story I like."

I rub my tired eyes and sigh. "Antonio, my dear, artless, beetleheaded, unripened slobberwit. Cannot you see? The Dim Avenger is going to play a crucial part in the story."

"A crucial part in the story?"

"Yes. Crucial. Why do you think we spent so much time developing the character and the relationship with Godfrey."

"I don't know," he replies obtusely.

"We cannot go killing off the major characters on a whim."

Antonio scratches his head, then examines the pate-crust under his nail. "Well, I don't want to advise you how to tell your story, because you're doing a fine job. All I'm wondering is when is Godfrey going to meet Mamooshka and . . . " He grins obscenely and makes a bawdy gesture.

"Shall I proceed with the reading?"

"O, please."

"I will not continue until you stop that indecorous pantomime," I assert.

Antonio smiles impishly and plops down on the bed.

I

THE FOP AND HIS DRUDGE

P urvious Grugno Papmero, a pasty-faced coxcomb and
the sixth son of the *podestà* of Carthusalem, stood posing in front of the great doorway to the House of
Verrazanno, dabbing effetely at the sweat on his upper lip.
Indeed, it was a scaldingly hot day in the city; but Purvious
had been protected from this heat all afternoon: he had been
carried through the streets in his luxurious palanquin, fanned
and misted continuously by Loutronio, his manservant, and
now stood under the cooling shade of a great umbrella held
by that same unctuous creature. Even so, Purvious felt terribly
cranky from the heat; he cursed Mamooshka under his breath.

"She should be made to come to *my* house," he whined.
"Heh! It's just too hot!"

Purvious was a notorious clotheshorse. Today, his slender
frame was dressed in an expensive suit cut from the finest silk.
His feet and hands were encased in the costliest leather made
from the skins of unborn goats. His codpiece was gilded like

The Podestà As A Youth

the proverbial lily. Unfortunately, he had absolutely no taste or style. Thus, all of the precious materials went to waste. The suit was a garish yellow decorated with great red pinwheels, the neck and wrists bordered with vast, absurd ruffles. His purple gloves and boots sported ludicrous tassels with tiny bells that tinkled when he walked (quite seldom) or when he gestured (all the time). The codpiece . . . well . . . let us say that the size of that object could only have been ordered with the most wishful thinking in mind. All together, Purvious resembled a very wealthy pantomime clown. His chalky pallor and rouged lips added to this impression.

Nevertheless, Purvious fancied himself the handsomest fellow in the city, quite possibly the country, perhaps even the world. He could stare at himself for hours in his dressing room mirror and practice making the coy gestures and wry smiles that had been taught to him by a cadre of insinuating Italian tutors—experts in the art of the courtier.

Though Purvious was the youngest of six boys, his mother doted upon him and spared no expense from her personal allowance to spoil him rotten. Why did she love him so, this cretinous scrub, this posturing jackanape, this self-satisfied bird-brain bereft of personality, wit, and flair? Quite simply, he was the only one of her children to be born without a hideous facial deformity, dubbed "The Papmero Snout." This nose was famous throughout the region for its grotesque resemblance to a pig's sniffer. The Papmero men, you see, did not possess nostrils like other humans; in fact, they were wholly deprived, dispossessed, denuded of nasal phallangi. Instead, they had two gaping, dark, hair-filled holes above their lip. It looked as if somebody had sliced off the tips of their nozzles, à la Tycho Brahe, with a dueling sword. Is it any wonder how, when compared to his swinish brothers and father, Purvious seemed an Adonis to his traumatized mother? (It might be recalled that during the early reign of our King

George, a pugified Papmero was wed to an inbred Hapsburg—they of the famous malformed bulldog-muzzle mandibles. Needless to say, their resulting offspring were miniature catastrophes.)

At first glance, Purvious appeared to be an attractive fellow in a girlish sort of way, with his high cheekbones, yellow, curling hair, and full lips. Indeed, this writer has often seen these effeminate, juvenile features develop into a handsome adult. Purvious, however, had passed that crucial age when a man's character is still malleable. His only companions had been oily-tongued servants and cringing courtiers. A life of lounging had stunted his mind and shrunk his heart. His father should have sent him away to a rough country where he could have served as page to some honest knight; through hardships and tests of courage, he might have learned the code of chivalry. But this was not to be. His soul was like a scroggling apple that withers in the heat of summer, yet remains living upon the stem, a mockery of the wholesome fruit growing around it. His wretched nature oozed from his expressions, eyes, manner, and voice, and ruined any physical beauty that might have existed. Purvious saw himself as a noble lord amongst men, a graceful gentleman with style and poise. Mamooshka Verrazanno, the object of his unwanted affections, saw him as a mincing toad, an uncouth looby devoid of substance and personality. Besides all of that, he had bad breath and toenail fungus.

Loutronio, Purvious' pinched-face butler, had served his master for ten years. In that time he had become an expert on potions for the remedy of obnoxious breath and salves for the cure of decomposing nails. Loutronio had been trained from birth in one of the finest manservant schools in all of Europe. He was a born lackeyjackal and lickspittle; thus, his employment with Purvious had been completely fulfilling. He was attentive to his master's every need, watching over him like a bird with chick. All the way from the *podestà's* palace, Loutronio had scampered alongside the palanquin, whisking his lord with a Chinese fan and spraying his face with rose water.

At this moment, he was concerned that Purvious might be suffering from heat stroke, so he ordered the exhausted bearers to blow gentle air onto their master's neck. Then Loutronio pulled a handkerchief, scented with essential oils, from a little box he wore round his neck and dabbed at his master's sweating upper lip.

"I knew Mamooshka before her father was lost at sea," said Purvious, regarding the Verrazanno crest above the gate (a chubby lad astride a porpoise). "She was a most wild, untamed girl. Both of us shared mutual friends but there was absolutely no love between us. She vexed me, Loutronio! She mocked me and chided me and belittled me in front of my friends with such skill and determination I was helpless to defend myself."

"O, master!" scolded Loutronio. "What fault could she find in yourself, my charming and most witty lord?"

"I told you once before, knothead," said Purvious. "She is very clever." He slapped at Loutronio's lip-mopping hand. "Oh, there were times I could have choked her dead! But I held myself back. I knew a day would come when I would settle the score with Mamooshka. And now, my day *has* come. Her sinister uncle, who inherited the family shipping business upon his brother's death, is indeed a wicked fellow. His strange and lascivious vices are well known . . . and he is respected for them throughout the city. He has wrestled with Mamooshka's spirit and broken it. For three years, she has lived cloistered, under guard, in this house. Now, her uncle has sent out word that she is of marriageable age, and the suitors have been prowling about like anxious dogs. Unfortunately for them, they will never be able to compete

with my grace, my intelligence, nor my lineage. I am the
podestà's son and it is manifest that I will be given her hand in
marriage. Thus shall I have my revenge! For in my house, the
sufferings, the berating, the humiliation she has spent in her
uncle's care will seem like a fond holiday."

"Delicious, lord Purvious."

"It is not out of cruelty that I make this pledge. For it is
inherent in man to break wild things and bend them to his
will. If women stop knowing their place, the natural laws
which govern our world will be thrown into disarray and
mankind will be subject to many great woes and . . . " He
paused, searching vainly for the proper *bon mot*, and ended
lamely with, "and such and such." Purvious' voice took on a
plaintive, pathetic tone. "Besides, I need the money: being a
Duke's sixth son is a wretched position to be in. I wouldn't
wish my hard life on the lowliest, grubbiest peasant. Five older
brothers, Loutronio! Five terribly healthy older brothers." He
held a dainty hand to his heart. Tinkle, tinkle, chimed the little glove-bells. "I'm weeping. Right here. Right inside here."

"My poor, poor lord," cooed Loutronio. "How coura-
geous you are."

"This is insufferable. I feel a cry coming on," said
Purvious. "See my tear? See it?"

"I do, my lord. It is a perfect, pearl-shaped droplet."

Purvious wept.

Whilst this insipid conversation was taking place, Godfrey
and Short Clog approached the Verrazanno house from a tiny
street called Monk's Alley.

"Zim Zam Street and our old home is beyond this corner,
Short Clog," said Godfrey coming to a stop. He was overcome
with a sense of trepidation.

"Master, I must away now to see to my father in the marketplace," said Short Clog. "I am anxious to know how he has
fared these three long years."

"Very well. I shall make myself known to my adoptive father's half-brother and learn what I can of the magician's foreboding words."

Short Clog scampered off in the direction of the bazaar. Godfrey took a deep breath, exhaled, then strode resolutely around the corner. When he entered the square in front of the Verrazanno estate, he saw the curious tableau created by Purvious and his minions. Godfrey at once took them to be a troupe of *commedia dell' arte* players: a yellow-clad, pale-faced Harlequin was bawling like a mad thing; four half-naked men, playing the parts of the clown's palanquin bearers, were blowing down his neck and sleeves; and a tall, prim-faced fellow, obviously the silly servant, or *zanni* character, was fussing at the clown's tears with a handkerchief.

Without cause or warning, Godfrey burst into tears. He bellowed like a moppet who had been scolded for stealing pie. Salty drops rolled down his cheeks. He glanced at the group in front of the gate and realized they were all staring at him: the bearers with curious eyes, the servant with a stern glare, and the yellow clown with an expression of amazed contempt. The clown let forth another choking gasp and again, Godfrey heard himself imitate the other man's sobs. The clown stomped his feet. "Why am I crying?" Godfrey asked aloud, and then the magician's words echoed in his head: "*If any man veeps, you must veep vith him.*"

"The villain parodies my tears!" proclaimed Purvious incredulously. "He fleers me! He's a fleering knave. A knave who fleers. I loathe him terribly. At this moment, I have discovered the man I hate more than any other on this earthly sphere. If I had sharp teeth like a wolf, I would chew him with relish."

"There, there, my lord," murmured Loutronio.

Godfrey realized with embarrassment that these men were not actors. He felt that he must apologize to the yellow-clad cove for seeming to mock him; so he strode up to the strangers and bowed low.

"Good day, sirs," saluted Godfrey.

"Good day," replied Loutronio in his most practiced snide tone.

Purvious stared up at the sky and sniffed angrily.

"Good day, sir," said Godfrey, addressing Purvious. "You too were included in my greeting."

Loutronio took a step forward and answered again for his master. His voice had an edge to it. "Good day."

Godfrey nodded toward Purvious. "Is your mate here a foreigner? A mute perhaps? I know much of this terrible affliction. Perhaps I can help."

Loutronio burst out angrily, "He is not my mate, nor a mute—he is my master, and with meager men he is mum!"

Godfrey bowed again. "I am indeed sorry to have presumed him to be of my own standing. Now, if you will forgive me, I will knock upon this door in front of which you loiter."

"We do not loiter, sirrah! We come to meet the master of the house."

"Then shall we make together through the portal, for, after knocking, I intended to pass within and meet the master of the house myself."

"It is not in the interest of my lord to pass through doors with men of unfamiliar origin."

"I apologize once again. Will you pass before me and I will enter straight up behind?"

"That will not do at all," said Loutronio acrimoniously. "My lord was here first, my lord shall pass through first, and you will not enter straight up our behinds. You will wait on the steps until after we have finished and departed and then you may play at your knocking game."

"I am sorry, but I cannot allow that to happen," replied Godfrey with absolute calm.

"Sir, you are in terrible danger of impending trouble!" answered Loutronio.

"Tell me something," asked Godfrey. "Are there any laws which say one man may enter a private home whilst another may not?"

"It is an unwritten law," replied Loutronio.

"May I see this unwritten law?" queried Godfrey.

Loutronio and Purvious turned to each other and rolled their eyes. *Was this fellow an utter rube?* Loutronio smirked and licked his lips.

"One cannot see an unwritten law," he said smugly, "because it is invisible to the naked eye."

"Ha!" exclaimed Purvious and lifted his chin toward the sun again.

But Godfrey was undeterred. In truth, he was feeling a little irked by these two stuffed shirts. His voice was full of pepper as he spoke: "If you have no solid proof of this unwritten law then I cannot accept it for I live in the world of truth and fact. Now, pass through the door in front of me, or with me, or behind me, or stand aside and let me be on my way, for I care not to waste dear time bickering over trifles."

"Trifles?" mouthed Purvious.

"Trifles!" spat Loutronio.

Godfrey strode to the great gate and knocked soundly on the portal. An instant later, a small door at the top opened, and a sad-eyed, slope-headed, unintelligent looking man poked out his head and stared morosely at Godfrey.

"Yes?" asked the servant.

"Hello, Drapslod," said Godfrey with a brilliant smile. He had always liked Drapslod, the doorkeeper, and he was glad to see him still employed after these three long years. "Please tell your master that Godfrey, adopted son of Zalman Verrazanno, wishes to see the master of the house."

Drapslod, without a hint of recognition on his dull face,

disappeared; the door slammed shut behind him.

"I see you are most welcome," snickered Loutronio.

He nudged Godfrey aside and was about to knock on the portal when, all at once, the doors swung open; Loutronio lost his balance, tottered on the steps with flailing arms, lurched, and finally, tumbled backwards onto the dirty, dungy street upon his deferential derriere.

14

THE HAIRLESS HALF-UNCLE

Standing on the threshold was Egelbun, an obscenely fat man with a pumpkin-shaped head. Upon his gourd was perched an ill-fitting wig of long blond hair. His blotchy cheeks were flushed as if from some strenuous activity. But in truth he had just come from gorging himself on roasted songbirds and jellied cow hooves. The remnants of his greasy meal coated his chin like mule slobber. His ferret eyes darted about nervously as he searched the small crowd for Godfrey. His glance flicked from the bearers (still blowing on their master) to Purvious (making a great show of bowing insignificantly) to Loutronio (picking dung off the seat of his pantaloons and scowling), and finally came to rest on Godfrey (who was staring in disgust at the fat man's oily face). Egelbun had never met his half-brother's adopted son; but since the handsome young man with the raven hair was the only person on the street whom he did not recognize, Egelbun took a chance that he was the one.

"Godfrey! Godfrey!" he shrieked as he minced up to him and made a great show of taking his nephew's hand and clasping it to his gelatinous bosom.

"That is I. Godfrey. Adopted son of Zalman Verrazanno." Godfrey pulled his hand away from Egelbun's moist palms, then surreptitiously wiped it dry on his pant leg.

"Is it so? Could it be so?" shrilled Egelbun. He tried to look pleased, but he was a very poor actor and his insincerity was quite evident. "But you are dead?" he added, attempting a gay laugh; it came out as a ghastly screech.

"Not dead," answered Godfrey. "I have been on holiday."

"How? Why?" asked Egelbun frantically. He regained his composure, smoothed his hair, and said lovingly, "The gods have answered my prayers!" He held a hand to his heart. "I am your Egelbun uncle, your brother's adopted half-father." He jerked, then flerked, then tried again. "I am your half-uncle's father, Egelbun, the adopted brother." He paused and scratched his head; the wig moved several inches back and forth. "I am . . . " Egelbun stared blankly into space.

"He is Egelbun, your half-adopted uncle's father," chimed in Loutronio, then frowned as he realized what he had said was not exactly right.

Purvious blurted out, "He is your aunt's mother's father's adopted cousin's . . . " then threw up his hands in disgust and said, "Oh, whatever!"

"You are my adopted father's half-brother, Egelbun," stated Godfrey placidly.

Loutronio, Purvious, and Egelbun cried out together: "Thank you!"

"I see you are a man of much discernment," said Egelbun in a sycophantic tone. "We have never met but I know of the love my half-uncle . . . "

"Brother . . . " corrected Godfrey.

"Brother had for you, his adopted father . . . " Egelbun

slapped himself in the face. "What a prize, sir! What a surprise! And how long will you stay in our beautiful city?"

"Just long enough to settle certain accounts."

"Accounts!" yelled Egelbun, his voice rising to a blore. "Accounts, you say! Aha ha ha! Accounts! Heigh-ho ha ha! Accounts! Eh?"

"To verify certain rumors," persisted Godfrey.

"Rumors!" Sweat poured from under Egelbun's wig. "O heh ha ha! O ho ha ha!"

Loutronio stepped forward and addressed Egelbun. "Sir?"

Egelbun turned and stared at Loutronio and Purvious. He slapped a hand to his cheek and said, "Ah! The Vizier's nephew."

"The *podestà's* son," replied Loutronio pertly.

"Eh? Certainly! Yes. How wonderful. I forgot you were coming. See here! My half-brother's adopted son." Egelbun paused, wondering if he had said it right, and coming to the conclusion that he finally had, let forth a tremendous sigh. "Wonderful, isn't it?"

"Ho, quite so," said Purvious, rolling his eyes.

"Yes. Yes," muttered Egelbun, eyeing Godfrey. "A handsome man he is too! Quite handsome! Very handsome. He will be a most welcome pest—" Egelbun jerked, coughed, "a most welcome *guest* in my house."

Purvious smiled slantendicular. "I seem to remember, dear Egelbun, that upon the disappearance of your late brother, the will stated that Godfrey, the adoptive son, was to inherit all of Zalman's vast fortune."

"Very true. So true. Did you know of this, Godfrey?" Egelbun looked as if he were going to be sick.

"Yes. He told me so the day before he left on his fateful journey."

Egelbun started to cough. "Fateful! O . . . (cough) Yes! (hack) Tragic!"

Purvious grinned maliciously and said: "When Godfrey could not be found, the estate passed on to you, good sir Egelbun. But now that Godfrey has seemingly returned, the household and all its goods shall legally pass back into his hands."

"Certainly! Certainly they will, good lord Purvious. Thank you for bringing up this delicate subject which would have taken me hours, no, perhaps days to poach . . . " Egelbun twitched again, "nay, to *broach* upon young Godfrey here."

"If indeed this is the true Godfrey." Purvious gave Egelbun an insidious smirk.

"What do you say, good lord?" asked Egelbun, perking up a bit.

"I say, I think, in all likelihood that this young so-and-so is a fraud." Purvious pointed a purple, tinkling finger at Godfrey. "I say, I think, perhaps he knew the true Godfrey. Perchance he was the one who killed him. Now he has returned in this guise to ingratiate himself into your house, gain your confidence, and steal everything which is rightfully yours."

Egelbun held a hand to his cheek. "You think so? You think so?" Without warning, he burst into a maniacal rage. "Impostor! Call the soldiers of the city!"

Loutronio motioned to one of the bearers who ran off down the street; in the same instant, Purvious drew his sword and held the tip to Godfrey's heart.

Egelbun's face turned the color of new-made blood pudding as he stared at Godfrey. "Charlatan! Criminal!" he fumed. "How dare you try to trick me. Why, I'll make you suffer for it."

"Don't run, scofflaw," Purvious jeered at Godfrey. "I've been trained by experts."

"I had no intention of running . . . " began Godfrey calmly, then without warning, his face contorted into a mask of rage and he blurted out viciously, "Slug Lips!"

Purvious let forth a diminutive gasp, a presage to tears.

Godfrey turned his head away, slapped a hand over his mouth, and mumbled an apology through his fingers.

"Do not listen to him, Master," cooed Loutronio to Purvious. "Your lips are like pert roses."

Godfrey lifted his hand from his mouth and spoke quickly—"I tell you, once again, in all honesty, I am Godfrey!"

"Liar!" snarled Egelbun. "Trying to steal my money! Trying to trick me! Twisting my words!"

Godfrey's hand flew away from his mouth as if possessed and made an obscene gesture at Egelbun. "Fatso!" he growled; then forced himself to yell out, "Not so! Not so! Bring members of the house staff before me. They will recognize my countenance."

"Do it!" said Purvious.

"Servants! Come forth!" commanded Egelbun.

The bearer arrived just then with two armed men: muscular city guards clothed in black leather. They grabbed Godfrey by either arm and held him tightly. (Egelbun blushed at the sight of this and forced himself to look away.) A moment later, Drapslod exited fearfully from the mansion's portal.

"You! Dripslob!" said Egelbun.

"It's Drapslod, sir."

"What?"

"Not Dripsop."

"I didn't say Dripsop. I said Drip*slob*."

"Drapslod, sir."

"I didn't say that either!"

"Dropcloth," said Loutronio. "That's his name."

"What is his name?" asked Egelbun with undisguised bafflement.

"Something like Draperies," replied Loutronio.

"Dogsod . . . or Dingleberries," piped in Purvious, then

gave up in consternation and said, "Oh, whatever!"

"You! What is your name?" raged Egelbun. "Tell me your stupid, pathetic name!"

"Whatever you wish it to be, sir," quailed Drapslod.

"That's right. Because I am your master. I can call you Dripslop or Drapsop or . . . Dicksock!"

"My mother makes them, sir," said Drapslod, brightening. "She has a stall in the market."

"Makes what?!"

"It's a thing one puts on one's potato-finger when one is cold," continued Drapslod.

"What is he talking about?" entreated Egelbun.

"Dicksocks, sir," said Drapslod shyly.

"So is that your name, then?" asked Egelbun.

"Not at all, sir. Which it is my mother makes them."

Purvious could stand it no longer: his sartorial interest had been truly piqued. He stepped forward and addressed Drapslod. "See here, peasant. What is this talk? I have never worn one of these items of which you speak."

"That's right, sir. It's something one only does when one is of the lower classes."

"Does she knit them herself?" asked Loutronio.

"Certainly."

"Are they drab or playful colors?" asked Purvious.

"Mostly drab, sir."

Loutronio was about to ask him if she used virgin wool, when Egelbun screamed, "What are you talking about, peon?!"

"That's right, sir," said Drapslod. "That's when your dick-sock comes in handy. After you've made water, it keeps the *pee* from dripping *on* your britches. No pee-on, guaranteed."

Egelbun slapped Drapslod on the side of the head.

"Headslap!" said Loutronio. "That's his name!"

Egelbun stared severely at Drapslod. "You there, answer me and answer me plainly."

"Yes, sir."

Egelbun made to speak, but he had completely forgotten what he had meant to ask Drapslod. He stood there with his podgy mouth opening and closing disgustingly.

"You were going to ask him if he recognizes me," offered Godfrey.

"Do you recognize this man as Godfrey, Zalman Verrazanno's adopted son?" asked Egelbun with a trembling voice.

"Hello, Drapslod," said Godfrey in a friendly way.

Drapslod peered at him, then spoke apologetically, "I'm sorry, sir, but I ain't never before seen you in me life."

"Kill him!" squealed Egelbun, pointing at Godfrey. "Kill him now!"

"Wait! There is some mistake!" said Godfrey.

"There is no mistake," raved Egelbun. "I will have your most delicate parts sliced from your body and fed to mangy, cankerous stoats and loathsome, unscrubbed Barbary apes. O, you will pay, you bastardly gullion!"

"I tell you, puffguts," replied Godfrey rudely, "this is a gross error on your part. If you had half as much brains as belly, what a clever cove you'd be."

Egelbun's face took on the aspect of an insane warthog.

"Perhaps he intended to rape your niece," cajoled Purvious. "Perhaps that is what his greedy fingers were after."

"I'll have you kicked by merciless men wearing pointy shoes!" ranted Egelbun, this being the penalty meted out in ancient Byzantium to presumptuous men who dared to wear prong-tipped sandals, the footwear of the elite.

"Mamooshka is here?!" asked Godfrey, who had no interest whatsoever in the sadistic sumptuary laws of the Eastern Empire.

"You durst not say her name aloud," threatened Purvious, who made a mental note to ask Egelbun, when time allowed, about this interesting form of execution. "I will see you dance upon nothing beneath the deadly nevergreen!"

"Then Mamooshka is here?" asked Godfrey, all aflame.

"So! You *did* intend to despoil the rose of Carthusalem!" stated Purvious triumphantly.

"She is the only reason I came here," replied Godfrey. "For her alone."

"I'll have you put in a sack full of rusty nails and dropped off a high place!" fumed Egelbun, this being the punishment in Milan for men who steal sacks of nails.

"I only speak the truth, and the truth shall win in the end," pronounced Godfrey.

"O, we'll see about that!" snickered Egelbun.

"Send for your niece," said Purvious with a twisted smile.

"Whatever for?" asked Egelbun.

"If anyone could recognize Godfrey, it would be her."

"No!" yelled Godfrey and thought, *I must not see her. The third shtipulation: 'Ven you see your true love, you vill be shtricken vith ze old curse.'* He addressed Purvious. "Please! I beg of you. Do not send for her! Take me to the dungeon. Anything but Mamooshka."

"Aha! He is a craven worm," gloated Egelbun. "He sees his end in it. Bring out Mamooshka!" he shouted to his servant.

Drapslod hastened into the house.

"It will be my great honor, master Egelbun," said Purvious, "to see this churl tortured and tormented in the most skilled ways imaginable." Purvious glared at Godfrey. "Do you cower, skulking fibber?"

"Not from you nor your threats, chalk-cheeks!"

Purvious let out an involuntary cry. "He insulted me! Called me 'chalky!' What gross impudence!"

"Shocking!" said Egelbun.

"Shameful!" said Loutronio and pinched Purvious' cheeks in an attempt to bring some color into them.

"What gall!" hissed Purvious.

"Great gall!" echoed Egelbun.

"Most galling!" agreed Loutronio.

Godfrey let forth a bizarre, squirrel-like yelp, and the others stopped their tantrums to look at him. They were all dumbfounded by the change which had overtaken both his physique and phyz. Gone was the confident, manly fellow who had demanded their attention. Instead, they saw a humpbacked, dull-eyed wretch. His head lolled on his shoulders as if his spine had been pulled from his body. His face had taken on a curious shape—a pathetic expression of subservient devotion mingled with abject dread. They followed his bedazzled gaze to the figure of a woman standing on the threshold: it was Mamooshka, and she had appeared at the gates so quietly that the others, with the exception of Godfrey, had not taken notice of her arrival.

Mamooshka was much changed from the last time Godfrey had seen her. She no longer carried herself with brazen self-assurance. Indeed, she was dejected and hung her head so low that all he could see was the perfectly straight, pale line made by the part of her hair, running down the middle of her head in a creamy furrow. From the instant he saw her again, he felt absolutely queasy with love, mortified that she would see him in his old, miserable form and not as the manly Gypsy.

"Ah, my niece, Mamooshka," wheezed Egelbun, for he was out of breath from his recent histrionics. "I regret to take you from your chambers, but an impostor has tried to infiltrate our home under the deviant guile of Dogfried. Fried Dog! God Dammit!"

"Godfrey," said Loutronio.

"Exactly! You must gaze keenly upon his countenance and cast the final verdict of his doom!"

"As you wish, honorable half-uncle," said Mamooshka

apathetically. She walked slowly toward Godfrey with her eyes focused on the ground.

Godfrey struggled wildly to be free.

"See how he fights so feebly against the powerful arms of those brawny men?" whispered Loutronio to Purvious.

"His harrowed nature thrills me," came Purvious' husky reply.

Godfrey had managed to squirm around so that his back was to Mamooshka.

"Turn him," commanded Egelbun. "Turn him thusly hither to us promptly."

The powerful guards spun Godfrey around and propped him up like a scarecrow.

The others watched as Mamooshka came to a stop directly in front of him. She was still gazing at the ground. Slowly, ever so slowly, she raised her head and stared indifferently at his face. Then, the slightest smile twitched at the corner of her mouth, and she said softly, "Hello, squirrel."

Godfrey groaned a reply.

"What's this, you know him?" asked Purvious in amazement.

"What do you say?" queried Egelbun.

"This is indeed the wretched Godfrey as I am truly the wretched Mamooshka." Mamooshka dropped her head, turned around, and walked back into the house.

The street was as silent as a tennis court during the plague. Loutronio stared in wonder at Godfrey. Purvious stuck a finger in his mouth and bit it anxiously. Egelbun trembled as if from cold and put a hand to his palpitating heart.

"Release him," ordered Loutronio reluctantly.

The guards let go and Godfrey dropped to his knees. He took a deep breath, then stood up straight. He was the Gypsy again, and he stared at everyone with a regal, hurt expression.

"I will leave now," he said at last.

"Wait, good uncle!" cried Egelbun.

"Nephew!" bellowed Loutronio and Purvious.

"Precisely!" muttered Egelbun.

"I will call again one day and we will resolve the differences between us," said Godfrey. He gazed up toward Mamooshka's tower room; then, turned and strode down the street.

As soon as Godfrey was out of sight, Egelbun pulled off his wig to reveal a pate as bald as a frog's belly. "What have I done? What have I done? The rightful heir has returned!" He chewed on the wig frantically.

"More like 'the rightful hair,'" said Purvious with a derisive grin.

"Brilliant, my lord!" praised Loutronio.

"I will be penniless once again!" moaned Egelbun through a mouthful of yellow mane.

"Do not fret, master Egelbun," said Purvious. "All is not lost. I may have a plan to rid you of this pesky Godfrey."

"O. A plan? A plan?"

"Yes."

"Anything! I will give you anything!"

A treacherous gleam shone in Purvious' eyes. "Anything is an offer I cannot refuse."

"Excuse me for interrupting, *signore*," says Antonio. "I am terribly enjoying the story, but I must go perform a duty and then I will come right back."

I have been so involved in reading aloud, that I had not even noticed the sun had set long ago. "I relieve you of your household duties," I respond benevolently.

"The task I must perform is relief in and of itself," says Antonio coyly.

"Quit talking in riddles, you silly lout!"

"I must water the grass!" blurts Antonio.

"That's the gardener's job, you oaf."

"No. I have to . . . you know," he says shyly, "water the grass. It's a genteel way of saying 'I have to take a piss.'"

"'Watering the grass' is what one calls a euphemism," I say.

"Yes," he nods. "I have to take a uffa-mism."

"No, no. A euphemism is a saying that takes the place of something else."

"I don't understand."

"For example, what is another way of telling me that you have to have a bowel movement?"

"Errr . . . I've got to make *stronzo*?"

"Antonio, thou simple soul. A euphemism is couched in such a way as not to sound vulgar. It is usually spoken in the presence of a lady."

"Ohhhhh! So . . . I would say something like...'I have to make brown linguini.'"

"Exactly!"

"Or, 'Excuse me, *signorina*, but I must squeeze the paint.'"

"Very artistic."

"'Pardon me, Madame, but the loaf that I've been baking is ready to come out of the oven.'"

"Rising to the occasion indeed."

"Well, I'll just go . . . drown some ants, ha ha! and then I'll be right back."

"I think that you should practice holding it," I suggest. "A test of fortitude."

"I don't believe that I can, *signore*," he says as he crosses his legs. "I've been sitting here listening to you for ten straight hours."

"What do you think the knights of the Middle Ages did when they were in the midst of battle?" I ask of him. "Do you think that when they felt the urge to moisten the shrub, they merely retreated from the fray, and galloped off the field?"

"I thought that they had a little door down there," he says.

"What do you mean, 'A little door'?"

"So that they could find relief as they rode."

"Have you ever tried to drain the pipe whilst sitting on horseback?" I inquire.

"No," he replies.

"Well it is damn near impossible, let me tell you. I can assure you from hard-won experience that it makes a terrific mess. The horse does not appreciate it much either. And in the first place, knights did not have little doors in their armor. Absurd. What would happen if that little door were to fly open in the heat of battle?"

"I don't know."

"They would be mocked silly, that is what would happen! Charging at Saracens with one's dangler to the wind. Ridiculous!

"Now da Vinci, great soul, when he designed his underwater diving suit, thoughtfully included a 'convenience' for the wearer. But pissing whilst swimming underwater in the quiet azure sea is quite different from pissing whilst charging at scimitar-wielding Mussulmen screaming like a pack of maniacal blue-painted Picts! Comical notion."

"What's a blue-painted Pict?" questions Antonio curiously.

"They were the barbarians that your Roman ancestors met in my homeland," I answer. "They painted themselves blue and charged into battle naked."

"To make the Romans laugh!" states Antonio.

"Whatever do you mean?"

"Well," he explains, "they probably painted themselves blue and ran into battle naked so that their enemies would start laughing really hard, and then, quite in a flash, when they were caught off guard, doubled over with laughter as it were, ha-ha-ing and tee-hee-ing, the barbarians would go—

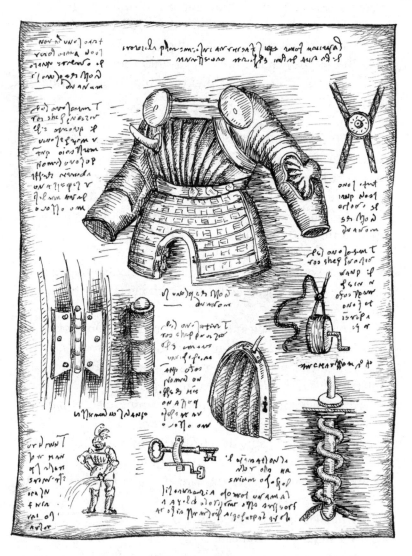

An Ingenious Design

thwack! Chop off their heads! Very sly, if you ask me."

"An interesting thesis. One best kept to yourself, however."

"Perhaps they had little locks that held the doors fast."

"What are you talking about?" I ask.

"The knights. Down below. On their crotch door," he replies.

"A lock? On the little door?"

"Perhaps."

"Antonio, imagine that you are riding through the deserts of Palestine. You are wearing eighty pounds of plate. Under that is a padded jerkin. Beneath that, pantaloons and shirt of thickest leather. Your hands are encased in mail gauntlets covered with a steel shell. In one metallic fist, you hold the reins. In the other, your broadsword. Under the crook of one arm, you are balancing a lance. Now tell me, thus outfitted and burdened, how in God's name are you to find your dainty little key amongst all of your articles of war, let alone maneuver said key into the trapdoor's minuscule hole, and then extricate your delicate carrot from its hiding place with those brutish steel fingers? Why, one would have to create an ingenious design for a suit of armor with an easy-opening, gear driven piss-portal, else the act would be as difficult as trying to unlock the chastity belt of a maiden with St. Vitus' Dance whilst wearing lead gauntlets."

"That was always one of my favorite stories," says Antonio with a smile.

"*The Blacksmith and The Dancing Lady*?" I query.

"Yes. My mama used to tell it to me," he says fondly.

"I have always been partial to it myself."

"Tell it to me now," he demands.

"In the midst of Godfrey's tale?"

"Why not? It will be like the lewd thing they act out during the middle of a play."

" 'Lewd thing'?" I ask.

"The *inter*-lewd," he says. "I'll be right back. And then you can tell me *The Blacksmith and The Dancing Lady.*"

I decide to humor the lad. Since he has been such an excellent listener, I give him a little reward. "You can use my chamber pot," I offer.

Antonio's eyes grow wide with excitement as he stares at the gleaming receptacle sitting in the corner of the room: it is one of the finest thunder mugs available—made in England by Chumble, Rattle & Co.—with porcelain bowl and ebony seat. "Really?" he asks.

"Be my guest."

He hunkers down on it, and a blissful smile appears on his face. "Now we can stay in the room until the tale is done!" he proclaims. "*Viva signore* Smythe!"

15

An Interlewd [sic]:

THE BLACKSMITH &
THE DANCING LADY

O nce upon a time, a knight named Baron Pierre de
Grimbouls was commanded by his liege lord the
King to take upon himself the mantle of a crusader and join a quest to regain the holy city of Jerusalem from
the infidel. Before he departed on this long journey, de
Grimbouls ordered the village blacksmith to fashion a belt of
chastity for his obscenely beautiful wife, Lady Penelope. The
blacksmith, whose name was Johan Longstaff, labored seven
days and nights to create an unbreakable, yet non-chafing
nest-guard of gold and silver. But when he brought the belt to
the castle and presented it to Pierre de Grimbouls, Johan
caught a glimpse of the Lady Penelope and fell deeply and sin-
fully in love with her; likewise, she was smitten by the handsome young smith, who in no way resembled her squat,
brutish, ogre-like husband.

Now it must be told that Pierre de Grimbouls was a member of that arcane order The Knight Templars and was an adept of the black arts of magic. He had studied in secret since his youth with a sorcerer who lived in a dank cave inside the hollow hills. Pierre de Grimbouls was possessed of many unnatural skills: he had the ability to speak to familiars in the shape of animals and the power to bewitch others with his honeyed voice; indeed, he had used all his dark wiles to convince the good Count Frutagar, Penelope's father, into giving him his daughter's hand, for the Count doted upon his only child and would have never, in sound mind, married her to such a wart-faced, vile-hearted man.

On the day that Longstaff brought the belt to his castle, Pierre de Grimbouls at once sensed the mutual liking betwixt his wife and the smith. On that account he had Johan thrown in the dungeon. Upon the lad's wrist he bade the dungeon master place cuffs of cold metal. Attached to these were lead-covered gauntlets. Having thus trapped and fettered the smith, de Grimbouls was confident that Longstaff would never be able to fashion another key to the chastity belt lock and, thence, partake of his wife's loin-treasure.

Furthermore, de Grimbouls took the key that fit the lock of the cuckold-proof cordon and put a clever spell on it: if the key came within six and one-half inches of the keyhole, it would turn molten hot to the touch and burn the holder's fingers like cruel fire. He also put a curse on Penelope: if the key came within six and one-half paces of her, she would become afflicted with Saint Vitus' Dance. Therefore, it would be impossible for any man to even hold the burning key, let alone fit it into the wildly undulating and oscillating lock which encircled the loins of the dancing lady.

Johan sat in the dungeon for many a week, and he cursed Pierre de Grimbouls for his untrustworthy and treacherous nature. He vowed vengeance. Therewith, one night the Lady

Penelope sneaked into the foul dungeon and spoke to her lover through a chink in the stone. Happy was he to hear her sweet voice in that accursed place. Happier still was he when on subsequent visitations she brought him dainties from her table and gave him a sharp stick with which he could poke through the chink in the stone and skewer the morsels. At first it was quite difficult for him to hold the skiver with his iron-mitted fingers. Through much persistence and friendly words of encouragement he mastered the tiny lance and became as dexterous with it as ever he was with knife and fork. He spent many a minute thrusting it through the hole, poking Penelope's prize; wherewith she cried:

"Oh! O! Hey Ho! Aha! Well done, sir!"

She came every eve to that dark place and they whispered sweet nothings until the red cock spoke. Whence they fell hopelessly in love. But under these hopeless circumstances their love seemed all for naught. But lo! The Lady Penelope's desire for young Johan became so passionate and inflamed that she took to the fever and consequently fell into a dire, fitful sleep that would not end.

Six months went by and word came to the castle from a road-weary messenger that the Baron de Grimbouls had died from the flux no less than five hundred miles from the gates of the Holy City. Lady Penelope's father, Count Frutagar, a knight in his own right, came to fetch his daughter from the Baron's castle: he wished to take her home and marry her to the gouty Duke of Penbrook and thus gain his enemy's allegiance. But when he found Penelope in that awful slumber, he feared to move her lest she die. He consulted with the late Baron's physician who explained to him that she was burning from a fire within her cursed loins. To demonstrate the heat emanating from that place he did cook an egg upon her chastity belt. Count Frutagar was taken aback by this uncanny heat and issued a proclamation that any young man who could place the enchanted key into his daughter's hole and unlock the belt would gain both her hand in marriage and a generous dowry.

And so it passed that a thousand men came to the castle from far and wide to try their hand at snatching the prize of both wife and marriage bounty. The first attempt was made by Allan of Tewsbury, a knight of the Holy Rood, and he cursed and screamed when the key caught fire in his fingers, burning through his glove like liquefied lead. Arnulf di Ceriseplucker, a suitor from Gascony, brought specially made tongs with which to hold the hot key; but howsoever he did try, he could not manage to slip the key into the hasp-hollow, such were the vibrations that wracked Penelope's body. For even as she slept, the Dance of Saint Vitus overtook her limbs. She shook with such force that her bed might have been a horse-cart being driven at full speed over the bumpiest road in Christendom. One thousand men tried various means of unclasping that cursed girdle. One thousand men failed in their quest. Count Frutagar fretted and moaned, for the physicians told him that his daughter would surely die within that night unless relief came.

Now it so happens that months previous to this day, a wandering dance master by the name of Wilfred The Shabby (on account of his slovenly attire) had appeared at the castle seeking employment. But he was thrown into the dungeon for soundly beating a young nobleman who had insulted his appearance. Wilfred The Shabby and Johan became fast friends. To while away the time in that loathsome place, Wilfred taught Johan how to dance. One of Wilfred's favorite capers was called "The Agile Goat." He had learnt it in his youth in the Highlands of Scotland. All night and all day they danced until the sweat poured from their brows and their legs ached from toe to hip. After several months of this prancing and shuffling they had dug a great hole in the floor. So deep was this hole that Johan noticed they had uncovered a cistern that ran the length of the castle walls. One night he decided to escape. He climbed this abandoned well to the floors above and found himself in the privy. He heard a great clamor emanating from the castle hall. The tumult was Count Frutagar, fretting and moaning his poor daughter's fate with a cry of "Alack-a-day!"

Into this commotion walked Johan. Covered in night soil he was, yet the Count's attendant noticed Johan's gauntlets outright. Thinking that he was a final, albeit filthy, suitor come prepared with heat-proof gloves, the attendant begged him to ungird the begirded dame. Johan took one look at his love, who was as pale as cream, and he burst into tears—such was his ardor.

The attendant brought him the key on a metal plate. Johan plucked up the tiny thing and held it deftly between his steel-capped fingers, such was the skill he had learnt whilst pricking Penelope's delectables. When he approached her she began to shake and twitch. He commanded the attendants to release her and stand her on her feet. And lo! Even with eyes closed, she danced the wild jig of Saint Vitus; and Johan danced along with her, such was the skill he had learnt from Wilfred The Shabby. He maneuvered the white hot key into the hole and gave it a full turn, unlocking the hated belt and sending it clanking to the floor amidst a riotous clapping of hands and gratulations from the spectators.

Count Frutagar was true to his word: the smith and his daughter were married the next day. Never was a pair so well matched, nor so in love, nor so happy to finally come together in holy union. Such was Johan's fervor to enter the marriage chamber, that his hand trembled fiercely with the key, and no less than a dozen times did he thrust it vainly against the lip of the lock; for which reason the Lady Penelope took it upon herself to finish the task: she grasped the key with her own hand, and guided it into the well-oiled hole where it fit like a hand in a glove.

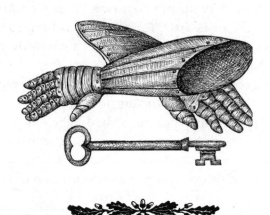

"That's a happy story, all right," sighs Antonio. "But what happened to Wilfred The Shabby?"

"Johan was so happy to be reunited with his true love," I explain, "that he forgot about the poor blackguard. When he finally remembered him, Wilfred was as dead as a door-nail—his corpse had rotted away and there was nothing left but his moldy, rat-gnawed bones and musty dancing shoes."

Antonio's jaw drops. Then his eyes well up with tears.

"I jest with you," I say.

"Really?" comes his plaintive query.

"Wilfred became the dancing master to Lady Penelope and Johan and fell in love with a slovenly kitchen wench who gave him beard lice, German measles, and Cupid's Itch."

"Now that's better!" replies Antonio.

16

THE LOVERS

Short Clog found Godfrey in his master's usual place—hiding in the orchard outside the walls of the Verrazanno garden. From his vantage point in the bough of an ancient apple tree, Godfrey could gaze longingly at Mamooshka's window without being seen: the gnarled tree limbs covered him like a cloak of woodsy fingers. Short Clog had known for years that Godfrey was in love with Mamooshka, though he never let on lest he embarrass the poor fellow. For that reason, whenever he approached the orchard (knowing that Godfrey was at his love-post), he made it his practice to call out loudly and create an enormous din. This gave ample time for Godfrey to climb down from his perch and pretend to be reading a book or watching a bird by the time Short Clog came into view.

"Master? Where are you? Master?" cried Short Clog blaringly.

"Here I am, Short Clog," answered Godfrey's dismal sounding voice. "I'm up in this apple tree."

Short Clog was nonplussed by this uncharacteristic reply. He walked hesitantly to the tree, gawped upwards and asked, "What are you doing here in this dark place, staring all moon-eyed at that window yonder?"

"I am a fool, Short Clog," said Godfrey sadly. "A fool to ever think my life could be changed for the better."

"You're not a fool, sir. And don't be sad. You have to take to heart those wise words my father always says: 'There's enough people in the world willing to kick your jewel-casket without you kicking it yourself.'"

Godfrey smiled and asked him how his father was getting along.

"Quite well in fact," replied Short Clog happily. "He saved up enough money scraping and picking to buy one Happy Cock."

"Indeed?"

"It's an inn, sir. He says we can stay at his place until we find lodgings of our own."

"Well, then. Let us stay there tonight. Please, go to the Happy Cock and make ready our rooms. I will follow soon enough."

A moth flittered around Godfrey's head, startling him from a reverie. He had absolutely no idea how long he had been staring into space, nor how many minutes had passed since the sound of Short Clog's plodding footfalls had faded into the distance. He realized that the air was full of the dusk songs of the crickets and frogs; the comforting smell of woodsmoke wafted in the air. The moth—a Gypsy moth—landed on Godfrey's nose. He crossed his eyes to focus on the creature. Then he gently brought his hand to his face, guiding the delicate insect to a perch upon his finger. The moth's antennae probed curiously at Godfrey's fingernail. Then it relaxed and preened its dusty wings.

"I have made a decision, dear little friend," he said to the moth. "I have made a decision just now and I think it is for the best." The moth seemed to cock his head. "I have routinely wondered about seemingly inconsequential events," continued Godfrey. "Many a time and oft, when I sat at my ledger, scribbling away at my father's accounts, something tiny would happen—an eyelash falling to the page, a gnat crawling across the hairs of my arm, a dust mote flashing in a beam of light— and this trifling event diverted my attention from my work with the power of a blunderbuss going off next to my head. I would ask myself, 'What did that mean?' and 'Why did that take place?' My father taught me that all things happen for a reason. And I've read many convincing spiritual books in which the writer implores the reader to believe that every one of the hairs on our heads (or wings, in your case) is numbered. God knows all, sees all, understands all.

"Now, sir moth, it is easy to believe that God watches over men of consequence, and circumstances of profound importance. It is plausible, is it not, to imagine Him casting His keen gaze over the creation of the world, Noah and the flood, Christ's long walk to Golgotha, Mohammed's desert ordeals? It is easy to believe that He is there to guide the King when he decides the fate of his subjects or the knight when he marches off to battle his foes. But why would God plan, or even care, for the trivial fall of an eyelash or the inconsequential plight of a gnat caught in the forest of hairs on a man's arm? Or you, dear moth. Why would he keep a watchful eye on your meaningless day of flower hopping? And most of all, why would he worry about a man like me, a nothing in a vast sea of nothings?

"I wonder about this question all the time, and occasionally, when the seed of a weed floats past my eyes . . . sometimes, this is enough to test my faith in God. For I question how a single entity could possibly perceive and care for the most infinitesimal parts of his creation? 'He cannot,' says a voice from within the darkest part of my soul. 'It is impossible that God is omnipresent.'"

Godfrey blew on the moth, and his breath sent the hairs on the insect's wings rippling like miniature fields of wheat. "I want to believe," he said at last. "I want to believe that He is watching out for me—and you. But I cannot. And so I have made my decision."

"What decision?" asked a gruff voice from below, jarring him from his contemplation; the moth danced away and vanished into the night. Godfrey's heart pounded furiously as he peered through the limbs. Standing next to the tree was the hooded figure of a man.

"Who is there?" asked Godfrey.

"Do you not recognize my voice? It is I, the Dim Avenger. Shall I climb up to your lair, or will you come down?"

Godfrey grasped the limb upon which he sat, hung for a moment, then dropped to the ground in a fluid, agile motion. "How long have you been standing there?" he demanded, feeling a little cross.

"Not long," said the Dim Avenger, scratching his clean-shaven chin. "Just a moment in fact. Just long enough to hear your resolve to 'throw away the scabbard,' as they say. So tell me. What have you decided?"

"I have decided to leave this place," said Godfrey in his most impassioned voice. "I have concluded that my hopes were nothing more than fanciful desires with nothing to substantiate them and no help from on high to guide me."

"Ponderous thoughts, I must say," replied the Dim Avenger, intending to prolong Godfrey's answer.

"A lifetime of pondering," went on Godfrey with disgust. "A lifetime of wasted dreams." He ran a hand through his hair, straightened his back. "But let us not dwell on my dreary thoughts. I am glad to see you again, new-met friend." He held out his hand, and the Royal Scamp grasped it manfully.

"Well met indeed," replied the Dim Avenger. "What are you doing here?"

"Hoping to catch a glimpse of an angel."

"At which place?" asked the thief, craning his neck from side to side.

"That window there," moaned Godfrey, pointing toward Mamooshka's balcony.

"Mamooshka?" The Dim Avenger's voice was full of shocked disbelief. "The evil Egelbun's niece?"

"Aye."

"How . . . how . . . how do you know of her?" stammered the Dim Avenger.

"In my youth, I saw her often. She never took notice of me, though. She does not even know I exist."

"And what do you want of her?"

"I am in love with her," answered Godfrey, clasping his breast with both hands. "So, I venture, I want her love in return."

The Dim Avenger turned his head away and let forth a strange gasp. "Love? With her?" he said in amazement.

"What care you whom I love?" snapped Godfrey, slightly perturbed at the Dim Avenger's strange reaction to his confession.

"You are . . . you are too good for her," spluttered the robber and stared, mystified, at Mamooshka's window.

"Whatever can you mean?"

"She's a witch," said the Dim Avenger softly. "Everyone says so."

"She is not!" said Godfrey as the stubble on the back of his neck ruffled like the hair of a boar-bristle brush. He took an aggressive step toward the thief.

"You should stay clear of that one," said the Dim Avenger pugnaciously. "She's a mantrap."

"Do not speak ill of her, I beg you," replied Godfrey with

a menacing tone. "I will be forced to sunder our untried friendliness."

The Dim Avenger let forth a dumbfounded, almost giddy laugh. "You'd be willing to fight me for Mamooshka's honor?" he inquired.

"Naturally," replied Godfrey. "To the death."

The highwayman put a hand to his mouth, attempting to hide a smile. He cocked his head to one side and stared at Godfrey with a peculiar, almost adoring look. Then, he shook himself from this trance, coughed manfully into his fist, and slapped Godfrey on the shoulder in a conciliatory gesture.

"I didn't mean to insult your lady-love," he said. "I'm just stating a simple fact about the sexes. Men need women who will lay down and say, 'Take me, I'm yours.'"

"That is primitive," said Godfrey with disgust. "Bestial."

"What does this Mamooshka possess that other women don't?" pressed the Dim Avenger.

"Fire in her eyes," moaned Godfrey.

"Oho! *How* romantic," said the Dim Avenger.

"Have you ever been in love, Sir Cynical?" Godfrey asked, then rested against the tree, sighed, and stared forlornly at Mamooshka's apartment.

"Never," answered the Dim Avenger. He plucked an apple from the tree and took a bite.

"Then you could not possibly understand," Godfrey said miserably.

"Women!" scoffed the Dim Avenger as he chewed with his mouth open. "You hold them up by the ankles and they all look the same."

"What a terrible thing to say!" blurted Godfrey, shocked by the scamp's lewd-talk.

"Have you ever been with a woman?" asked the thief.

"Ack!" replied the accountant.

"I take it that's a 'Nay'?"

"Nay, I have not," he said. "I am saving myself for my true love."

"You're pure of body as well as spirit!" said the Dim Avenger, and tossed his half-eaten apple to Godfrey, who snatched it deftly from the air. "Well, I'm not," he continued. "I've cooked hot nuts with more of the wanton creatures than I can count on my fingers and toes."

"What did you hope to gain from these wicked actions?" asked Godfrey, and he took a hesitant nibble from the apple.

"Pleasure," answered the thief. "Pure and simple."

"A man and a woman," began Godfrey in the venerable tone of a wizened vicar, "must not share one another unless there is true love between them. It must be consecrated in God's eyes or it is an unseemly, unholy, scurrile concern, without love or happiness."

"I've loved every woman I've ever poodled!" cried the Dim Avenger passionately. "And they've certainly made me happy." He stared into the distance and rubbed his hands together, as if rolling a doughy thought between his palms; and thus began:

"There is a certain marriage of spirits which takes place during a tawdry, adulterous union. The action of the love-making itself represents a miniature version of matrimony. Listen. You meet her in a dark and unseemly inn. She sits on your lap, and you joke and jest. There is a burning desire to join with her in that first meeting. You feel her body, her warmth, and imagine the pleasure held there. Later in the night, the two of you steal hand in hand to the barn like new-lyweds. In the greasy straw your passion seethes and grows until it is a desperate urge. You join together and satiate your mutual needs with many exclamations of love. When it is done, you lie together in silence. Ten minutes pass, like ten years in the life of a married couple and you both find your-selves thinking, 'Who is this person I am with?' and 'Whatever have I done?' Ennui overcomes the former mood. In this after-math, you both feel a new insatiable urge which is to divorce yourself from this other person and be on your separate ways."

"I pity you and your hollow meetings," said Godfrey.

"I pity you and your naïveté," replied the Dim Avenger.

"I only speak how I feel." Godfrey took a last, lingering look at Mamooshka's window, then forced himself to turn away. "I must depart from this place," he said in a throaty voice and heaved the apple into the darkness. He made to leave, but the Dim Avenger stopped him with an outstretched hand.

"Where will you go?"

"Far away. Maybe to the east. Perhaps to the west. The south . . . "

"The north?"

"It does not matter. It does not matter."

The Dim Avenger's fingers clutched his arm in a fierce, swordsman's grip. The robber's eyes, shaded by his hood and mask, stared desperately into Godfrey's. Just as Godfrey was about to let forth a painful cry, for his arm was smarting something fierce, the Dim Avenger blurted out desperately, "That fat uncle of hers is trying to marry her off to the *podestà's* pasty son, Purvious!"

"The deuce you say! No. That cannot be," protested Godfrey. "The pasty *podestà's* son?"

"No. The *podestà's* pasty son," explained the Dim Avenger. "The *podestà* is sort of a marbled salmon color."

"The mottled *podestà's* pasty son! How do you know?"

"Mamooshka is a friend of mine."

"Halloo!" Godfrey was flabbergasted. "A friend? Of yours?"

"Don't worry. I'm not her fancy man," pledged the Royal Scamp. "I assure you, our relationship is platonic. There is a love between us but it is only the affection . . . that close relatives feel."

"Does she wish to marry this *podestà's* pasty son?" asked Godfrey as he felt the blood rush to his face.

The Dim Avenger turned away and the thief's fingers clutched the air as if they were choking an unseen villain. "She'd rather swallow poison," he said, his voice cracking with emotion. "She'd rather be picked apart by a thousand vicious marmoty things. She'd just as soon crawl with naked body upon a million sharp and jagged objects. She'd more readily have hot burning tools of torture thrust into every pore of her body and twisted like corkscrews until her sinews were un-knit, her bones undone, her heart ripped out and thrust into the mouths of hungry eagles, pecking and scrabbling for her miserable bloody flesh!"

"She doesn't care for him then?" asked Godfrey hopefully.

"You could say that."

Godfrey exhaled an enormous sigh and smiled radiantly. "This is a great relief." His gaze turned longingly to Mamooshka's balcony. "When I saw her last, she looked so full of despair. I must think of a way of saving her."

The Dim Avenger clapped hands together and jumped up and down excitedly. "You could kidnap her!" he said gleefully.

"I could not do anything untoward like that. Nothing against her will."

"I don't think she'd mind too much." The Dim Avenger stepped closer to Godfrey and smiled flirtatiously. "A handsome fellow like you. She might enjoy it."

"You . . . ummm . . . flatter me," replied Godfrey shyly.

"You're really a rather charming man. There is a certain purity which radiates from your face which is not completely unattractive." The rascal came even nearer and put a gentle hand on Godfrey's shoulder.

"Oh, well, thank you," replied Godfrey modestly.

"Why do you turn away?" asked the Dim Avenger.

"I have something in my . . . ear," answered Godfrey and took a step back.

The thief stroked his chin thoughtfully, then said, "Come back tomorrow night and I'll arrange a meeting."

"I could not!"

"What are you afraid of?"

"I must not see her!" grunted Godfrey. "I will not be able to speak. I will change. Into something stupid and mealy-mouthed."

"You can't be serious."

"But, I am!" he bellowed mournfully. "It is a curse, you see? I am cursed."

"You are in love, dear, dear boy." The Dim Avenger stared at the ground pensively, then snapped his fingers. "Hulloo! Here's an idea. I will be the go-between. You tell me what you want to say to her and I will relay it to Mamooshka."

"You would do that for me?" asked Godfrey suspiciously.

"It's an adventure. And I love adventures," cooed the scamp. "Besides, I would thoroughly enjoy sabotaging the pasty Purvious' attempts to woo Mamooshka, not as if she's even about to be taken in by that . . . rotten toenail, that scab, that cringing dollop of dung. Perchance together, you and I can win her love, and then we can elope."

"The three of us?" replied Godfrey, laughing at the Dim Avenger's inclusion of himself into their elopement plans.

"I mean . . . *you* can . . . the *two* of you can elope." The Dim Avenger laughed nervously.

Godfrey beamed and said, "Dim Avenger, you illuminate the dark places in my heart." Impetuously, he embraced the gloam-time mugger in his arms. But it was a strange sort of clasp. He had meant to wrap the thief in a hearty, hail-fellow-well-met bear hug. Instead, without thinking, he placed one hand around the Dim Avenger's waist, and the other behind his hood and brought the other man's head to his chest. Oddly, The Dim Avenger complied with this eccentric embrace and seemed to actually . . . well . . . melt in his arms. The highwayman was several inches shorter than Godfrey, and so he fit quite snugly in his arms. Godfrey felt the fellow's limbs wrap around his waist and squeeze. A trembling sigh, an almost girlish gasp escaped the lips of the Dim Avenger, and Godfrey thought, *What pleasant yet un-natural longings I surprisingly feel for this hooded man.*

The Dim Avenger, as if sensing Godfrey's dilemma, jerked and pulled away. The two cleared their throats with manly coughs and cracked their knuckles.

"So!" rasped the Dim Avenger. "What is your first message for the lady?"

"I do not know." Godfrey searched his brain for something poetical to say, but he was too nervous to think.

"Can you sing?" asked the highwayman. "Because Mamooshka loves singing."

"I can sing," he said.

"Oh, most excellent. Listen, I'll climb up to her room right now and tell her to step out onto her balcony. Then you can serenade her."

"Thank you, friend."

The Dim Avenger slapped Godfrey on the shoulder, somewhat too vigorously, then climbed over the garden wall and scrambled up the grape arbor to Mamooshka's escarpment.

Godfrey watched as the Dim Avenger slipped into the chamber. He heard the sound of a foot stubbing into a piece of furniture and something like chair legs skidding across the floor and, oddly, *Mamooshka's* voice crying out in pain. Then a lamp was lit and the room glowed to life. A few moments later, Mamooshka stepped onto the balcony and stared into the night. She was dressed in her nightgown and the silk hugged her lovely body. Her hair was tousled from sleep. The Dim Avenger was nowhere to be seen.

Godfrey felt himself convulse, and he quickly averted his gaze from Mamooshka to counteract the effects of the dreaded *shtipulation*.

"Who stands there in the darkness?" asked Mamooshka with a note of fear as she squinted into the shadows.

"I . . . I do," gasped Godfrey. "A Gypsy." He took a position under the balcony so that he would have no chance of seeing her.

"Will you reveal yourself to me?"

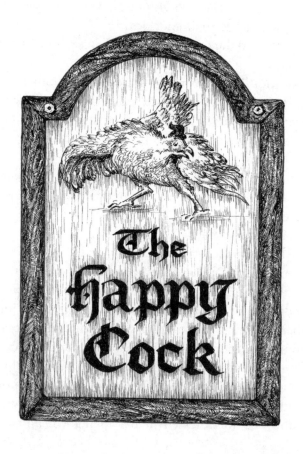

"I would . . . but I cannot."

"My friend tells me you have a song?"

"I . . . do."

"Then let me hear it for I am sad, and lonely, and alone."

Godfrey began his song, and his lovely voice made Mamooshka shiver with joy and desire.

The next morning, the tall, sloe-eyed Gypsy—his hair wild and unkempt and his clothes glistening with dew—wandered into the courtyard of the Happy Cock at the moment the inn's mascot quit his sunrise crowing. Godfrey's eyes were dark-rimmed and heavy from lack of sleep, but his smile was as blissful and serene as a pasha upon waking in his love-chambers. Godfrey held a night jasmine between two fingers . . . a flower given him by Mamooshka. He put the blossom to his nose and took in a giant draught of the heady fragrance.

A window opened on the second story of the main house and Short Clog's head popped out. "I was worried about you, sir! You didn't come home last night."

Godfrey laughed. "Oh! I was . . . you know . . . " His voice trailed off into love-struck gibberish. But this babble, although incomprehensible, was quite different from his old affliction: it was more like a happy, preoccupied mumbling. Short Clog, however, with his uncanny ability to understand almost anything Godfrey said, grasped his meaning completely.

"You slept in the woods and watched the sunrise. That's nice, sir." Short Clog's features took on a worried expression. Had his master finally lost his mind?

"And . . . well . . . you know . . . after I talked to..." his voice trailed off into gabble.

"You met the lady Mamooshka?!" interpreted Short Clog. "Talked to her?!"

Godfrey expelled happy gibberish.

"You spoke for hours!"

Godfrey let forth an immense sigh.

"You're in love, sir!"

Godfrey nodded joyfully. "I am in love!" He reached into his pocket and took out a folded letter. "Here! I have a missive for you to deliver."

Short Clog climbed onto a rope that hung from the eaves of the inn and slid nimbly to the earth, landing spryly on his feet. He gave Godfrey a jaunty bow. "I am at your service," he said gallantly.

Godfrey smiled. He had never seen his uncoordinated servant so adroit. "Take this letter to Mamooshka for me. Let your legs move with utmost post haste to the House of Verrazanno. Guard it with your life."

Short Clog stared at him earnestly. "Master, I will pretend I hold the reputation of my sister in my fingers." The servant grasped the letter delicately between two digits, took three steps forward, caught his foot on a wheelbarrow, and fell face first into a pile of horse s - - t.

"You may think that last part is funny, *signore,*" snaps Antonio, "but I have fallen face first into many piles of s - - t and when it happens to you firsthand, it isn't so humorous."

I respond to Antonio's complaint with a chuckle, followed by a mirthful wheeze. And then I cannot contain my laughter. It wracks my body with cheerful, cachinnating convulsions. I snort and guffaw and nearly split my sides. If there were an aisle nearby, I would roll in it.

"Let's get on with the story," gripes Antonio.

17

THE SCHEMERS

Whilst Godfrey was extricating Short Clog from the equine ejectamenta, Egelbun, Purvious, and Loutronio stood scheming in a courtyard at the House of Verrazanno.

"How goes your plan, my lord?" asked Egelbun anxiously; he was actually wringing his hands in the attitude of a morality play sinner.

"It is a very nice little plan. A neat, tidy, scrumptious plan." Purvious smoothed the supple hide of his purple goatskin jacket like a cat grooming himself contentedly in the sun.

"Very tidy, my lord," chimed in Loutronio, gazing smugly at his master.

"Tidy? Yes? Tidy?" Egelbun mopped the sweat from his fat head.

"It is a very, mmm . . . intricate plan," said Purvious.

"Ah, yes. Complex, my lord," added Loutronio.

Egelbun looked worried and asked why it was complex.

"Do not worry, Egelbun," said Purvious. "All you have to do is stand by and look stupid."

"Play the innocent?"

"More or less." Purvious narrowed his viper's eyes. "Has a magician been found?"

"Not yet! I have sent my man . . . " Egelbun paused and foraged in his barren brain for the name of that damn, impertinent, impossibly named little brute. Finally he said, "Dogsnot. Yes. I have sent Dogsnot a-searching."

"Good and most excellently fine," purred Purvious.

"Please tell me," coaxed Egelbun, "I'm aching to know. What is the plan? I have not slept this past night for my anticipation gnaws at me." His voice became a whine. "It is intolerable that I, a wealthy man, should suffer. Look at me shaking all over. Look at my hand. See how it shakes." The obese flesh of Egelbun's hand jiggered upon his knuckles like congealed pudding fresh from the mold.

"Do not worry yourself, tender merchant, for I will soon relieve you of much of what burdens you." Purvious curled his lips into an evil grin. "First of all, half your estate. And secondly, your niece's hand. As well as the rest of her, for that matter."

"Ah! You made a funny, my lord!" croaked Loutronio and giggled obnoxiously.

Egelbun was confused. "Hmmmm? What are you talking about?"

"Those are my conditions for taking care of Godfrey," said Purvious and snapped his fingers.

Loutronio held forth a scroll and Egelbun smiled painfully as he read the terrible words written upon it. When he had finished, he let out a strained laugh and rolled his meaty lips in his fleshy fingers (a hideous habit that had turned the stomach of many a dinner guest at his table). He looked at Purvious and realized by the young man's snakish stare that the words on the scroll were not a joke. Egelbun shrieked piteously, pulled off his wig—twisting it in his fingers as if it were Godfrey's neck—and mumbled deranged oaths of outrage under his breath in the manner of the proverbial cheese-fearing lunatic who was forced to make buffalo mozzarella for the Pope.

"Pray, sir," asked Purvious with acid on his tongue. "Is something not to your liking?"

"Hmmm? Eh? What?" queried Egelbun distractedly.

"The marriage contract?" reiterated Purvious.

"Oh, it's very pretty. Beautiful handwriting."

"Will you sign it?" asked Loutronio.

"May I think about it for just an eensy teensy while?"

Purvious turned on one slick heel. "Come, Loutronio. Let us leave this unhappy hippo to his own wallowing."

Purvious and Loutronio each lifted a leg as if to walk away, but Egelbun cried out, "Wait! Please! I have but a few questions, that is all!"

"Speak," said Loutronio.

"Half? Half? Half of my estates?" brayed Egelbun.

Loutronio raised his eyebrows pertly. "My master could ask for more, more, more," he mocked, "if less is what you mean by half, half, half."

"I'm a lonely soul," replied Egelbun, sagging to his knees. He truly was about to cry. After all, he had leaped through such hoops of fire to inherit his half-brother's estate. And now, because of this nasty nephew Godfrey and this scheming *podestà's* boy, all of it was on the verge of ruin. Or at least half of it.

"Good day," said Loutronio, as if to take leave again.

"May I hear the plan first?" begged Egelbun. He beseeched the two with hands folded like a supplicant. "Prithee please? Let me first hear the plan. Then I will sign."

"Very well. Here it is," said Purvious. He took a deep breath, raised his chin, cleared his throat. "I will persuade Godfrey, in such a way to, in essence, kill me."

Egelbun's face brightened, and he struggled to get back on his feet. This didn't sound all that bad. "Do tell," he importuned, newly enervated.

"Once I am dead, " continued Purvious, "Godfrey will be taken away to prison. Since he has murdered a member of royalty in cold blood, he will be put to death at sunrise the next day and that is that."

"Where do I sign?" yawped Egelbun.

"And once he is dead," stated Purvious, "I arise from my grave—Lazarus-like—and marry your niece. I'll also take over half your estates."

Egelbun's face dropped like an old blanket falling off a bed. "Could you repeat that last part a second time? The resurrection idea?"

"Loutronio. Knife, please."

Loutronio pulled a wickedly sharp-looking blade from his bodkin and handed it to Purvious. "Here you are, my splendid lord," he said as he held out his hand, palm upward.

Purvious ran the blade along his servant's hand, cutting a thin, shallow slit in the skin. Blood seeped from the incision, but Loutronio simply smiled obsequiously.

"Thank you, my lord," said Loutronio.

Egelbun felt queasy, grabbed his paunch, and staggered slightly. He had met and made fête with some unwholesome fellows in his time, but these two were obscene.

"You're welcome," replied Purvious, and then asked coyly, "Do you love me Loutronio?"

"With all my heart, lord."

"Then you wouldn't mind if I killed you?"

"Not at all, my lord and master."

Purvious thrust the dagger into Loutronio's stomach, and the servant crumpled to the stone floor like a puppet whose strings have been cut.

"Wasn't he the president of the Servant's Guild?" asked the stunned Egelbun.

Without warning, Purvious turned on Egelbun and jammed the dagger into his blubbery stomach.

Egelbun's eyes—popping out of his head as if somebody had hit him on the back of the skull with a scaffold board—stared in horror at the dagger handle protruding from the folds of cloth covering his pudgy guts. A blood-curdling yawl escaped from deep in his throat. He dropped to the floor like a wineskin full of lard and lay there kicking.

A moment later, Loutronio, no longer dead, jumped nimbly to his feet and brushed himself off. He and Purvious gazed at Egelbun (who was still in wild death throws) with unparalleled jocundity.

"It's a trick dagger, Egelbun," said Purvious with disdain.

Egelbun opened one eye and peered up at the two. Then he clutched his body, feeling for a wound.

Purvious pushed the blade on the dagger in and out of the handle to show him how it disappeared into a hidden slot.

Egelbun slowly got to his feet. He did not bother brushing off the twigs and moss that begrimed his expensive robe. He was so mortified at being made the fool and so furious at Purvious and Loutronio and so relieved, oh, yes, so thoroughly relieved that he was still alive, that he could hardly speak. All of a sudden, he cast up his accounts on the floor. After he was done, he wiped his mouth, turned to the others, and said:

"Lovely trick."

Loutronio snickered cruelly and Purvious sniffed the air pretending to smell something stinky. "Somebody had better change his under belt," said Purvious, and this sent Loutronio into a gleeful snigger fit.

Egelbun feigned laughter but inside he was full of hateful rage.

"After Godfrey is executed," continued Purvious in narration of his plan, "a magician—that's your charge—under our employment will resurrect me from the grave. Everyone will rejoice at the miracle. I will gain a wife and properties and you will be able to retain your . . . " he gestured at Egelbun's gut, "your greatness. So what think you?"

"Oh, yes. Mmmmm . . . " hummed Egelbun.

"Does it make sense to you or must I put it all together in one slowly spoken paragraph?" huffed Purvious.

"Mmmm . . . " said Egelbun, as he imagined Purvious in that particular level of Dante's *Inferno* where flatterers go (the eight level, *Malebolge* by name), in which the sinners are upside down in *stronzo* with their arses in the air, eternally farting the most hideous stink-pots in all of Gehenna. In his fantasy, Purvious' face would be shoved into one of those flatulent bung holes by powerful, merciless goblin hands for a malodorous eternity.

"I provoke Godfrey into a duel," Purvious went on, oblivious to Egelbun's seething spleen. "We fight. He kills me with this fake dagger. We pretend my death. After Godfrey's true demise, we have our hired magician bring me back from the unknown regions. And then we have a very real wedding. At your expense."

"I like it," said Egelbun and he chuckled at the sound of Purvious' plaintive caterwauls echoing in his mind.

"Use my quill," offered Loutronio.

Egelbun tittered dementedly as he took the quill and signed his name with a flourish.

"Who," asks Antonio during the pause between chapters, "was the 'cheese-fearing lunatic who was forced to make buffalo mozzarella for the Pope'?"

"You have never heard this fable?" I ask with disbelief. "It is common knowledge in these parts and dates back to the late fourteenth century. I was told the tale by Pietro Serrafini, the cheese merchant round the corner."

"Never in my life," responds Antonio. "But it has pickled my interest, and I long to hear it."

"Piqued your interest, you mean?"

"Pardon?"

"It has piqued your interest?"

"I *would* have a *peek* at the story, indeed."

"No . . . what I'm trying to say is . . . " I give up with my attempted explanation, chew the end of the quill, and take a deep breath. Then I flip to the back of my notebook where I transcribed the fable told to me by *signore* Serrafini one rainy day whilst we sampled wine and cheese at his shop. I clear my throat and begin with:

"Once upon a time, during the Black Death, in fact, there was a young cheesemaker whose entire family died from the pestilence. This young man, thinking that bad cheese was the culprit, gave up the practice of cheesemaking all together. He was so overcome with grief that he did not notice that half the village had perished. Even his bitter enemy, Enrico the bread maker, who scorned cheese and would take not a morsel of it with his supper, had become a home for maggots. It so happens that the cheesemaker's name was Marco. A further consequence of all this death is that Marco went mad; in his madness he beat himself with the fibrous ladles used to skim the cheese; in doing so he attracted the attention of some wandering mendicants who were dressed as giant crows so as to ward off the plague. One of them beheld Marco and asked of him through his beak, 'Why with woven cheese skimmer doth thou strikest thyself?' And Marco did not reply. Another of the holy men asked him, 'Why dost thou wear nothing but a raiment of cheesecloth about thy loins?' And Marco did not reply. The third and final crow beat Marco with his staff until Marco replied, 'Cheese is the culprit! Cheese is Death.' The sanctified crows shuddered for none of them ate any cheese at all as it was a part of their vow not to partake of anything tasty. They had been living off of gruel and salt and black bread for lo these twenty years. Now here was proof that their wearisome diet had indeed saved them! For were they not alive whilst the brothers of the neighboring abbey who indulged in mozzarella and feta and parmesan and gorgonzola and even curds derived from the milk of cloven-hoofed goats, had subsequently perished outright at the start of the plague?"

Antonio is fidgeting with his toes, harvesting the gunk beneath the nails, and flicking the vile goo onto the floor. I tell him to stop, because he is distracting me from my reading. He informs me that this story is not nearly as interesting as *The Blacksmith and The Dancing Lady*. He questions whether or not cheese in and of itself is an exciting enough device to carry a plot. He adds that it would be more zestful if, rather than a mere cheesemaker, Marco was a zany, slapstick knight or a bawdyhouse gigolo. He also suggests that I throw in the odd maniacal Moor . . . the occasional drunken, licentious monk. Perchance, even an entire chapter that takes place in a pushing school. I tell him that if I had wanted advice from toe-jam plucking groundlings I would have asked for it. And furthermore, if he wants to hear the rest of Godfrey's tale, he will keep his lip buttoned!

He responds with a chastised grin.

Since Antonio is uninterested in the story, I will cease and desist. Pearls before swine, you know. But for the dear reader, understand that this has just been a small taste of the adventures of Marco. The fable is over a hundred pages long. I will summarize the dénouement.

After many long journeys, Marco was brought before the Pope who had heard that Marco was a skilled cheesemaker. The Pope's cheesemaker had long since perished from the Black Death and this Pope was desiring, nay, craving with utmost cheese-lust for a taste of delectable buffalo mozzarella. Marco refused point-blank to make the cheese. The Pope threatened to put him in the Iron Maiden. But even the unholy dread of this fiendish torture did not sway the cheesemaker. The Pope then ordered that Marco be subjected to that most heinous of dungeon perversions: the Happy Gopher. Faced with this gruesome, painful and downright embarrassing death, Marco relented. Whilst he stirred the buffalo milk in the vat and skimmed the top and worked the doughy cheese in his fingers, Marco screamed and gibbered and cried and shook like a lunatic.

"I want to tell a story," says Antonio a little testily. "I want to tell the story of *my* adventures. They're much more interesting than that ass-face Marco."

"I have heard your story, Antonio. It's shorter than Napoleon's pant leg and about as interesting as infertile dirt. You were an apprentice of some rude trade who joined the Italian army to fight with the French. They turned you into a latrine digger and beat you with a leather thong. You finally ran away during the Peace."

"That's just the boring old story that I told you, to trick you into hiring me," he replies petulantly. "If you knew about my true adventures, you never would have taken on such a man of the world."

"Oh, really?"

"Yes. Truly."

Since Antonio has been such a devoted and unwavering listener to my tale of the Gypsy, I have decided to humor him by putting his brief biography to paper (though he cannot grasp the written word and no one else will ever want to read it). I tell him to fetch my writing equipment: the portable bed-desk, paper, quill, and ink. He demands that I use red ink for his tale because, "It's all about lust and blood and reddish things." I make a great show of sharpening the quill and selecting the paper. Antonio's excitement is barely contained. He stands on the carpet, scuffing his toes across the nap in a curious dance. His manner reminds me of a dog which has just made *caca* then kicks up the grass with his hind legs.

I raise the quill over the paper, give a miniature bow and say, "You may begin."

18

The Clock Sniffer's Tale

"I am a true bastard," says Antonio.

"Pardon?" I reply.

"I am a true bastard," he repeats. "That is the first line of my story: 'I am a true bastard.' My story begins with that fact. And what is a *true* bastard as opposed to a *false* bastard, you might ask? Well, a true bastard is somebody whose *mother* doesn't even know who his father is. Now my mother wasn't a whore, exactly. She *did* take money for copulatory [*sic*] activities, but she would have done it for free if the men weren't willing to offer her restitulation [*sic*], bless her heart, the kind woman. So it was more of a hobby than a small business. I was apprenticed at a very young age to a master Clock Sniffer and—"

"Prithee, what is a Clock Sniffer?" I interject.

Antonio smiles smugly and crows, "You wealthy, educated men don't know everything, do you?"

"I have never heard of a Clock Sniffer, " I snort and add for good measure, "And I believe that you made it up."

"Is this *my* story or *your* story?" he asks.

"It is your story, but I'm not about to write down a pack of lies."

"It's no more unbelievable than a Tongue Scraper!"

"I have read about scrapers of tongues in books, Antonio. But never have I read about sniffers of clocks, and—"

"A Clock Sniffer," interrupts Antonio with a hint of spleen in his voice, "is . . . an expert whose job it is to sniff clocks!" He crosses his arms and nods his head, as if that has answered my question.

"And why, pray, would anyone want their clock sniffed?"

"Clocks are expensive, are they not?" he asks with a patronizing tone.

"Yes."

"And you wouldn't want anything living in your expensive clock, would you?"

"*Living* in them? Like what?" I laugh. "Wee little clock people?"

"Mice," he says.

"Mice?"

"We checked to make sure that mice weren't living in the clocks!"

"And how does one do that?" I query.

"By sniffing it!" cries Antonio. "We sniffed the clocks."

"For the scent of a mouse?"

Antonio bursts into laughter. He shakes his head and slaps his thigh. "For the scent of a mouse!" he cries. "Oh! That's a good one! Have you ever smelled a mouse?" he asks disparagingly.

"It is not exactly a pastime of mine," I reply.

"Well, mice don't smell," chuckles Antonio. "They don't smell at all."

"Do you sniff for their dung?" I ask.

"Dung!" bellows Antonio. He slaps his thigh some more.

"Have you ever smelled mouse dung?"

"Only when I get a whiff of your breath," I say, *sotto voce*.

"Tell me, good *signore*," inquires Antonio with the patronizing tone of a professor asking a rhetorical question of his most learnless and backward student, "what does an old clock smell like?"

"Confound thee, man!" I scream. "Quit asking me if I have smelled these obscure scents. I have smelled all sorts of things in my life, from yellow roses to turpentine. But never in my existence have I inhaled the guts of a clock!"

"Well, an old clock smells all musty, don't it?" replies Antonio with impatience. "And what does mouse dung smell like? Well, I'll tell you, so you don't have to work it out— mouse dung is all musty too! So if you're sniffing a clock for mice, and you smell something kind of musty, it could be mouse. Or it might just be the old damn clock its own self!" He flops on the floor, slaps his fat palms to his cheeks, and stares at me, shaking his head.

I scratch my chin and take a deep breath. "All right then," I say. "Prithee, what does a clock sniffer sniff for?"

Antonio lets forth an enormous guffaw and glances around the room, calling on an unseen audience to observe my ludicrous question. "What does a clock sniffer sniff for?" he asks the invisible observers. "Why, cheese, of course!"

I let forth an involuntary laugh. I cover my mouth so that he cannot see my mirth and urge him on with a wave of my hand. "Please continue."

Antonio crosses his arms. "Are you going to keep interrupting my story?"

"Only when the hilarity of your commentary or the audacity of your mendacity provoke an involuntary replication."

"Good," he replies. "Now then. Where was I? Ah, yes. I had been working as master Angelo's apprentice for seven years. During that time I had shown my worth on several occasions. Once, I found a whole mouse colony in the Count Querini's giant cuckoo. The Count had a huge collection of clocks. Swiss grandfathers and . . . English chronometers. Viennese mantle pieces and German pendulums. He even had an old fashioned Roman water clock, an antique thing it was, and I sniffed out a whole hive of water bugs that were living at the bottom of it. The Count and I became the best of friends and . . .

"I see the look on your face, *signore*. You're saying to yourself, 'Antonio only befriended this old man so that he could sniff his lovely clocks in secret.' Well, you're wrong! He was like a father to me. The father I never had. On my day off, I would go to his villa where he taught me to ride a horse and do sword tricks. But the Count was an old man, and eventually he died. And on his death bed, he bequeathed me with a golden broach in the shape of a nose—it was a reward for my services to him—and I wore the nose proudly for the better part of a year until I lost it playing dice with an apprentice dog buffer. And that was when my luck changed for the worse. Soon after, I developed a sinus infection which would not go away. I tried every remedy on earth, but still my nose remained as stopped up as a corked barrel bung. After six months of my sickness, master Angelo petitioned the Guild to void my contract and I was cast into the street with nothing more than the clothes on my back and a pouch which contained only a rag for my snot and a dirty piece of string with too many knots in it to do much good.

"For months and months, I lived behind a dung heap next to the stables. Not a minute did pass in which I did not curse my fate. When recruiting officers from Napoleon's army came to the city, I went and heard their speech in the *piazza*. They told of the glories of the French troops, and how we could be a part of that glory, if only we would take up arms and enlist in the Italian corps. They didn't care that I couldn't smell worth a damn. 'The only clock in this army is the sun,' they said. 'When it comes up, it's time to attack, and when it goes down, it's time to attack some more!' Well, the French made me one of them dragoons, and . . .

"I can tell by the look on your face that you can't believe it! Well, I'll admit that I'm an average horsey rider. But I will tell you, *signore* Smythe, it was my swordplay that convinced them. Yes! You see, the Count taught me a trick whereby I'm blindfolded and I grasp a sword in either hand. Then a whole gang attacks me and I fend them off from both sides. I actually cut three soldiers in half and one right down the middle. Oh, it was disgusting! If I hadn't been blindfolded, I would have puked at the sight of all those guts and brains on the grass; but the Frenchmen, who are used to eating their horrible French food, didn't even bat an eyelid. The recruiting officer was so impressed by my carnage, he put me in command of a whole spittoon . . . err . . . what? Ah, yes . . . I mean, a whole *platoon*.

"Many battles did I fight. Many Russians did I maim and kill. My name became famous throughout the army. Whenever I was stationed near a great manor or castle, I was always invited to the big dances which they call 'ball parties' up north. All the fancy ladies wanted to see me—'Antonio, the Italian Butcher.' At one particular castle in Prussia, I was introduced to the most beautiful woman I had ever looked at. Her name was Princess Vurstenhaufen and her skin was as pale as a fish. A pretty fish, mind you. And her hair was as yellow as nice German straw. She noticed me staring at the great clock in the hallway. (I longed to sniff it to see if it contained mice.)

" 'Why, sir, doth thou stare at the clock with such longing?' she asked. 'Doth thou doubt it keepeth good time?'

" 'Nay-eth,' I replied. 'I doth not-eth care-eth what-eth time-eth it-uth is-uth. I only admire the beauty of it-uth.'

" 'If I were a clock, would you stareth at me that way?' she asked.

"'If you were a clock, I'd open your back door and sniffeth your gears,' I said. I was about to add, 'And see if you smell like cheese,' but I noticed that she had turned bright red, like the color the knob of your *cazzo* makes when you see how hard you can squeeze it. She grabbed me by the hand and took me . . . nay . . . dragged me up to her room. I cannot tell you the things that we did for she had no clock in her room, but I performed many of the same duties I did for the Count's timepieces, only upon her person.

"After it was over, we lay on the bed exhausted, like two lonely shepherds who have chased a shy ewe all over a mountaintop on a summer day. The Princess told me that she loved me more than her husband, the General. At that moment, the bedroom door was flung open and there he was! His sword was drawn and he had a horsewhip in one hand and he screamed something in that terrible German tongue. Even though I couldn't understand the words, I knew that I was in deep s - - t. I fended him off with a gilded chair for as long as I could, but the whip struck me here on the chin where you can still see the scar. See it? Well, the only way out was through the window, so I jumped out and landed on a soft, fat man who was making water against the wall. I was forced to steal the clothes of a tanner's apprentice and I ran all the way through the woods to the road, which is where you found me, begging for a ride back home, smelling of the dogberries the tanners use to cure the leather hides.

"There! That's my tale. And I hope you put down every word of it. I plan on learning to read someday and I'll be vexed if what I've told you just now isn't on this page. For I'll have a hard enough time remembering it tomorrow, let alone fifty years from now."

19

THE ARGONAUT

During the time that Egelbun, Purvious, and Loutronio were plotting Godfrey's death, a tall, barrel-chested man in a dust-covered mantle was walking north toward Carthusalem on a lonely dirt road. He stopped and leaned against an ancient oak tree and wiped the sweat from his brow. He had traveled many miles and gone through more adventures than the wily Ulysses to get to this place; he relished the sight of the familiar towers rising from behind the city's great walls. He was much changed since he had departed from his home three long years ago. *Verily, even my children will not recognize me*, he mused. For what used to be puffy and pale from leisure was now tanned and chiseled from hard living. In addition to a mustache, he now wore a long forked beard. His body, formerly rotund, was today muscled and lean like a soldier's.

A very short man wearing a hood strode up to the tree, tripped, spilled the bladder of water he had collected from the river, sighed, and turned back toward the river to try once again.

"Stay," said Thomas to his servant. "I can wait until we make the public fountain at the great bazaar. Pray, Gurditta Singh, faithful foreign servant. Come and gaze upon my city. It has been many years since I last viewed its fair towers and gilded roofs." The orange light of dusk illuminated the buildings in an ephemeral glow.

At that moment, the Dim Avenger strode up to the tree. The thief was carrying a large sack over his shoulder. He stopped and stared at Thomas with a nefarious leer.

"Ahoy!" exclaimed Thomas jovially. "What say you, good fellow traveler, on this dusky evening?"

"Your money," hissed the thief.

"Pardon?" asked Thomas.

"Give me all your money or I'll kill you."

"I am sorry, my dear scoundrel," replied Thomas without fear. "But you have opened an empty chest, stepped into a vacant room, peered up at a starless sky. I am in distress. There is a wolf at my door. I am at low tide. I am broke."

The Dim Avenger bowed. "Good sir, I believe your words and offer you my service, for it is my habit to steal from the opulent and give to the bereft."

"Who art thou, Royal Scamp," asked Thomas, "that I may speak to you as man to man, not cloaked person to cloaked person?"

"It is my custom to first ask of my victim or my recipient his name," said the Dim Avenger.

"I must tell you that it has been my long-held custom to remain anonymous in my vast wanderings; it is difficult for me to reveal my name to a stranger." Thomas' tone was growing more and more annoyed as he spoke. "Especially one who threatens first to rob me, then shortly thereafter to benefit me, and all the while keeps his name from me."

The Dim Avenger replied peevishly, "It is I who stand in the position to receive your name first since it was I who first asked it."

"On the contrary," stated Thomas, "it is always proper for an inhabitant of a place to tell a stranger his name since he is, in a broad and general aspect, acting *in spiritu* as a host of his city."

The Dim Avenger clapped his hands triumphantly. "There you are caught! For I do not associate myself with that stinking vile rattrap of a place. I spit on it and its bloated population of snivelling reprobates." He spat.

"Has the city changed so since I have been away?" Thomas asked with wonder.

"It depends on how long you have been gone. Three years have passed since Zalman Verrazanno, the great merchant, was lost at sea. Since that time his evil half-brother, Egelbun, has taken over his properties and the city has turned into a foul and sinister place. 'Where one rat abides . . . '" the Dim Avenger trailed off, leaving the all-too-familiar platitude incomplete.

Thomas steadied himself against the tree. "Holy Christ! The deuce you say! Not Egelbun, that lousy cur! That good-for-naught-flap-ear'd-knave! The lands and titles were to have passed to Godfrey, the good adopted son of Zalman Verrazanno."

"How do you know this?" asked the Dim Avenger suspiciously.

"I . . . I was a friend of Zalman Verrazanno," replied Thomas. "I was his secret confidant and partner. I was on board the ill-fated ship which bore him to distant lands and his untimely death."

The Dim Avenger took a step back and asked softly, "Then it is true that he is dead?"

"Very true. I saw him perish with mine own eyes."

The Dim Avenger's shoulders drooped. He seemed about to swoon, then leaned on his sword for support. He stared into the distance, and after a long pause asked, "If you were such a good friend of Zalman Verrazanno, why do I not know of you?"

"If I do not know who *you* are," asked Thomas, "how am *I* to know why *you* do not know of *me*?"

"Tell me something secret about Zalman Verrazanno that only he and his close friends would know. Then I will trust you."

"May I be so bold as to ask of you the same?"

"I asked first," whined the crook.

Thomas stroked his beard and peered at the highwayman with keen eyes. Then he sniffed and said, "Verrazanno had a daughter."

"He still does," replied the scamp.

"And this daughter had a pet rabbit whom she loved with all her heart," continued Thomas.

"Aye?" The Dim Avenger's voice trembled with excitement.

"And this rabbit had a name."

"Aye? Aye?"

"The rabbit's name was . . . " he paused for effect then said, "Lord Frou Frou!"

The Dim Avenger jumped up and down, laughing girlishly. "Yes! Yes! How very true! Lord Frou Frou was the dear rabbit's name!"

Thomas stared askance at this strange fellow. The Dim Avenger caught the curious glance and stopped his uncharacteristic cavorting.

"May I ask you how you know this creature's name?" asked Thomas.

"I am a friend of Mamooshka's," replied the Dim Avenger defensively.

"Yes," said Thomas dryly. "You are the sort of friend she would acquaint herself with. What led you, a seemingly intelligent young man, to adopt such a wasteful life?"

"My own father is dead and . . . " the Dim Avenger's voice cracked and stopped.

"Did you love your father?" asked Thomas with compassion.

"I loved him with all my heart," answered the outlaw sincerely. "Though he treated me like a child."

Thomas sighed. "Alas! 'Tis the manner of all creatures with those whom they adore and seek to protect from the evils of the world."

"You seem to have suffered, dear fellow. Your sigh tells a tale of sorrow."

"Suffered?" said Thomas, more as a statement than a question. "Oh, yes. I suppose. You see, I was a wealthy man, much like my friend Verrazanno. I had become bloated with luxury and fat with pride. And when all of that was taken from me, I nearly lost my mind."

"Please, would you tell me your tale?"

"Dear boy, that would take a week."

"The abridged version, then."

"At least a day."

"The summarized account, perhaps?"

"You really wish to hear it?"

The Dim Avenger nodded his head. "But please begin with an account of my . . . " he paused, coughed nervously, "an account of my *friend* Mamooshka's father. Tell me how he died."

Thomas shook his head woefully. "I cannot lie. His last moments were shameful."

The Dim Avenger let forth a distraught exhalation at this revelation. He seemed to lose his balance, but Thomas and Gurditta Singh were quick to help him to a seat upon a rock.

"We had been sailing for three days," began Thomas, after the Dim Avenger had recovered from his bout of swooning. "The weather had been fine. Both Verrazanno and I loved the sea as we always felt rejuvenated upon the water. We enjoyed sitting in our cabin and reading books, eating figs and other dainties, and listening to the hard work taking place on the deck above. The crew was the usual lot of grim men, but those kind of fellows make the best sailors. We thought nothing peculiar about their looks or actions. If we had been paying attention, however, if we had not been living in our isolated little world, if we had been attuned to undercurrents flowing around us, we would have caught the wry looks and strange smiles that were directed at our persons whenever we left our bepillowed cabin to come onto the deck.

"We had been napping on that third day when I awoke to the sound of the lookout crying, 'Sharks!' I thought nothing of it and went back to sleep. Several minutes later, the door burst open and our room was filled with sailors. All of them carried great gleaming knives. They grabbed us quite roughly and pushed us onto the deck. The captain, poor man, was already bound and gagged upon the poop, and his terrified eyes implored me most piteously. 'Mutiny!' I cried. 'How can this be? Master Verrazanno pays you better than any merchant in the city.' In response, the leader of the gang brought his fist against my cheek. 'We've found a better master,' said the pirate with a leer. 'One who will make us all rich.' The mutineers grabbed us and bound our hands. 'Take the ship,' cried Verrazanno, 'but leave us alive.' 'Ho, we'll leave you alive,' said the leader. 'That was part of *his* plan.'

"Then, dear boy, these cutthroats, these monsters brought out three buckets brimming with blood and guts and splashed us with this goat's gore. Aye. You shudder because you can see it coming, can't you? So could Verrazanno. He screamed like a madman. 'Sharks!' he cried. 'Not sharks!' (For as you may well know, Zalman was terrified of those ocean demons and had nightmares about them the whole of his life.)

"Those coldhearted buccaneers giggled and capered upon the deck, mocking his tears and sobs. 'Dear God!' shrieked Verrazanno. 'Anything! Name your price!' He would have sold his soul to the devil to escape that hideous death and it pained my own soul to see him cower so poltroonishly in the face of disaster.

"They hoisted the three of us, the captain, Verrazanno, and me, onto the railing, then dropped us like goat dumplings into the sea. They had not bound our feet, better so that we would tread the water like living bait for the water beasts. Verrazanno and I were both fat men and we were able to hold our heads above water quite easily, kicking with just our legs; but the captain was as slender as a stick, and he thrashed wildly about to keep from sinking. His ferocious flopping instantly brought the sharks to him. The noise of those creatures tearing into his flesh is a sound that I will never forget. The carnage brought a dozen of the monsters and soon the water was churning with their gray hides and his blood. We could hear the sailors screeching and braying with glee at this hideous show. I waited with blind terror for the jaws to find me next. I pulled desperately at the ropes binding my hands, but I could not break their hold. Verrazanno was the next to die. Fortunately, it was over quickly.

"In that moment, I gave up hope of ever living, and said my final prayers. Strangely, my life did not flash before my eyes. Only the faces of my children appeared in my mind. The regret that I would never see them again pierced my heart more wickedly than any shark's tooth. When I saw the dorsal fin heading toward me, I closed my eyes and let myself begin to sink.

"What happened then? How do I stand here before you? Listen and be amazed. I had resigned myself to death and

Damnation and Salvation

hoped that I would drown rather than be chewed upon by those terrible fish. The next moments have become a blur in my mind. I felt an animal's hairless skin against my flesh and sensed that my body was lifted from the water. I had the sensation of moving through the waves, as if I were a tiny boat propelled by some unseen force. The voices from the ship had grown distant and were becoming weaker and weaker with every second. I finally opened my eyes and what did I see? A black eye without pupil staring back at me. It shot a spray of water into my face and I realized that it was blowhole. My hands, still bound, were in the jaws of a porpoise and it clutched the rope like a horse's bit. This kindly beast had rescued me from the sharks and was spiriting me away to safety. Why did he save me? I don't know. I did not have the strength to even ponder this question at the time. All I knew was that I had quite literally escaped the jaws of death.

"What did you say, dear lad? Yes. Later on I came to the same conclusion. The porpoise was an angel sent by our Heavenly Father himself—my guardian angel. Gurditta Singh, give the young man a drink of water. There, my dear Royal Scamp, you looked parched. Perhaps we should wait . . . well, if you insist, I will continue with my tale.

"The porpoise brought me to a calm inlet, then gently rolled over, letting me slip from his grasp. With a skilled and mighty snap of his mandibles, he cut through the ropes that bound my hands. 'Thank you, sir porpoise,' I said to him. 'I owe you my life.' He looked at me with one laughing eye, clicked and screeched merrily, then dove under water and was gone. My trials did not end with my deliverance from pirates and ocean devils, however. For the porpoise, savior though he was, knew nothing of the landscape of men and had left me in one of the most notorious hellholes in all the world: in the land of Ozkack pirates! I had not been on the shore for more than an hour before I was captured by slavers and put to work

in a galley. O, those first weeks were hell on earth. I confess
that I actually cursed God for sparing my life, only to be put
into this state of cruel bondage. In the first days, the flesh on
my hands bubbled up like poorly primed paint and the oars I
held were slick with my own blood. My shoulders and legs
and spine ached from morning until night. And that was not
the worst of it. For the ship was lorded over by a wicked man
who took a keen disliking to the tender skin upon my back;
he whipped me until my flesh was a lacework of welts and
scars.

"Gurditta Singh, please take this piece of cloth and fan the
young man. He looks a little pale.

"A year of this misery I endured. My body grew as lean
and muscled as it had been in my youth; my heart became as
hard as a rock. At first I received the strength to live from hat-
ing God for taking everything away from me. I cursed him
every moment of my waking hours. But when I slept, I dreamt
of home and my children, and what joy they had brought me.
These happy dreams kept me from completely losing my
mind because my waking life became nothing more than a
continuous nightmare. All during that time, I pondered who
was the 'him' who had turned our ship's crew against us. It
became my obsession. I vowed to live only so that I could find
this villain and kill him.

"And then the storm came—the greatest storm that I had
ever seen in the middle earth sea. It dashed our ship upon the
rocks with such force that the very chains that bound me to
the wooden seats were ripped from their ring bolts. Even
though my legs and arms were still manacled, I had grown so
powerful from my constant exercise that I was able to swim
the hundred yards to shore in spite of that extra weight. I did
not tarry on the beach but headed straight inland: I had had
enough with water and wanted nothing more to do with it.

"Soon I was in another kind of sea—a sea of sand. I wandered for weeks in that parched place, a region so dry it makes a mummy of you. I lost so much weight that the bracelets that encircled my hands and feet slipped off without my even noticing. The people of that desert bury their dead in the sand with only their faces showing; often did I pass an unseeing countenance peering up from the dunes like a wizened death mask of shriveled fig-skin. When I finally reached a small caravan town, I was near death with exhaustion. But a kindly holy man took me into his care and nursed me back to health. I became his helper and learned the ways of the desert . . . and the life of an ascetic. He taught me how to sit in silent contemplation and forget about the world and my past. He told me not to worry about my family nor lost wealth nor revenge. For the first time in my life, I had no desires. I had no possessions. I craved nothing except to look into that place inside myself, a place that I had never glimpsed before.

"I might have stayed with the old man forever but he died. With his passing, all of the old nagging worries came flooding back. What of my son and daughter? What has happened to my belongings? Who was the 'him' that brought about my ruin?

"I became a camel-driver with a caravan that was making a journey across the great wastes to the home of Hannibal. From there, I believed, I could gain passage back home. The trek took two long years, and many more adventures did I have along the way: bandits and oases, lost maidens and djinns. I could rival Scheherazade with my tales. But however interesting those anecdotes may be, they do not concern us now. In short, I made it to the land of the Ethiopes. There I did gain passage on a merchant vessel from Gezan heading for Corfu. Yet halfway across the Mediterranean, the captain and his crew attempted to put me in chains and thus sell me again into slavery! I slew them all with my sword, shouting with great wrath in the language of the Arabs: *Lami, ianon ancati telethe elphi seraphi: vualla anemaiati chelp menelchelp.* Which translates roughly as: 'O, foolish ones, I was going to give you three thousand ducats, by God, but I won't give them now, you curs, sons of mongrels!' And so I took the ship for myself and piloted it home alone, a little worse for wear but so much wiser."

The Dim Avenger shook his head slowly. "Your story, coming from the lips of any other man, would seem fantastic and unbelievable; but I trust the unvarnished truth of your words, just as I am certain of the honesty in your eyes. Pray, tell me your name."

"They call me . . . Thomas the Wandering Merchant. Tom for short."

"Well, Tom, I am known only as the Dim Avenger."

"What, are you stupid?"

"I must give consideration to changing my name," said the Dim Avenger under his breath, then replied in a strong voice, "Listen, Thomas! Any friend of Zalman Verrazanno will be in peril in that city. Even now, the *podestà's* pasty son is conniving with Egelbun to kill off Godfrey and marry Verrazanno's sweet and kindly daughter to himself."

"The *podestà's* pasty son! Godfrey! Egelbun! Mamooshka . . . " Thomas frowned with disbelief, " 'sweet and kindly?' "

"For these three long years she has been kept cloistered in a dank room with no one but herself for company and she has indeed changed," said the thief. "Godfrey has been missing from the city since the day Zalman Verrazanno left and only last night returned; he is his old, helpless self. And as for Egelbun, it is my opinion that he—the depraved brute—devised his own brother's death."

"Yes. I have come to believe that he is the 'him' I have been seeking," said Thomas. "I must go to Mamooshka and have words with her."

"Fie! She's just a woman!" said the Dim Avenger with disgust. "What help could she give you? Listen! I have a newly-met friend, known only as 'the Gypsy,' a strong and virile gentleman, quite capable of many manly deeds and manners. To him you should go and ask help."

"But in the light of day I might be recognized as . . . errrr . . . Zalman Verrazanno's old friend."

"Go in disguise! Just now, before coming upon you, I robbed a most foul and pathetic man who pretends to be a magician. This mountebank has been going about from village to village, duping poor rubes with his false medicines and seeming powers. I struck him one great blow upon the head and whilst he was unconscious, stripped him of his clothes. Here in this bag I have his cloak and hat and articles of pseudo-magic. Put on his costume and play his part, for a magician is always welcome and accepted and looked for in such unnatural cities as Carthusalem. Go to the Inn of the Happy Cock and there you will find the Gypsy."

"I will take your advice, Dim Avenger. Come, Gurditta Singh, help me into my costume."

Gurditta Singh sneezed and his hood was thrown back.

The Dim Avenger was stunned, for Thomas' servant bore an uncanny resemblance to . . . "Short Clog?!" he exclaimed with disbelief.

As Thomas put on the magician's outfit, he spoke: "Nay, this is not Short Clog, good Godfrey's faithful servant, but a man bearing an uncannily similar visage to that same fellow. His name is Gurditta Singh, and I saved him from a cruel master in a distant land. He does not speak our language though he understands certain things. Is it not strange how he mirrors Short Clog's features?"

"Strange indeed. Until we meet again, Tom, the Wandering Merchant and Gurditta Singh, faithful foreign servant. Adieu to the two of you."

The Dim Avenger ran off into the darkness. Almost immediately, Drapslod scurried up to Thomas and bowed.

"Good evening, sir, are you a magician?" asked Drapslod.

Thomas instantly recognized the House of Verrazanno's ancient doorkeeper. "Drapslod!" he exclaimed happily, then remembered angrily that he was supposed to be incognito and that he had probably ruined his disguise.

Drapslod fell to his knees, looked toward Heaven, and cried joyfully, "Here must be a magician, for he has just conjured my own name, a task which the greatest lords of the city in combination could not do!"

Thomas spoke softly to Gurditta Singh. "This is a servant of the House of Verrazanno. He doesn't smoke me in this fashion. He thinks I am a thought reader." Thomas turned to Drapslod and spoke in a deep, mysterious voice. "You there! What does your fat master . . . " he paused dramatically, "Egelbun wish of me?"

Drapslod gasped at the mention of Egelbun's name. "Most knowledgeable sir, my master has been looking far and wide for a magician to come to his house and perform certain tasks for him."

What a stroke of luck this is, thought Thomas. *I will go to the House of Verrazanno and see firsthand what that wicked Egelbun is about. Then, I will instruct Gurditta Singh, with certain gestures and the few scarce words we share between us, to make way to the Happy Cock and deliver a message from me to the Gypsy.* He fumbled in the pocket of the magician's cloak and pulled forth an unmarked papyrus scroll. *I will write the note on this blank screed-roll taken from the magician's mantle. How shall I begin? Ahhh, yes . . .*

Dear reader, I hold a piece of that very scroll in my fingers! It is the secret scrap that I keep on the special shelf between two panes of glass (and this covered by the thick swath of velvet to protect it from the sun). It is about the size of my palm, the color of a sun-dried leaf. Under a magnifying glass one can identify the fibers from which it was pressed: reedy papyrus and the stiff hairs of a goat. I hold the magnifying lens to the surface and grasping the parchment with my special padded tweezers, gently turn it up so that I can see the words, "I, a wandering mer . . . (tiny hole, space for two letters, almost certainly 'c' and 'h') . . . ant in the guise of a magician . . . " which runs into the torn edge of my magnificent fragment. Is that not undeniable proof of my tale? Is it not? Wait, there is more! Gently, ever so gently, I rotate the fragment to reveal the most significant evidence of all, the most wondrous secret held within this enigmatic document (that I value more than if it were the Holy Shroud of Christ itself): the mark that entirely verifies the veracity of my story.

"Antonio, draw the shades," I call out. The room is cast into darkness, lit only by the eerie glow of a single candle: this flame burns eternally in front of a bust of Plato on my desk. I cover the fire with the lantern I commissioned from those cunning Murano glass blowers. An ingenious design: extreme heat without the burning properties of the flame. With trembling hand I hold my precious document to the glass, and the invisible symbols embossed thereon appear like a road sign etched in stone emerging from a mist. The cabalistic letters, black as tar, display the remaining segment of their hideous message: ". . . does hereby consign his soul to Hell for eternity." My heart beats like a chased fox. The darkness is too much!

"Antonio!" I cry. "Light! Light!"

Antonio pulls back the shades and once again the room is suffused with heavenly sunbeams. Yet even as the evil words begin to fade, one can still see a lovely, looping *f* of the word "frey," the remaining part of Godfrey's signature that, long ago, was inscribed under the invisible text of this unholy contract. One *can still see* that the name was signed in blood.

"Antonio! Wine!"

20

THE HELLHAG

The so-called magician who cured Godfrey of his affliction—the impostor who claimed to be Short Clog's uncle—sat on the ground with his back to a small cedar. His arms were stretched around the trunk and his hands tied together at the back, thus locking him to the tree. Upon his balding pate was a fair-sized lump. He was dressed only in his small clothes.

He had been awake for several hours, staring into space, lost in thought. But he was so still and silent that he had virtually become part of the landscape. A rabbit hopped from the undergrowth, sat in a patch of sunlight, and nibbled on some grass at the man's feet. Since there was no one else nearby, and the false magician was longing to voice his predicament, he decided to address the rodent.

"You observe before you an old man," he began, sans accent. "Beaten and robbed. Abandoned in this humiliating posture. But I am not as I appear to be."

The rabbit perched on its haunches, stared curiously at the speaker, and groomed the fur around its eyes.

"In reality," continued the fettered monologist, "I am Azfall, second lieutenant of the assistant to the Lord of Demons. I know this sounds absurd, my dear rabbit, and you probably think that I am mad, but I am telling the truth. Probably the only honest thing I've said in a thousand decades. For, you see, I was sent to this world to steal the soul of a good man. Having completed my task, I set out to do the many little ruinous things that are in my power and authority (under the auspices of the Evil One) to commit in this world of fools. Once I had Godfrey's soul, I should have made straightway to Hell and received my reward. But I was greedy. There were so many creatures here to corrupt, so many plagues to spread! I collected a pouch full of contracts whilst I was here. Human souls, the most valuable item in the universe, mind you, bought for trifles: power, wealth, revenge, satiated lust. I created tyrants and made merchants rich, killed true love out of jealousy and warped innocence.

"Now Godfrey was a different sort of proposition. Before he came to this dung heap of a world, he was a Lord in the Kingdom of God. Do not ask me why he was forced to take on this gross physical form. I do not know the rules that apply in that other domain. All I know is that he was intended to bring light and happiness to this dark globe and that is where I came onto the scene. Know that my Overseer plays a strange game with Godfrey's Lord. It is a game that they have played since He was cast down from that high place, eons ago. It is a balancing act. A chess match. A tug of war. My task is to even the odds. To thwart the good.

"So, when Godfrey was a child, I took him from his rightful place. He was meant to be a Gypsy king, one of those happy wanderers who banish bleak reality with their songs and stories and give hope to those with impoverished imaginations. Godfrey was supposed to instill the denizens of this sorrow-sick planet with hope and joy, and raise their heavy heads and hearts heavenwards to a better place. That is why I snatched him from his cradle and left him in a reeking stable amongst the most low-minded and venal pariahs I could find: a merchant family. And what's more, I took away the one attribute that mattered most to him: I stole his voice. Then I left him for several years and pursued other subjects. Time and circumstance were my tools to bend him to abject misery. Finally, all I had to do was offer him the gift of speech. Brilliant in its simplicity. Elegant in its subtlety. Rich in its cruelty. Quite original.

"Now, after being fleeced of my clothes wherein was hidden the papyrus scroll upon which was signed, in blood, his soul, I am undone." The Demon took a deep breath and stretched his arms. His sinews creaked, his muscles bulged, and the ropes snapped like thread. He stood up and rubbed his wrists.

"Actually, I enjoy a challenge. Is it not a struggle which

builds and strengthens one's character? Perhaps my dark Lord is testing me. Perhaps he is setting me this trial to make sure I am worthy of his ranks." Azfall smiled. "I feel better." A hand strayed to the lump on his head and he winced at the pain. "Except my ears are still ringing from that blow upon my head. Even though I am a demon at heart, this body in which I travel is quite human. I am, howbeit, gifted with several strengths of unnatural origin. Now I need a new persona."

The demon stroked his nose pensively. "Perchance a wandering mendicant? Or a doctor of theology?" He smiled wickedly. "Nay. Hold! I have it!"

Azfall's entire body convulsed, and a horrid sound—the cracking of bones and the tearing of tissue—emanated from his shuddering form. The rabbit, had it not been transfixed by the demon's fiendish power, would have bolted long ago; but the sound of Azfall's magical voice had bewitched the poor animal and all it could do was stare with terror at the incomprehensible metamorphosis taking place before it. The demon's flesh fell from its body like old clothes to reveal the form of a beautiful, naked woman. Her face was Botticellian in its perfection. Her long, curling hair shone like the tresses of an Arabian princess. Her breasts . . . nay, I will not think of them for in doing so would put me in mortal peril. Needless to say, she was the kind of woman who would make a departed Pope gambol and swagger.

"The Temptress!" she said with a laugh, and her gaiety was both cruel and seductive.

Just then, a wild boar, snorting for truffles, forged through the underbrush and startled the poor rabbit out of the spell. The rabbit bolted into the woods. (It did not stop until a fortnight had passed, and from that magical day forth had more adventures than any hare from Aesop.) The boar, however, was neither scared nor repelled by the demoness. In fact, he was fascinated by the strange, malodorous smell that wafted from her devilish skin. Despite her ravishing form, there was no disguising the stench of Hell.

"Snort," said the boar.

"Hello, my comely brute," said Azfall.

"Grunt," replied the pig.

"Prepare yourself for a transmutation," said the demoness and waved her hand in front of the animal's snout.

The boar twitched and grunted and slobbered and screeched. It too shed its skin. From the pile of smoking bacon and tusk emerged a short, stubby man bearing the striking resemblance to none other than Short Clog! The newly-made minion instantly ran to Azfall and, with arduous maneuver, attached himself to her svelte leg.

Azfall kicked the little savage away. "Sit," she ordered.

The pig-man sat obediently on his haunches.

"You answer to the name 'Short Clog,' said the demoness. "Can you say that? 'Short Clog?'"

"Stinky *caca*!" replied the demon spawn.

"Short Clog!" repeated Azfall.

"Grubby poo poo!" answered the pig-man.

Azfall sounded out the name, "Sha-"

"Sha-"

"Ort!"

"Sn-Ort!"

"Ka-"

"Ka-poo poo!" screeched the swine-goblin. He rolled on the ground, scratching his dainties, laughing maniacally.

"Very good," said Azfall sardonically, and she gave him a good swift kick. "Just keep your little mouth shut and listen to me. I will go to the woods outside of Mamooshka's estate. You will proceed to an inn: the Happy Cock. There you will find Godfrey. Bring him to me. Do you understand?"

Hog-fellow nodded his head vigorously.

"Bring him to me without delay," continued Azfall. "Not only will I have Godfrey's soul, I'll have his virginity as well."

"This was a very good chapter!" exclaims Antonio. "That diabolo is a proper minx! A right *buona roba*. I'd enjoy eating her supper-dish at the banquet of love. How will Godfrey ever be able to resist her devilish beauty?"

"Perchance he will not be able to resist." My voice is laden with doom. "Perchance he will succumb."

Antonio smiles and raises his eyebrows. "Now *that* would be a story. Trapped in Hell with a comely succubus."

"Hell is not a pleasant place," I declare. "It is full of evil smells, tormented souls, and searing heat."

"*Signore,*" laughs Antonio, "you have just described Firenze in July."

"My dear boy, Hell is a very bad place. Heaven is where you should aspire."

"In the next chapter," he says, "the demon should sport her dairy."

"Pardon?" I reply, shocked at his coarse language.

"I think that you should describe her bosom," he says with a leer. "Something along the lines of . . . 'Like two majestic pumpkins, her baubles were bursting to be free of her gown.' What do you think of that? Poetical, no?"

I shake my head disdainfully. "Not all men are attracted to women who possess gargantuan . . . errr . . . torsos."

"Like two massive wheels of parmesan hanging in a cheesecloth sack, her thingamabobs strained against her chemise."

"Your similes, Antonio, are thoroughly vulgarian."

"Like two . . . "

"If they were to be described as anything," I interject before he can construe another revolting comparison, "I would say that they looked like perfectly proportioned honeydew melons, ripe and pliant and ready for the handling. Now, let me carry on with the story."

21

An Exchange of Missives

Short Clog, bearing his master's laboriously written love letter to Mamooshka (grasped delicately between his finger tips as if it were the maidenhead of his dear sister), entered the bazaar from the north gate.

At the very same instant, approaching in exactly the opposite direction, was the loyal Gurditta Singh, carrying Zalman Verrazanno's message to the Gypsy. Gurditta Singh was also lost to the world, focused upon his important mission.

Their paths were like two sides of a triangle that must inevitably intersect at the apex. Do not question the reality of this convergence. Do not cast it aside as mere coincidence. I know that the city was large and full of many streets and the odds of these two bumping into each other was next to impossible. But these identical servants were drawn together by unseen forces that go beyond our meager ken. Think of all instances when a simple decision could have altered the course of history. What if poor King Harold had stood one small inch to the left at the Battle of Hastings? The arrow that pierced his eye would have merely grazed his scalp and those homicidal Normans might have been given a decent thrashing. Or consider the Duke of Medina Sidonia, he who led the Armada against the English. If the Duke had simply looked outside his window on that fateful morning of their Channel crossing and said, "The sky looks a trifle sinister; mayhaps we should weigh anchor the day *after* tomorrow," I might be writing this story *en español*. They had no choice in the matter, however. They were steered by invisible winds.

Pray, let us turn our attention back to Short Clog and Gurditta Singh so that I may prove my thesis. Not only did our messengers play a part in the greater arc of our tale, but their own lives had been destined from birth to collide. At the moment, they were both running through the bazaar as fast as their duck legs would carry them. A casual observer, looking down upon the scene from a rooftop vantage, would see no danger of these two meeting. Indeed, Short Clog's route took him close to the saffron-seller's stall, whilst Gurditta Singh's course had him pass near the ostrich-egg dealer on the opposite side of the lane. In a trice, they would scurry by one another without incident.

But what is this? A mad Gypsy moth just flew up the nose of a cart horse! This event is not unique: bugs find themselves in the nostrils of horses with great regularity; but this horse was particularly timorous of flying insects, especially when they were up his snoot. Recently, he was much aggrieved when an enraged wasp lodged itself in his muzzle and stung him most cruelly. Believing that the moth was a terrible wasp, the horrified horse started forward, reared violently, then bucked like a colt. The cart he was pulling—a cart stacked precariously to the top with wine barrels—lurched out of control. Hogsheads tumbled off and onto the street.

Short Clog, lest he be flattened by one of these barrels dodged to the right. Gurditta Singh, in a similar predicament, sidestepped to the left. Their foreheads met behind the wagon, making a noise akin to wooden mallets striking together.

"Ooof," groaned Short Clog.

"Fooo," grunted Gurditta Singh contrariwise.

Both landed painfully on their rumps and dropped their letters in the process. For a moment, their heads swam and their ears rang. Then they dusted themselves off, *picked up the other's note,* and went their separate ways with no more acknowledgment of the meeting than if they had walked into a wall. (Or a mirror, suggests Antonio.)

22

THE HAPPY CLOCK

Godfrey lay on the bed in his room at the Happy Cock and mused upon his life. For his entire discontented existence, up until the moment he was cured by the magician, he had felt as if he were inhabiting the wrong body . . . as if his soul had been forced into another man's mortal coil. But now, for the first time in his being, everything seemed perfect! Heretofore, he had been weak and ill. Now he was strong and hale. Until that fateful meeting, he could not even speak. Now he was a regular Demosthenes. He used to think of his features as hideous and deformed. But now . . .

Godfrey studied his face in a looking glass with awe. His thoughts went back to a startling incident which had taken place after his unfortunate meeting with Purvious and Egelbun: he was wandering in the marketplace, thinking morose thoughts, when he caught a glimpse of a fierce, handsome man staring out from a small window. Godfrey turned and looked at the stranger and was frightened to see the man's dark eyes glaring back. Godfrey smiled, raised a hand in apology (gaping into another person's private chamber was incredibly poor manners). Curiously, the intimidating man returned his warm smile and waved his own hand at exactly the same time. And that is when Godfrey realized, with amazement, that he was not looking through a window into a room, but gazing into a mirror that hung upon a wall, and the stranger staring back was himself!

An even more momentous event had occurred since that revelation in the bazaar: for the first time in his life, he had spoken to Mamooshka . . . really talked to her. He had felt a yearning pouring from her voice and knew that she favored him. Well, actually, it was the Gypsy for whom she had affection. But was not he the Gypsy and the Gypsy him? It was true she had not actually *seen* him—only heard his voice from under the balcony; but he knew that if he could appear to her in the guise of the Gypsy, she would be captivated by his other self's *sprezzatura* . . . just as the Dim Avenger had been.

He peered at himself in the mirror, felt his nose and chin and tugged on an earlobe. "Yes," he said aloud. "I am the Gypsy." It was not a mask that could be pulled off. It was not an illusion. The only problem now was getting past the *shtipulation*. He had to discover how to keep the face of the Gypsy—his genuine visage—when he was with his true love. Otherwise . . . otherwise it was all for naught.

A knock on the portal returned him to reality. He opened the door to find who he thought to be Short Clog standing in the hall.

"Have you already delivered the message to Mamooshka?" asked Godfrey with awe. "You run like fleet-footed Mercury, though I see no winged sandals on your modest trotters."

Gurditta Singh, on his mission from Zalman, handed Godfrey the note that he had mistakenly picked up after bumping into Short Clog—the note which Godfrey had written minutes before.

"Mamooshka's reply?" asked Godfrey. He took the note and held it to his breast. "Short Clog? Does the world look clearer and brighter to everyone who is in love?"

Gurditta Singh, who spoke nary a word of Godfrey's language, shrugged his shoulders.

Godfrey unfolded the note, read the first couple of lines, frowned. "Uhhh . . . good friend. Why have you brought back the note I sent you to take to Mamooshka?" came his puzzled question.

Gurditta Singh smiled timidly and thought, *What sort of curious message did my master Thomas have me bring?*

Godfrey laughed. "I would ask if you forgot your way to the House of Verrazanno but I know, for certain, you once lived there too." Gurditta Singh shook his head. Godfrey became concerned. "What is wrong, dear friend? Have you been frightened into speechlessness? Has someone scared you? Threatened you?" Gurditta Singh pointed emphatically at the note. "The note? Is something wrong with it? Did I misspell a word?" Godfrey read aloud: " 'My dear heart Mamooshka, I will come this evening to our secret place, your Godfrey.' No, nothing wrong here."

Gurditta Singh started to walk away, but Godfrey's powerful voice stopped him in his tracks:

"Wait! Where are you going?"

Gurditta Singh pointed in the opposite direction.

"Back to Mamooshka's?" asked Godfrey. "Well, then. Do not you think you will be needing this?" Godfrey handed the letter back to the messenger.

Gurditta Singh took it hesitantly, then offered it back to Godfrey. Godfrey, his patience wearing a little thin, snatched the letter from Gurditta Singh's hand, folded it once, twice, thrice; then placed it firmly in the servant's palm, and closed his fingers over it. "Now go and stop this silly game," he decreed as he sat down, stared out the window and sighed.

Gurditta Singh was altogether confused. His master Thomas would be angry with him if he didn't complete his task, but this fellow here was obviously deranged. Or perhaps . . . perhaps the letter wasn't properly presented. Gurditta Singh had once been the court Nose-picker to a Mughul prince, and this lord would not let Gurditta Singh dig into his princely nostril unless Gurditta Singh's fingernail had been first dipped in gold.

It's all in the presentation, he considered. He turned his back to Godfrey, hurriedly wrapped the letter with a piece of string from his pocket and put the letter back into his cloak. Then he faced Godfrey again, smiled, and cleared his throat dramatically.

"What now?" asked Godfrey peevishly.

Gurditta Singh made an elaborate show of opening his jacket, taking out the note, bowing, and handing it to Godfrey with a flourish.

Godfrey noticed the string. "What's this?" An expression of insight flashed upon his brow. "Aha! I see now. You gave me the wrong note. *This* is Mamooshka's reply!" Godfrey held the letter lovingly in his hand, kissed it, smelled it, then rubbed it on his cheek; and Gurditta Singh smiled jauntily, thinking his plan was working brilliantly.

"Mark how her paper does smell of her?" said Godfrey. "Good Short Clog. Come. Give it your nose." He held the note out for Gurditta Singh who drew back. "Go on. Have a smell. Why will you not smell it? There, good man. Is not that divine? Like lilacs! Or rose petals!"

Gurditta Singh inched away. If Godfrey was so enraptured by the smell of something that he had carried in his sweaty old cloak, he worried what the crazed man would do were he to actually get a whiff of pure Gurditta Singh?

Godfrey carefully untied the piece of string. "I will save this delicate ribbon amongst my most cherished belongings." He wrapped the string into a loop, and placed it in his pocket. Slowly, he opened the corner of the note and peeked at it. Without warning, he let forth a cry (Gurditta Singh jumped a foot off the ground) and handed the note back to the poor lackey.

"Dear friend, I cannot bear to read it," moaned Godfrey. "Our meeting last night was like a dream. I sang to her. Then she came to the wall and we whispered through a crack. Sweet were her words and with the sound of them how my heart did race. I am terrified through and through: afraid perchance she will have changed her mind—afraid perchance she does not wish to see me again! Please. You must read the missive for me."

Gurditta Singh stared at the note in his hand, wholly perplexed.

"What does she say?" asked Godfrey. "Please. The anticipation is destroying me!"

Gurditta Singh cleared his throat, paused, then started to fold the letter back up again.

"What are you doing?!" cried Godfrey. "Give that back! Some friend you are."

Godfrey snatched the note away, unfolded it, and read it with shock. "Why this is the very same note I wrote and gave to you to take to Mamooshka!" he cried—again in a rankled voice. "Short Clog! You are trying my before now seemingly unlimited patience." Godfrey folded the letter, stuffed it into Gurditta Singh's pocket, and pushed him out the door. "Deliver this letter now and be quick!"

Gurditta Singh, on the verge of frustrated tears, walked slowly down the stairs and disappeared into the street.

A few minutes later, the pig-goblin who bore the spitting (or snorting) image of Short Clog (and Gurditta Singh for that matter), appeared at Godfrey's door, hiccuping dementedly. The demon-spawn clutched a glazed beer mazer in one hand, and his chin was covered with slaver. He squealed with inhuman gibberish.

"Come again, dear fellow?" asked Godfrey, baffled at the bizarre and quite sudden drunkenness of his servant.

"Gaaaw-Da-Freee. Gurgle shneegle nyuck," said the boar-entity.

"Hulloo!" bellowed Godfrey, smacking himself on the forehead. "I just now realized! The note I wrote to Mamooshka I signed from 'Godfrey.' Not from 'the Gypsy.' So that is what you were trying to tell me! What a fool am I. How could I have been so preoccupied as to almost give away my secret? Hand me the note and I will destroy it, for Mamooshka must not know that the Gypsy and Godfrey are one and the same."

The goblin was busy gulping down beer and sloshing the brew all over his face and the floor. Godfrey probed the creature's pockets for the letter. "Come, slovenly Short Clog, give me the note." The goblin belched. "Short Clog, give it to me!"

Without forewarning, the creature hit Godfrey over the head with his beer mazer and Godfrey collapsed to the floor. His head wobbled about, and his eyes were dazed and bewildered. The goblin poured the rest of the beer onto Godfrey's face and snorted with glee.

"You have wounded me, friend," mumbled Godfrey. The goblin started to drag him away. "I presume you know where we are going. A physician, perhaps?"

Loutronio entered the room at this moment and curled his lip at the odd scene before him. "Good Godfrey," he said condescendingly, "I come from my lord Purvious to deliver a message."

"Ah! Purvious' fart catcher," said Godfrey. "Stop your dragging for a moment, Short Clog. We have a visitor."

Godfrey got free of the goblin's grasp, stood up, staggered over to Loutronio, and leaned against him. Loutronio supported him with a disgusted expression on his face, for Godfrey reeked of beer, and his undignified servant was now rolling on the floor like a pig, snorting and scratching himself.

"My lord wishes to apologize for his rash behavior of last night," said Loutronio with a scrunched-up nose. "He wishes to meet with you and show you signs of . . ." The goblin chose this moment to demonstrate uncouth affection in the manner of an amorous cur upon Loutronio's leg. "Signs of love and respect," continued Loutronio and gave the troll a good swift kick with his unoccupied foot; the porker scurried away and hunkered down in the corner. "Come to the House of Verrazanno this evening and there you will be treated to much kindness."

"I thank you most courteously," replied Godfrey politely. "I will be there."

Loutronio let Godfrey drop to the floor. Then he quickly left the disgusting inn and its revolting guests.

The pig-thing, who possessed inordinate strength, easily hoisted the now unconscious Godfrey onto his shoulders, and carried him out of the room.

The House of Verrazanno

23

THE
CROMNYOMANCER

Thomas, disguised in the magician's garb, entered the House of Verrazanno from the servants' entrance and followed Drapslod across the cool inner courtyard toward the main house. The marble floor felt like water from a mountain stream on his leathery feet, and he relished the small pleasure it gave. He had reminisced about this lovely abode so often during his wanderings and hardships he had begun to think that perhaps his days in Carthusalem had merely been an apparition. But here he was, listening to the splashing fountain, enjoying the delicious smells wafting from the kitchen, and gazing at the intricate black shadow patterns cast by the marble screens upon the clean, white floor. He had rested in the cool shade of this courtyard during his fevered dreams and had pretended to sun himself in the garden during his darkest, coldest hours. It was so very strange, then, to be back in these familiar surroundings and yet not be able to announce his presence with joy. He knew, however, that Egelbun was dangerous; this he had learned the hard way. If he were going to trap the brute and expose his evil deeds, he would have to be very clever.

"This way, sir," said Drapslod as he led Thomas into the main room where guests were received.

Egelbun was lounging on a giant silk cushion, picking morsels from a massive tray using a solid gold lazybones. His cheeks were covered with slurp and crumbs. A vast array of servants scurried about him, performing repulsive tasks upon his body. One little man was cleaning the gunk from under Egelbun's toes. The toe-picker's face was twisted into a hideous grimace from the appalling smell of his work. A tall, slender man stood behind Egelbun pulling the vermin from his blond wig with giant tweezers. He too wore an expression of barely disguised disgust. Two more servants stood on the opposite side of the room working a great fan that whisked air onto Egelbun's puffy flesh. They were drenched in sweat, and their swollen tongues lolled about in their parched mouths in the manner of exhausted mules.

Egelbun looked up as Thomas and Drapslod entered. A sharkish smile appeared on his lips. "So! You are the magician that my servant Dicksocks has brought me. What are your services?"

"I am a mystic, mainly," pronounced Thomas dramatically. "I practice sooth and such."

"The duty I wish you to perform is necromancy."

"As you wish, most excellent and graceful lord. The raising of the dead is one of my skills."

Egelbun clapped his hands, and all of the servants (with the exception of the poor fan workers) hustled out of the room. "Where do you come from, good man?" asked Egelbun.

"Another place with names which are difficult to pronounce in your tongue," answered Thomas; and thought, *forked tongue, that is.*

"Can you tell fortunes?" asked Egelbun with a rapacious gleam in his eye. For like all avaricious people he was impatient about everything and even ached to know the future.

"Prognostication is one of my gifts," offered Thomas with an insouciant wave of his hand.

"Do you not fear the punishment in Hell for those who would presume to see the future?" asked Egelbun with a frolicsome tone.

Thomas knew that Egelbun was obsessed with Dante's *Inferno*. It was the only book the scoundrel had ever studied. The animal had never bothered to read the next two books, *Purgatory* and *Paradise*, but was content to dwell upon perdition and all of the gruesome tortures suffered therein. He was like those crackpots who visit Bedlam on a Sunday afternoon merely for a caper, or those fiends who never miss a public hanging, just for the pleasure of it.

"You will be forced to wander forever with your head on backwards," said Egelbun with a stupid laugh, "for daring to look forward into destiny."

Thomas had read Dante too. But *his* favorite book of the *Divine Comedy* had always been *Paradise*, where the traveler ascends to the Empyrean, the highest region of Heaven, and is reunited with God and surrounded by angels of the blessed court as they sing a glorious song of serenity. *But,* he mused, *if there is a Hell such as Dante has described, I hope that Egelbun suffers the torments of the Chasm of Thieves, where swindlers are entwined by writhing serpents whose bite contains an agonizing venom that consumes the miscreants in a ball of fire, burning them to cinders, and thence to rise anew, only to endure the agony over and again.*

"Why are you grinning?" asked Egelbun.

"Forgive me, my lord," said Thomas at once. "Your hair is so radiant and lovely, I was brought to mind of Jason and the famed Golden Fleece of Colchis."

Egelbun vainly fluffed his wig. "What sort of prognostica-
tor are you?" he asked.

"I am learned in the lore of cromnyomancy."

Egelbun sloshed to the edge of his seat. "Cromnyomancy?
I have never heard of this. What is it, prithee?"

Thomas reached into his robes and pulled forth a massive
onion—as big as a cantaloupe. "Cromnyomancy is divination
by means of onion skins," explained Thomas and presented
Egelbun with the bulb. "It is an ancient lore from Roman
times."

Egelbun took the onion as if it were a precious crystal ball.
"What do you see in these onion skins?" he asked Thomas
with wonderment.

"You must peel the skin yourself," said the magician.

Like a greedy child unwrapping a present, Egelbun tore off
the dry, outer-layer, then regarded Thomas eagerly. "Well?" he
asked.

Thomas moved his head from side to side and stared at
the onion skins on the floor. He mumbled an incantation
under his breath, then touched his forehead. "I'm looking
into your heart," said Thomas as if reciting a charm.

"Yes! Do tell!"

"I'm looking into your soul," chanted Thomas.

"Come on. What do you see in me?" demanded Egelbun,
biting his fingernails with anticipation.

Thomas cocked his head to one side and frowned.
"Food," he said with a wearisome tone.

"What?" cried Egelbun angrily.

Thomas made his voice sound mystical and prophetic. "I
see much food being eaten."

"This is a metaphor of prosperity," said Egelbun with glee.
"Please continue."

"You must peel deeper," ordered Thomas bodefully.

Egelbun pulled apart the first layer of the onion flesh and

squinted with pain as the vapors from the bulb stung at his eyes. "This hurts," cried Egelbun petulantly. "My eyes are burning. See how I weep?"

"*Lacrimae simulatae,*" muttered Thomas, quoting the Latin phrase for "crocodile tears."

"What was that?" demanded Egelbun sharply.

"I see a little room, in a dark place," continued Thomas quickly. "A nasty, dank hole with bars on the window and you sitting on cold stone, weeping."

The onion made Egelbun squint and squinch his face comically, and Thomas nearly burst out laughing at the man's ludicrous expressions. "Indeed!" cried Egelbun, rubbing his eyes with his knuckles. "This image of the prison is a symbol of my caged and fettered soul. I am a lonely man. I'm really rather sensitive. But nobody has seen this inner me until now. What else, good cromnyomancer?"

"Another layer," commanded Thomas.

Egelbun dug into the onion, hissing with pain and choking on his own tears.

"I see a white-faced man," continued Thomas.

Egelbun strained to see Thomas through his red eyes. "A clown? Someone mocking me! A malicious chider?"

"Nay! A man pale of face!"

"Death?" screamed Egelbun. "You see my death?"

"Pasty," said Thomas, but Egelbun's eyes were blank. "Son." Egelbun shook his head. "*Podestà.*" Egelbun scratched his wig. Thomas sighed. "The . . . "

Egelbun finally pieced the words together and cried excitedly, "The-*podestà's*-pasty-son, Purvious! What is he doing?"

"I cannot see anymore," said Thomas and feigned exhaustion.

But Egelbun had worked himself into a fevered pitch. "Tell me more," he appealed. "I must know."

"I cannot!"

Egelbun's face contorted into a mask of ire. "I order you to tell me, you vile stinkard!"

Thomas smiled slightly. "You must eat the onion!" he said.

"Eat the onion?" asked Egelbun with disgust. "Raw? Like some sort of Gypsy beggar?"

"Now!" bellowed Thomas.

Egelbun shoved the entire onion into his mouth and chewed frantically, gagging on the bitter knob.

"I see a knife in the back of a good man," said Thomas after a long pause.

Egelbun gasped and spoke through a mouthful of onion. "Treachery! After bringing the death of Godfrey, he plans on killing me, a good man! What else? What else?"

So that's it! thought Thomas. *They plan on murdering Godfrey, the true heir to the Verrazanno estate.*

"What else?!" screeched Egelbun.

"That is all for now."

Egelbun sat back in his chair and rubbed his greedy guts contemplatively, burping obscenely. "So. It all makes sense." He glanced at Thomas and smiled. "Magician. You may wander freely about the servants' quarters until tomorrow when you shall be needed."

"As you wish."

Thomas went back to the courtyard and sat by the fountain. *O, how I long to cast off these garments and assume my true identity,* he thought. *But I must wait until all the facts have shown themselves and the evidence is incontestable. Then I will have my revenge. Now, I must go to the Happy Cock and make sure good Godfrey is warned of these evil plans against him.*

24

THE TEMPTRESS

The homunculus-pig staggered through the woods with Godfrey on his back. The wild boar-man was not used to carrying humans (or anything, for that matter) and, what with the tremendous amount of beer he had swilled earlier in the day, he was feeling rather sick. He stumbled into a meadow, dropped his burden onto the ground, and reeled into the thickets to search for a nice bog to retch and wallow in.

A moment later, Short Clog entered the scene (having just delivered the wrong note to Mamooshka) and walked directly into Godfrey, accidentally kicking him in the gut. Short Clog looked down and realized that it was his own master whom he had punted and cried out, "Master! What has happened to you?" He propped Godfrey up and slapped his cheeks.

Godfrey slowly opened his eyes and stared groggily at his servant. "Hulloo there, dear friend. Where have you brought me to?"

"I haven't brought you anywhere. I've just now stumbled upon you."

"Come now," said Godfrey irately. "No more silly games. Where are we?"

"A meadow, not fifty yards from the Verrazanno estate."

"And where is the note I gave you?" Godfrey held out his hand for the note.

"I snuck over the wall," replied Short Clog, "and left it in the secret place in Mamooshka's room."

Godfrey sat bolt upright and spoke with exasperation. "After I told you to give it back to me?"

"You never said such a thing!" protested Short Clog. "You told me to take it to her and off I went on my errand. Which I accomplished most successfully, I might add."

"Why do you torment me so?" groaned Godfrey, holding his head. "You hurt my noggin!"

"I do?" asked Short Clog.

"You did. At the Happy Cock. Unprovoked, you struck me with a glazed mazer."

Short Clog, addressing his unseen audience, spoke in an aside: "My master, so deep and rich in love, has lost all his sanity. By Gad, he is mooned with it! I must play along with him so as not to upset him the more."

"To whom are you speaking?" asked Godfrey.

"Nobody at all, master," replied Short Clog. "But . . . I suppose I did hit you with a mazer."

"Whatever for?"

"You had a great big spider on your head and I was killing it dead."

"Could not you have used something softer?"

"I could have, sir." Short Clog chewed on his lip thoughtfully. "I might have used a hungry starling, but there wasn't one at hand."

"And why did you carry me out here upon your back?" asked Godfrey.

"On my back? Well, hmmm . . . " mused Short Clog. "Well, it's just something one does when one is of the lower classes, sir. I can't rightly explain it."

"And why did you kick me just now?"

"Errr . . . that was my clumsy attempt at showing affection, I suppose."

"Well, next time, perhaps a pat on the back would suffice." Godfrey struggled to his feet and faltered in his steps. He felt an unsettling sensation tingle over his flesh. An ill-smelling wind blew into the meadow. The sun passed behind a cloud, casting a lowering murk over the world. In that instant, six terrifying lizard-goblins raced from the undergrowth and seized Short Clog in their scaly hands. They were no bigger than monkeys but possessed herculean strength. Their faces contorted into evil grimaces as they pulled the amazed Short Clog into the dark forest; the abduction was over in a trice. When Godfrey looked up, his servant was nowhere to be seen.

"Short Clog?" he called out.

"Hello, Gypsy," said a sultry voice.

Godfrey snapped his head around and laid eyes upon a woman—as naked as a fountain nymph—who had appeared in the meadow seemingly from thin air. She bore an uncanny resemblance to Botticelli's Venus, from that delightful work in which the goddess of love was painted floating across the water in her shell-made boat. Whereas Botticelli's *donna* was pale, blond, and innocent, this nude "S*ignorina* In Meadow" was her exquisite opposite: olive-skinned, sable-haired, with the unflinching, immodest gaze of a public house wench; and she was the most tantalizing creature Godfrey had ever seen.

"Aack" said Godfrey as he felt a pleasant tingling in the cods. "Where is my servant, short man, and friend?"

"Do not concern yourself with that obnoxious runt," said Azfall. Her full lips curled into a lusty smile, and the tip of her tongue stuck out between her front teeth. "Think only of me."

"Who are you? Why do you fill me with foreboding?"

"Not foreboding. It is longing you feel. I am your Gypsy queen."

How alarming, thought Godfrey. *I feel an overpowering urge to do that which is unprudent with this woman.*

"I can read your mind," she said. "You find me desirable."

"'Snipples! I cannot, for I . . . errr . . . love another?"

Godfrey did not sound the least bit convincing.

"Love has nothing to do with it," said Azfall. "This is about lust."

"But love is everything," said Godfrey. "Without it, we are empty shells. There is a Latin phrase . . . a particularly suitable phrase that I am trying to think of," he continued with mounting desperation, for he could not pry his feasting eyes from her ideal shape, "which completely expresses the intertwined natures of 'love' and 'fidelity' and their importance to a meaningful relationship between man and woman; but the bloody quote has entirely slipped my mind! Dear God, but you're fetching."

"*Libido dominatur,*" said Azfall. "'The passions win the day.'"

"I'faith!" said Godfrey. "That was not exactly the quote I was thinking of."

The demoness came slowly toward him, and it seemed as though she glided across the ground like a spirit . . . or a deity. She stopped so close to him that he could feel a powerful heat emanating from her body—hotter than a blazing hearth. This further aroused his baser instincts. Naughty images, rivaling the obscene antics of those rascals from Bosch's *Garden of Earthly Delights* (where unclothed sinners sport on the grass and chew giant pomegranates; reprobates ride bareback on goats, pigs and other creatures; and flowers are stuck into most inappropriate places), raced through his mind.

"Sh-sh-shells," stuttered Godfrey and gulped the clam-sized lump in his throat. He was already imagining her covered with treacle.

"Pry me open and you will find there is much pleasurable flesh within," she said.

"I do not seek pleasure, only respite from pain," said Godfrey. Against his will, his hand reached out and wrapped itself around her waist and pulled her to his trembling chest.

"Assuage your suffering in my arms," whispered the lovely monster.

"The hurt I have can be cured by only one doctor's care and you are not she." Godfrey stared at her heaving bosom and made a sound akin to a rutting camel: "Geeeyarrrrr."

"Do not fight it," she urged. "Simply give in."

"Temptress," said Godfrey as his lips seemed to pull away from his face with a mind of their own and reach out for the mysterious woman's mouth. He tried to pull back his head, but the lips were winning the battle.

Azfall hauled him in and greeted his mouth with a trick that she had learnt whilst stealing souls in France.

Godfrey pushed Azfall away and wiped his mouth with disgust. "Un-tongue me! 'Steeth, 'Stailbone, and 'Stoes! A carrion-bird would balk at your crow-baited breath!"

Azfall was taken aback. She cupped a hand to her mouth and exhaled, trying to smell her own reechy odor.

Suddenly, the Dim Avenger stepped from behind a tree where he had been secretly watching this earthy scene. He wiped hot tears from his cheeks. When he spoke, his voice was choked with grief. "Gypsy. I see now your prattling words of chastity and love are false."

Godfrey smiled. "Dim Avenger! In the nick of time! Let us begone from this evil place."

"Why don't you stay?!" the bandit cried. "Clap lips with that fleak till cockshut! Play poop-noddy with that poplolly till the sun comes up at swallow-fart! I know I would!" The Dim Avenger's lower lip trembled piteously, and then he wept.

"Friend," said Godfrey, as he himself shed scalding tears. "What is wrong?"

"You betrayed true love!" keened the highwayman.

"For some reason I was defenseless," explained Godfrey. "I was witch-held. Eyebitten." He put a hand on the Dim Avenger's arm.

"Let me go! Let me go!" shouted the Dim Avenger. "You're never going to see Mamooshka again. I'm going to tell her . . . right now . . . that you're just like all the other philandering cocksmen in this world." And with that, he ran into the orchard and was gone.

"Dim Avenger!" called Godfrey forlornly. "What have I done?! What have I done?!"

Godfrey looked around the meadow and realized that he was alone. The lewd wench had vanished.

Without warning, Short Clog stumbled back into the meadow. His hair was a-tangle—bits of bramble and sticks clung to it; and his clothes were ripped and sullied. He resembled a poorly costumed wood elf from a rude village production of *A Midsummer Night's Dream*.

"Lizard-goblins, sir," said Short Clog with a dazed voice. "I was assaulted by lizard-goblins."

"Come," ordered Godfrey. "I must find Mamooshka before it's too late!"

"Terrible creatures with gnashing teeth and crooked fingers," said Short Clog. "Farting and spitting!" He collapsed on the ground.

"Can you walk?" asked Godfrey. Short Clog's head rolled back and his tongue wagged about disgustingly. "I need you now. Come. Onto my back." Carrying Short Clog pig-a-back, Godfrey headed in the direction of the Verrazanno garden. "You are rather heavy for such a short fellow, aren't you then?" he said through clenched teeth.

After five minutes of hauling Short Clog, Godfrey had slowed to a laggardly walk. His mouth was parched and his back ached. Short Clog, however, had perked up and was staring at the world with the wide-eyed wonder of a child.

"The world looks much different from this height, sir," stated the servant. "I question what my life would have been like had I been born tall instead of short."

"That is difficult to say," replied Godfrey.

"Perhaps I would have become a great tyrant," said Short Clog wistfully. "Someone people looked up to."

"Being tall has certain benefits and its own disadvantages," reasoned Godfrey.

"Ah, well sir, I'm sure it does but I'd wager being short has more contras than pros."

"Tall people are always knocking their heads into lintels."

Short Clog sighed. "What joy I'd experience banging my skull on a lintel for once. What rapture I'd feel striking my noggin on a beam."

"When you are tall, people are always asking you to reach a high shelf for them."

"I'd feel honored grasping a high shelf."

"Tall people become bent with old age," logicized Godfrey.

"Which us short people get even lower to the ground," Short Clog deduced.

"Tall people fall harder."

"When you're short, everyone can see the pate-crust on top of your head without even trying."

"Are you well enough to walk on your own yet?" asked Godfrey, for his knees were buckling.

"I would, sir," answered Short Clog, lying through his teeth, "but one of them goblins bit me in the shin and my leg feels all numb and insubstantial."

"Hulloo," said Godfrey. "Here we are at the garden wall. Can you see Mamooshka?"

Short Clog peered over the high stone wall that surrounded the Verrazanno estate. "I see her!"

"How does she look?"

"Fretful."

"What do you mean?"

"Well, she's throwing plums against the wall, and every

time one of them splats, she grumbles, 'the Gypsy.' "

"Tell her you come from him."

"Are you sure?"

"Do it!"

Short Clog waved his hands above his head and called, "My lady!"

Mamooshka stopped her plum-chucking and glanced toward the voice. She was surprised to see Short Clog at the top of the wall from the shoulders up. "Short Clog. Have you grown?"

"I come from the Gypsy," he replied tentatively.

"Go away," she screamed and hurled a plum at Short Clog's head.

"I obey," said Short Clog and turned to go. His master, though, refused to leave; Short Clog bobbed precariously on Godfrey's shoulders as Godfrey steered him back to the wall.

"Tell her that your master needs to speak with her," ordered Godfrey in a hushed tone. "Tell her that you come from Godfrey."

"I come from Godfrey," called out Short Clog as a rotten plum hit him square in the kisser.

Mamooshka's face brightened. "Godfrey! Where is he?"

"Hereunder my hinder parts," replied Short Clog as he wiped the maggoty fruit from his mouth.

"Tell him to come through the gate," commanded Mamooshka.

Short Clog climbed from Godfrey's shoulders to the top of the wall. He sat and watched as Godfrey entered the garden through the gate, marveling at the transformation: one moment, his master was the magnificent Gypsy; in the next instant, he was the wretched Godfrey again, all hunched and twitching. Mamooshka ran to Godfrey and embraced him.

"Squirrel," she said, "you are in desperate trouble. Purvious and my uncle wish to kill you."

"Squap, squawk splat," replied Godfrey.

"He says," said Short Clog, "'I do not fear them because they are wicked men. God will be on my side.'"

"I sent a friend to help you," said Mamooshka.

"'Guppies,'" Short Clog replied. Godfrey shot him an exasperated look and corrected him. "Oh!" said Short Clog. "He said, 'the Gypsy.'"

"Then you have met him?" asked Mamooshka.

"'Yes, we have become like brothers,'" quoth Short Clog.

"I hate him!" spat Mamooshka vehemently.

Godfrey twitched in silence for a moment, then took a deep breath. "Ee ruvs ooo," said Godfrey and held up his hand to keep Short Clog from trying to translate for him.

Mamooshka's eyes doubled in size. "What did you say, Godfrey?" she asked in amazement. "I thought I understood what you just said."

Godfrey mustered up all his strength, and spoke again. "He roves you wid allllll his haaaart."

Mamooshka laughed joyfully. "Squirrel . . . you said, 'He loves you with all his heart.' You've never spoken before in your entire life!"

Godfrey let forth an enormous sigh and rattled off a sentence of excited gobbledygook.

"'The Gypsy has been teaching me how to talk,'" interpreted Short Clog.

Godfrey started to speak, realized he was too spent to try, and simply gestured for Short Clog to take over.

"'You are the sun on his face,'" said Short Clog with passion. "'The air he breathes. The earth beneath his feet.'"

Mamooshka smiled and turned away. Then she gasped. "I almost forgot about the Gypsy's missive!" She took a folded note from her pocket. Godfrey realized that it must be the letter he had sent signed 'Godfrey' and he barked with fear. "What's wrong?" asked Mamooshka.

Godfrey spoke in fast gibberish.

"He says, 'Don't eat that note, it's poison.'"

"Whatever do you mean?" asked Mamooshka with a frown.

Godfrey glared at Short Clog and answered her question.

"O, sorry, master," said Short Clog and turned to Mamooshka. "He said, 'Don't read that note, it's the wrong one!'"

Mamooshka became furious and ripped open the letter. "A note to his lover, perhaps?" Her voice trembled as she read, "'I, a wandering merchant in the guise of a magician, have been given your name by one Dim Avenger . . .'" She paused and her look became full of concern. *What has happened to Thomas?* she thought, and turning to the others said, "Well, this is indeed the wrong note."

At this point in the tale Antonio cries out, "Wait! I don't understand. How did the note that Thomas wrote end up in Mamooshka's hand?"

I give him my sternest glare and ask him if he has really been paying attention or just taking this opportunity to drink my wine and daydream. He protests heartily and tells me that he is thoroughly enjoying my 'recountation,' that the writing is 'bang-up,' and can he please have another glass of vino? I indulge him. He is an excellent audience, however limited he may be.

"Antonio, do you remember when Thomas wrote the note to Godfrey?" I ask.

"Errr."

"He had just put on the wizard's garb and had reached into the pocket—"

"Aha, yes!" interjects Antonio. "The parchment upon which Godfrey's soul was signed in blood."

"Very good. Now, Thomas gave the note to his servant Gurditta Singh."

"Hee hee."

"Why do you snicker?"

"It's a funny name. Did you make that name up?"

"Damn your impertinence, Antonio! I did not make any of this up, you rogue. It has all been told to me by the old Gypsy minstrel and verified from manuscripts and diaries and firsthand accounts told secondhand."

"I'm sorry."

"Here, let me top off your glass."

"Thank you!"

"It is good wine, is it not?"

"Oh, yes."

"Dear God! Smell it first. Take your time."

"Smells good, *signore!*"

"Now swirl it in your mouth."

"Shrrlllluurrrp."

"When you die, Antonio, and if you go to Heaven, the wine that you are slurping is what the water from God's heavenly stream will taste like."

"That's something to look forward to!"

"So. Back to the note," I say.

"Gulp. Ah, yes! The note."

"Thomas gave the note to Gurditta Singh. And Gurditta Singh bumped into Short Clog. Each dropped the note he was carrying and it was picked up by the other. Your face is as blank as a freshly gessoed canvas."

"So . . ."

"Gurditta Singh picked up Short Clog's note. And Short Clog . . . come on!" I urge him.

"He picked up Gurditta Singh's note?" replies Antonio hesitantly.

"Yes!"

"So . . . Ummmm . . . "

"When Short Clog bumped into Gurditta Singh, both dropped their missives. Short Clog, by a fortuitous mistake, grabbed the note which Thomas had written to the Gypsy. On the back of this piece of parchment was a seemingly blank surface. But in fact, it contained the hellish document, written in invisible ink, signing Godfrey's soul over to the demoness. Short Clog then delivered it to Mamooshka, thinking it was the love letter from his master."

"Oh! Oh! I get it! So Mamooshka is holding the hellish contract. And Gurditta Singh still has the love letter."

"You are a regular Leonardo."

"The tile maker across the bridge?"

"No, the scientist."

"Can I have another," he bisects his sentence with a hiccup, "another . . . sip of vino?"

"Yes. Go ahead."

Sophia appears at the door and wrinkles her nose. "Dear God," she says, "it smells like a pig sty in this room." She looks particularly appealing today. She must have just come from beating the laundry at the river: the sleeves of her chemise are pushed up to reveal her strong, smooth forearms, her long skirt is pulled through her legs and tucked in the waist to keep it out of the dirt, and her hair is held under a quaint, fetching turban, fashioned hastily from a dish towel. I am reminded that Leonardo da Vinci's mother was a peasant woman, and she most certainly had the wholesome, strapping features of our Sophia. I have been told that after da Vinci died, his half-brother Pietro set out to experiment with nature by attempting to recreate his dear deceased elder sibling. He went to the home village of Leonardo's mother and paid a hardy young shepherdess of similar visage to said genius' mother to bear his own child. Indeed, the spawn of this tryst, a boy, grew up to be an accomplished artist, though, admittedly, nowhere near as brilliant as his famous uncle. I have often fantasized that if I were to breed, it would have to be with a woman as fine and healthy as Sophia, else the child would turn out to be a misshapen wreck. Just the thought of this fills me with an irregular tingling in the gingambobs, a feeling I have not experienced since my youthful pining for Sarah. Mercy! What has come over me?

"You two are disgusting," says Sophia as she goes to the window and pulls back the curtains. Antonio and I, like wraiths in a barrow, recoil from the light of the sun. "You haven't left this room for days!" She smacks Antonio on the head with one of her giant palms. He winces and crawls under the bed. "You have work to do, *troglodita!*"

"The story!" cries Antonio's muffled voice. "He must finish telling the story."

Sophia picks up the full chamber pot and flings the contents out the window. Then she scoops up the numerous empty plates that have accumulated on the floor—the remnants of our hastily eaten meals. "The *dottore* is here for your *clistere* and bleeding," she says to me and gives a haughty stare.

"Well then, *signorina*, send him away," I command.

"He's down in the kitchen drinking all of the wine," she hisses.

"Then kick his fat arse out of the house!"

Sophia gives me a strange look. I sit up in bed and meet her gaze. My heart is beating so strongly, it makes my nightshirt billow and tremble. After a long, delirious moment, she breaks the delicious contact of our eyes, turns away, and straightens her gown. "As you wish, *signore* Smy-thee." Her hips swish appealingly as she leaves the room.

"Is she gone?" asks Antonio.

"Yes."

"She likes you," he says.

A bark of sardonic laughter erupts from my mouth.

Antonio's head appears from under the bedstead. His hair is covered with the dust that collects beneath the mattress on the floor. "No, I do not lie," he insists. "She's secretly in love with you."

"Whatever are you talking about, you unholy fibber?! Why would a creature like that be in love with me?"

"She finds Englishmen attractive. She thinks your accent is charming. Besides all of that, you treat her like a lady and call her *signorina*. She had a very hard life before she was employed in your house: her father beat her and men used her roughly. She loves you because you are gentle with her. And how do I know all of this? Because I overheard her speaking to Gabriella next door when they were hanging the clothes on the line. Gabriella said that you looked like a blond weasel and Sophia beat her and pulled her hair."

"Rubbish!"

"The Hungarian doctor has asked her to be his mistress."

"Dear God! That despicable quack!"

"Sometimes Sophia sits outside the door and listens to you read out loud from the story. And how do I know this? Because I can smell her scent of lavender."

"She does?"

"'Well, this is indeed the wrong note,'" quotes Antonio, content to lie on the floor.

"Pardon?" I am still thinking about Sophia's hips. Her hair. Her eyes. I imagine a man using her roughly and feel a hot anger surge through my body. Faith! If a man were to use her roughly in my presence, I would skewer him through the heart, be he shriven or damned!

"That was the last line that you read. 'Well, this is indeed the wrong note.' Mamooshka had just opened the letter. Please continue."

The scent of Sophia fills the room; it indeed smells like lavender. How could I never have noticed this before?

"Read!" pleads Antonio, kicking the mattress from below.

Mamooshka was still holding the letter from Thomas in her hand. "Will you see the Gypsy tonight?" she asked.

Godfrey nodded his head.

"'Aye,'" said Short Clog.

"Give him this note," ordered Mamooshka, "and tell him to meet me back here at sunrise tomorrow." She wrote her own note below Thomas' message and handed it back to Godfrey. "Thank you, dear brother." She kissed him on the forehead. The smell of his skin sent a strange thrill through her body—a feeling that she couldn't explain. Then, without thinking, she kissed him on the cheek. Her lips became flushed and hot. Sans warning, she kissed him on the lips, and both of them felt a searing heat flood through their flesh. After a moment, she pulled away and stared at the sky in embarrassment.

"Remember," she said. "Whatever you do, stay away from Purvious and Egelbun. Go straight away to the Gypsy for he will keep you safe. Now I must be off. I have much to do." As she walked away, she glanced back over her shoulder at Godfrey; her brow was shaped in a perplexed frown.

As soon as she was out of sight, Godfrey transmuted back into the Gypsy. He read the note with a glowing smile.

"What does it say, sir?" asked Short Clog.

"It says," he paused and placed a trembling hand over his heart. "It says, 'I am yours.'" He kissed the note, and spoke wistfully. "If only I really were the Gypsy."

25

The Monomachists

When Godfrey and Short Clog stepped back through the garden doorway into the orchard, they were greeted with a jarring sight: Purvious, Egelbun, Loutronio, Drapslod, and two of the *podestà's* personal guards barred their way.

"Hulloo," said Godfrey. "What are you all doing here?"

"Forgetting something, sirrah?" asked Purvious nastily.

"I do not think so." Godfrey caught the menacing glare of the guards, noticed their drawn swords, and turned to Short Clog. "Come, Short Clog, let us go partake of that tongue scraping you have been speaking of."

"Right, sir."

They turned to walk away, but the massive soldiers grabbed the backs of their necks in vice-strong hands.

Loutronio took a step forward and addressed Godfrey formally. "Sir, I came to your lodgings today expressing many niceties and friendly words. You were supposed to meet my dear lord Purvious and master Egelbun this evening to make up for your harsh words of yesterday."

Godfrey snapped his fingers. "Oh, *that*! Well, all is forgiven."

"Not anymore," replied Loutronio. "You have just now insulted your dear uncle Egelbun."

"I am hurt," said Egelbun, pretending to pout.

"By attempting to molest his precious Mamooshka," continued Loutronio.

"I have never done such a thing!" cried Godfrey.

"Bitterly hurt," said Egelbun and bared his incisors like a wolf.

"Hence my master Purvious," explained Loutronio testily, "has graciously accepted to champion the honor of Mamooshka and has challenged you to a duel."

Purvious commenced the dueling stretches taught to him in childhood by his fencing master; he had never been an apt pupil, however, and he looked more like a frail, cloddish ballerina warming up for a toe dancing recital than a *beau sabreur* preparing for combat.

"This is absurd," said Godfrey.

"Do you accept?" asked Loutronio, ever a stickler for the details of courtly ritual.

"I cannot," stated Godfrey.

"And why not?"

"I have no good reason for wanting to kill Purvious. Besides, killing is a sin."

"Then I will run you through where you stand!" exclaimed Purvious. He jumped gawkily, thrust his pretend sword at an imaginary target, then spun on one heel.

"I cannot let that happen either," said Godfrey.

"Then you are in a quandary. Ha ha!" cried Purvious. He repeated his silly-looking practice.

"Listen, good fellow," said Godfrey calmly. "If I kill you, which in all likelihood I could, you would be dead and the weight of your death would bear heavy on my shoulders. Not to mention the fact that I would be taken to jail and executed at sunrise. I know the laws of this city quite well."

Egelbun tore off his wig and stomped the ground. "O what a learned beast!"

"Then," said Purvious in an overwrought tone, "I shall be forced to stick my sharp knife in your softest places!"

Godfrey smiled benignly. "As I said, that would not do for there are many things yet left on this earth I wish to accomplish before I pass to the other realm."

"Then what do you propose we do?" asked Purvious, attempting to affect a challenging tone.

Godfrey lifted his chin, thought for a moment, then nodded his head. "I will defend myself, never once cutting you with keen blade, until you, Purvious, are totally exhausted, spent, and unable to continue."

This outraged Purvious. "Ha! Ha! I have been trained by master swordsmen."

"And I have Gypsy blood coursing through my veins, thou *gadje*," replied Godfrey, raising one eyebrow balefully. "So let us begin at once that I may be on my way before supper."

"What outlandish braggadocio!" cried Loutronio.

"What effrontery!" screeched Egelbun.

Purvious snapped his fingers aggressively. "Egelbun. Weapons!"

Egelbun took out two short daggers from the folds of his cloak. He handed one to Godfrey and the other to Purvious.

"You made sure of the daggers?" Purvious asked Egelbun, *sotto voce*.

"Quite sure," replied Egelbun, his voice quivering with baneful mirth.

Purvious and Godfrey faced one another and saluted.

A half hour later, Purvious' scheme to dupe Godfrey into "killing him" was not going as planned. During the previous thirty minutes, Purvious had been hurling his body at Godfrey like a demented monkey, exposing himself to hits at all times. In spite of this, Godfrey stayed true to his declaration and had not scratched his opponent, nor had he received a cut from Purvious' deranged attacks.

All of this activity had exhausted the pasty son of the *podestà*. His thin hair hung in lank locks upon his forehead. His silk fencing outfit was absolutely ruined with perspiration stains, and his face was as white as a new-laid egg. Godfrey, on the other hand, had barely broken a sweat.

"Swine," gasped Purvious. "You dog. You monkey-turd." Then he shrieked and "attacked" once again.

"Fribble-faced lout," replied Godfrey with a thoroughly bored voice. He deflected Purvious' feeble strokes and knocked Purvious' dagger to the ground. "O, give it a rest!" scolded Godfrey, for he was quite fed up with this ludicrous game. "That's about the hundredth time you've fumbled your dagger."

Most of the witnesses to the fight had long since fallen asleep out of sheer boredom. The two guards were propped up against one another, napping beneath the shade of a tree, one of them having visions of harem girls whilst the other fantasized of harem eunuchs.

Short Clog was taking a siesta on a patch of moss. He kicked like a puppy dreaming of cat-chasing. Actually, he was dreaming of chasing the buxom saffron seller from the bazaar. But every time he got close enough to touch her, she turned into a giant bota bag and sprayed him with vinegar.

Loutronio was slumbering standing up—a neat trick he had learnt in courtier school—and he swayed gently with his arms at his side, a peculiar smile upon his lips, like a man who has been bewitched by a forest spirit. In Loutronio's reverie, he was being presented with the Servant's Guild Emblem of Honor: a golden medallion designed by the great

Foppa; it gleamed with the radiance of a miniature sun.

Egelbun and Drapslod were the only ones still awake. As it was Egelbun's evening snack time, Drapslod held a massive tray on his head from which Egelbun plucked tasties, stuffing the tidbits into his greedy gorge.

Only Drapslod was following the duel. It had been an odd sort of fight in his modest opinion. He had been witness to many chivalric contests (he was once a cup bearer for the Duke of Milan); this duel between Godfrey and Purvious had turned out to be the most unsatisfying fray he had ever seen. It was like watching a bored matador toying with a senseless, decrepit, albino calf. He longed to see Godfrey skewer the *podestà's* son; the servant's face was fixed into a rigid, hopeful grimace.

Purvious, disarmed for the hundred and first time, raised his arms and screamed in exasperation, "Kill me! Kill me!"

"No," replied Godfrey emphatically.

Purvious screwed up his mouth and looked toward the sky as if searching for an insult that would provoke Godfrey to action. Finally, he raised his eyebrows and made a mocking sneer as if to say: "I've got it!" He laughed maliciously, then goaded Godfrey in a schoolboy singsong, "Godfrey has a farty bum. Godfrey has a farty bum."

"Now, that's not much of an insult, is it?" admonished Godfrey with out and out contempt. "Cannot you do better than that, you untutored little turd?"

Purvious' lower lip trembled with indignation. "What's wrong with 'farty bum'?"

"We are supposed to be fighting to the death," explained Godfrey. "Calling me 'farty bum' is just not much of an insult. In the first place I do not *have* a farty bum so it is meaningless to me. Give me something to work with at least."

"Like what?" pouted Purvious.

"Oh, I don't know."

"*Tout de suite*, monsieur clever," taunted Purvious. He was on the verge of tears. "Teach me how to insult!"

Godfrey passed air through his lips—an expression of bored contemplation. After a pause, he laughed softly to himself. "All right, try this on for size. Come on and fight, you pus-faced-dandipratt-son-of-a-scapegallows-heathen."

"Hmmmm," said Purvious. "I like that one."

"Or keep it plain and simple," continued Godfrey. "Is that your breath, or did a dog just vomit in a thunder pot?"

"Extraordinary," exclaimed Purvious.

"How about this . . . *I ad Graecum Pi*," cursed Godfrey.

Purvious frowned. "I don't understand that one. It's Greek to me."

"It *is* Greek, you dolt," said Godfrey. "I just abused you in another language which is a double insult since I've proven that you are stupid *and* a monoglot."

"But what does it *mean*?" asked Purvious.

"Literally, it means 'Go to the Greek Pi.' The symbol for Pi resembles a gallows [π]. Thus, I told you to 'Go hang yourself.' In your case, my dear fellow, I am reminded of the words of Seneca when he said: 'Leisure without reading is death.' If you had spent your dissolute, wasted youth reading books, and filling your mind with the wisdom of the philosophers rather than traipsing about like a colorblind-cunny-thumbed-mother's-loll, perhaps this intended meeting of monomachists might have led to the *physical* death of one us, rather than the *metaphorical* death I am suffering from this excruciating boredom."

"Well . . . you're a *painus anus*! That's Latin for—" Purvious stopped. Godfrey was walking away! "Hey! Where are you going?"

"I'm worn out," said Godfrey. "I'm going home."

Purvious stomped in a circle. "Heh," he whined. "What is a mono-gluteus-glotticus, or whatever?!"

Godfrey stretched his arms with exhaustion (carelessly holding the knife straight out in front of him). He turned his head to Short Clog and said, "Short Clog. Wake up. It is getting late and—"

Catching Godfrey off-guard, Purvious ran at him with arms raised, stuck out his puny chest and impaled himself onto Godfrey's dagger. Godfrey shouted in horror and let go of the hilt. Purvious fell to the ground grasping the blade's handle protruding from his bosom. Godfrey backed away. Everyone who was asleep came to attention.

Purvious' eyes went wide with shock and his face contorted in agony. "*Pi,*" he wheezed. And never again in the history of the world was spoken as solemn and enigmatic a final word from such a frivolous and pointless man.

"No!" cried Godfrey.

At a signal from Loutronio, the guards grabbed Godfrey and put him in manacles. Egelbun turned away and clapped his hands happily.

Loutronio tossed a sheet over Purvious. "Wonderful job, lord," he whispered to the dead body. "Very convincing. See you tomorrow." And turning to Godfrey said, "You will pay for this cowardly act!"

Egelbun could hardly contain his laughter. "You blackguard!" he shouted at Godfrey. "You villain! You will *die* for this!" He snuck a swift kick at Purvious' corpse.

"Dicksock," said Egelbun to Drapslod. "Help Loutronio take the very dead lord Purvious to the crypt. I will notify the authorities." He turned to Godfrey. "And you, you usurper! Meditate, monk-like, in your prison cell, for the moment when your head is made separate from your body."

Short Clog, unnoticed by anyone, ran into the woods.

At the same time, the equally disregarded Drapslod picked up the trick dagger that Egelbun had given Purvious and hid it in the folds of his shirt.

"Antonio, it has grown dark whilst I have been reading. It is time for bed. And I need to go talk to Sophia about . . . ummm . . . household sundries."

"What?"

"Bed time. Sleep time. Dream time."

"But sir!" protests Antonio. "The story."

"What about it?"

"When will I hear the rest of it?"

"It is pretty much over."

"Well . . . keep reading. Please!"

"My eyes are tired," I say.

"Well . . . let me read it then!"

"You cannot even read. And besides, it is written in my own special code. Backwards."

"Backwards?"

"I write backwards, in a mirror. Like Leonardo."

"The baker?" asks Antonio stupidly.

"Da Vinci! Noodle head."

"Da Vinci Noodle Head? The pasta maker?"

"Antonio . . . "

"You can't stop now," he declares with emotion. "I must find out what happens to Godfrey. And Mamooshka. And Thomas. And even that *diletto* Short Clog. Dear God, you can't stop now."

"You are enjoying my story then?"

"O, yes!"

"Really?"

"Terribly."

"Before you seemed to be under the impression that I was making all of this up. That it was untruth."

"I believe it now."

"I am not so sure."

"Let me light the oil lamps. Christ in Heaven, where are those damn wicks!" He runs around the room, harum scarum, looking for the lamp fuses.

I pull on the cord that is connected to the kitchen. Several agonizing minutes later, Sophia enters the room dressed in her sleeping clothes. Her disheveled appearance is remarkably captivating.

"*Signorina* Sophia," I say. "Please bring me some food. I am famished."

She gives me an odd look. In the three years she has known me, I have never once requested provisions. She has grown accustomed to my diet of broth and bread.

"Food?"

"Start cooking and don't stop until I say so."

"What kind of food?"

"The kind that you eat." My mouth is already beginning to water. Our Sophia is a regular gourmand. "And absolutely no beets," I add for good measure.

26

THE CAGELINGS

G odfrey had given up all hope. His dreams were dead. He would never clasp Mamooshka in his arms again nor hold their barefoot children on his lap nor grow old and become a wise grandfather. And he would not ever be reunited with his natural parents—those nameless but beloved Gypsies who made him. Godfrey was so despondent that he didn't even mind the rats (as pushy as tour guides at the Duomo), who scrambled over his body and wrestled at his feet. He had done everything possible to avoid hurting Purvious but had killed the knave anyway. Would God forgive him for this accident, or would his soul be consigned to Hell for eternity? Well, all would be revealed when the sun rose on the morrow. All questions would be answered with the swing of an ax. It didn't seem right, though, this ignominious, lonely death. How cruel to spend one's last night on earth in a cold, damp, terrible cell. It didn't seem apropos to the path his journey through life had recently taken.

Perchance, that is the lesson we all must learn, he thought. *How many poor souls have passed from this earth with desires unfulfilled . . . with no one taking notice? We all die alone, after all.*

"We both lose our heads at sunrise," said a voice from the darkness.

Startled, Godfrey sat up and peered into the black. "Who's there? I thought I was alone."

An old man leaned forward. His ancient face was barely illuminated by a patch of starlight streaming through a small window cut in the stone above.

"Only me," said the old man, and he smiled warmly.

"Why are you in this dungeon, aged one?" asked Godfrey.

"I was in the wrong place at the wrong time," explained the old man. "Blamed for something that I did not do."

"O, the injustice of it all," said Godfrey.

"At least they put us together so we could share this last night with another soul."

"Yes, let that give us cheer, old friend."

"What did you do to deserve this horrid death?" asked the old man.

"It does not matter," replied Godfrey. "My whole life has been a jest; this is merely the final irony."

The old man launched into a terrific bout of weeping. Godfrey felt a strange stirring in his soul. He started to cry . . . not involuntarily . . . not because of the magician's *shtipulation*, but because of something more profound. He felt a brotherhood with this poor man, the likes of which he had never before experienced. In that instant, the other man's sorrow seemed more important than his own, and Godfrey forgot his own plight all together. It was a staggering feeling—a thrilling, dizzying sensation. It was as if he were watching the world from a great height, entirely detached, free of selfishness. His own death no longer mattered. His only goal was to console this poor, grieving man. And then he realized that here was one of those little moments he had so often pondered: distant, tiny, like the gnat caught in the hairs of his arm, or the dust mote catching fire in a shaft of light—seemingly removed from the eyes of God. He understood that his life would have been worth living if he could simply mitigate this being's suffering. Perhaps that was the only reason he had been put on this earth: to act as this man's angel; to help him through this terrifying ordeal. He moved next to the old man and held him in his arms.

"What is wrong, friend?" asked Godfrey softly.

"I have failed in my quest," sobbed the old man. "And now my ill-used life is over."

"Do not be afraid of death. There is nothing to fear."

"I am not afraid of death. I am afraid of what will happen *after* death: when I must face Him."

"Have you done something terrible to incur His wrath?"

"I . . . I . . . O, you would not believe me if I told you."

"Please. Tell me," pleaded Godfrey, his eyes full of mist.

"Do you really wish to hear my story?" asked the old man, brightening.

"Very much. Very much, old sir!" answered Godfrey with sincerity.

"I am an angel," stated the old man and peered at Godfrey to see if he would scoff.

"An angel?" asked Godfrey.

"Not a very good one, though," continued the old man. "I was sent to earth in this garb of human flesh to save a good soul from a demon. Now that I have failed, my place in Heaven is . . . well, let us say, insecure."

"Is Heaven a nice place?" asked Godfrey, and attempted to see the angel's eyes in the meager light of the cell.

"Then you believe me?" queried the angel.

"Of course," replied Godfrey with sincerity. "I don't see any reason why you should lie about such a thing at a time like this."

Godfrey's cellmate smiled wistfully, closing his eyes.

"What is Heaven like, you ask? It would take a thousand life-times to describe."

"Well, we only have a couple of hours, Sir Angel, so maybe you could just hit the high points."

"Heaven," began the angel, shifting on his haunches to make himself a little more comfortable, "is just like everyone thinks it is going to be, only a billion times better. But wait! I am jumping ahead of myself. I must start at the beginning. I must begin with death.

"When we die, our soul leaves this husk we call our body and flies straight up through the sky, hovering over the world, bobbing there like a cork on the end of a fishing line. You see, young man, even though our body is dead, our spirit is still linked to the Earth by a golden rope of memories and attach-ments. This is called our *Corporeal Vinculum*. Death is quite a shock to the soul because the soul has become completely mired in this body and has totally forgotten its former exis-tence in God's kingdom.

"As we float in this strange predicament, motionless above the continents and oceans, our entire lives play back to us like a performance in the theatre. We see the tragedy and the comedy, the pitiful and the sublime . . . the great absurd show of our lives. In this panorama we perceive the villains who wronged us and the heroes who helped us. Passing before us are all of those whom we loved and hated and even those minor characters whom we really did not care about. We actually relive all of our good deeds and bad deeds and in-between deeds. All of our fears and dreams and hopes and desires flow past in a great recapitulation. Our entire life his-tory is replayed in less time than it takes for a heart to beat or a moth to flap its wings. Then, quite simply, it is all tallied up like purchases in the market. If the good outweighs the bad, you go to Heaven. If you led a virtuous life and were kind to others, detached yourself from worldly emotions and desires and if you had faith in God and followed His instructions . . . voilà! Your scale slides to the right and you have earned the passage to Heaven.

"In that instant, a magnificent thing occurs: the Pilot Angel appears from behind the moon, and she cuts your *Corporeal Vinculum* with her Star-Knife; she puts you on her back and takes you through the secret corridor that spans the Black Abyss of Nothingness, right up to the shores of Paradise.

"If, however, you led an immoral life and were cruel to others, if you were attached to worldly emotions and desires, and had no faith in God and disobeyed all of His instructions, then—kerplunk! Your scale slides to the left and you will go to Hell. You will not be greeted by the Pilot Angel. Instead, a dozen hideous demons will materialize at your side like burning comets and chew your soul to shreds with their shark-like teeth. All the while, you scream with terror and they laugh cruelly at your piteous pleas for mercy. Finally, they pull you down into the pits of perdition where you will be assigned a punishment: for example, if you were a murderer, you might be covered in oil and set alight like a giant torch to illuminate Satan's heinous hall for ten thousand years."

"Dear Jehovah, no!" exclaimed Godfrey.

"Are you all right, young sir?" asked the angel. "You look as though you were about to faint. Och! I forgot. Purvious. What a shame. It was not really your fault, you know? O! Injustice! Well, let us not dwell on Hell, that wicked place! I was supposed to tell you about the Lord's Dominion, not its contraposition. So . . . where was I?"

"The Pilot Angel," said Godfrey, anxious to change the subject from the human torches.

"Yes, thank you. The Pilot Angel, lovely creature with hair like sunshine, takes you upon her back and carries you across the Black Abyss of Nothingness. You must cling tight to her locks lest you fall. Some rueful souls, so partial to the world

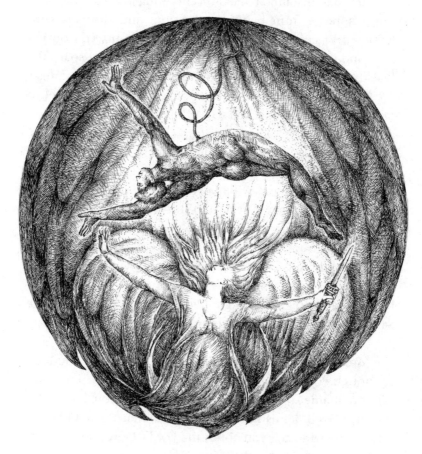

The Pilot Angel

that they have left behind, willingly leap from the Pilot's back;
they become the accursed ghosts and specters that haunt this
orb, lost spirits who are trapped in between this plane and the
next. The Pilot flies like a giant glowing swan through this
eternal sea of darkness. In the distance you can see a point of
light, like a single star in a night sky. Soon, the point of light
grows bigger and bigger. It is the size of a marble, then a
melon, then a boulder, then a lake. All at once, the entire sky
is refulgent with the light of ten thousand suns. The Pilot
lands on the shores of Heaven. Your old human eyes would
have been blinded and shriveled by the light that shines in
this place, but your new celestial eyes can see everything with
perfect clarity. Indeed you feel like a man who has spent all
his life at the bottom of a murky ocean and has floated to the
surface of a sunlit pool.

"The inhabitants of this land wander about in pure ecsta-
sy, drinking from springs of nectar, singing songs in praise of
Him, gazing in wonder at His heavenly kingdom. The white
buildings, carved from thought by an unseen hand, rise like
mountains toward the multihued sky. These monuments and
palaces and temples are so beautiful as to make the Taj Mahal
or Versailles or the Duomo look like muck heaps cloyed
together by dung beetles. The great prophets are here too.
There are Mohammed, Buddha, and Christ, as well as many
great teachers that you have never even heard named. There is
a constant music that plays in the air, sweeter and more
thrilling than anything of this world. Compared to it, the
finest Vienna symphony sounds about as pleasant as howling
cats engaged in back-alley coitus, or a goblin's fingernails
scraped across a slate board. The chosen ones are given free
rein to travel about this kingdom: it is their reward for their
virtuous life. The pleasures there are indescribable."

"I am astonished," whispered Godfrey.

"After many thousands of years," continued the angel,

"the soul becomes restless even in this Valhalla and sets out across the Vast Plain of Bliss to God's Palace. Arriving there, the soul is greeted with all of the honor and love bestowed upon a prodigal son. For this is indeed the soul's true home, and this arrival merely a return from a long absence. The soul is brought to His seat where many secrets about the universe are revealed, such as . . . "

" 'What makes the sky blue?' " asked Godfrey with excitement.

"Of course," smiled the angel.

"And, 'Why must babies sometimes die?' "

"It is on the top of the list," replied the angel.

"Or, 'How many angels really *can* dance on the head of a pin?' "

"That one I can answer for you myself," replied the angel. "The number is six hundred and sixty-six."

Godfrey clapped his hands. "Wonderful!"

"Then you are given a duty to perform by Himself," said the angel. "Some are sent to other worlds to act as prophets, to lead the sinful back to Him. Others, like myself, are assigned to act as guardian angels and protect good souls. For, you see, He is always at war with His brother, His opposite, that rascal Lucifer, the Arch Fiend, who is fighting to fill his kingdom with more followers than God.

"There is much more that I could tell you, dear boy, about that wondrous place. I could describe the Golden Forests of Joy, and the Bottomless Ocean of Rapture, or about flying from place to place on the gentle winds like a glorious bird, and lounging with the inconceivably beautiful Houris in the Gardens of Euphoria."

"What is a Houri?" asked Godfrey.

"It is a woman . . . nay . . . a goddess," replied the angel huskily, "who is so inscrutably pulchritudinous she would drive a mortal out of his mind with lust. Thomas Becket, that virgin saint, had he but seen one of these dames merely through opaque glass, would have burned his hairshirt in a trice and plunged in headfirst like a good 'un."

Godfrey exhaled a tremendous sigh. "Why did I have to ruin my chances?" he said wearily. "If only I could have entered God's court and kneeled before His throne. I would give up all of the pleasures you have mentioned, just to see His face."

"Your innocent, thoughtful manner reminds me of the youth I was sent to save. If only I could have found Godfrey Verrazanno before that wicked demon."

Godfrey jumped as if he had been stung by ten dozen wasps. "Godfrey Verrazanno?! Why that is me and I am him!"

"You trifle with me," said the angel, but his voice was filled with hope.

"I was left in a stable," asserted Godfrey. "Zalman Verrazanno adopted me. On my forehead is a birthmark. You cannot see it in this light but—"

"I know of this birthmark: it is in the shape of a crescent moon."

The angel peered at Godfrey's forehead and shouted, "You are him and he is you!"

"My guardian angel," said Godfrey thoughtfully. "I always knew I had one, somewhere." He contemplated all that the angel had said, then asked a bit peevishly, "Where were you, anyhow?"

"Waylaid by demons!" moaned the angel. "You are a prize in Hell: your virtue, twisted and made dark, is of value to them. I was sent here to thwart their evil schemes but I have failed." The angel looked at Godfrey and his mien was full of sorrow and pity. "I found you too late because it has already captured your soul. Please forgive me. Forgive me, dear Godfrey."

"*It* has captured my soul?" asked Godfrey. "Whatever can you mean?"

"The demon. My antithesis," explained the angel. "You signed away your soul to a demon."

"Where and when did this occur?" asked Godfrey in amazement.

"In the forest. Three years past."

"But I did no such thing!"

"Your annoying little servant Short Clog brought you to an old man in the forest, did he not?"

"Yes. But he was merely a magician who gave me back my voice. What of him?"

"That was no magician," said the angel. "It was a demon in disguise."

Godfrey's stomach lurched toward his gullet and the skin of his forearms prickled with goose pimples. "A demon?" he asked softly.

"He demanded that you sign a contract."

"Yes."

"An invisible contract," said the angel.

"It was merely a statement of liability," said Godfrey.

"No! It was a soul-pact. If the papyrus is held to a fire, these fiendish words become visible: 'Godfrey Verrazanno does hereby sign away his soul in blood for all eternity in exchange for regaining his voice.' This is what is written on the hateful scroll."

Godfrey slumped against the wall. Suddenly, he could not breathe. His forehead and cheeks flushed. Memories of the meeting with the magician came racing back: the old man's affected accent, rancid breath, devilish eyes; and the scroll utterly bereft of words. He knew in his heart that the angel spoke the truth. *How could I have been so foolish?* he thought miserably. *I, a man steeped in the ways of commerce, duped into signing a blank contract!* Through clenched teeth he muttered, "Fraud."

"Oh, deceit is part of the game," said the angel with the

worldly air of an urbane advocate. "The methods it used are wholly incontestable in God's court."

The image of the temptress appeared in Godfrey's mind's eye. "And the dark-haired woman in the meadow?" he asked.

"A stunningly beautiful woman?" queried the angel.

"I would not say 'stunningly' beautiful," replied Godfrey. "And I'd sooner kiss the fetid mouth of a full-fledged leper than merely peck her cheek."

"They were one and the same," said the angel and sighed miserably.

"Bloody, bearded, bullocks!" said Godfrey and pounded his fist into his palm. "What a gull am I!"

"'Snuts!" cursed the angel.

"He . . . she . . . it tricked me!" stammered Godfrey.

The angel put his hand on Godfrey's shoulder and said solemnly, "All is lost."

"That is simply not fair," whined Godfrey, turning away from the angel.

The angel paused for a time. Then he spoke in a grievous voice: "You will spend eternity in Hell, roasting in fire as the disgusting stench of that accursed place singes your nostril hairs with its noxious odors, while hideous goblins poke spiny things in your tender bott—"

"It's unfair!" blurts Antonio furiously. "I don't like the way this story has turned out. Not one bit."

I tell him—between bites of fresh baked bread with toasted cheese and tomatoes, oozing with olive oil—to sit down and be quiet so that I can continue the story. He tells me that he does not want to hear it anymore and walks petulantly to the balcony.

"You tricked me!" he says with vehemence and expectorates onto the street, eliciting the angry cry of a pedestrian on the avenue below. "*Scusa,*" apologizes Antonio lamely.

"What do you mean? Tricked you?" I plop a whole handful of fat, green olives into my mouth and spit out the pits, one by one as I denude them of flesh. It is a habit that I learned from Antonio.

"I thought this was going to be a good story. One with a happy ending."

"But life is not that way," I reason as I slurp giant spoonfuls of minestrone soup. I try to hide my excitement from him. This is the first time I have ever seen the laconic Antonio filled with such passion. This is the power of the Gypsies! He has become *Antonio Furioso*! "Look at your pitiable biography," I say, prodding him to even greater heights of passion. "Born to an impoverished family. Wasting your entire, fleeting youth attending to a sickly derelict like me. You will die just as poor, stupid, and unsatisfied as the day you were born."

"Stories aren't supposed to be real!" he mewls.

"But this is not a story. I told you that before. I am writing down history. It actually happened. I cannot change it to suit your tastes."

Antonio slumps to the floor and cradles his head in his hands. "Why *do* babies have to die?" he asks plaintively. His voice is as high and reedy as a child's.

"Come. Sit on the bed," I reply consolingly. "I am not done with the story. This is not the end."

Antonio comes over, flops on the bed, and lies on his back with one arm covering his eyes.

"Here, Antonio. Have some of this very satisfying risotto. And, please, do not jump to conclusions."

"While hideous goblins poke spiny things into your tender bottom," droned the angel. "Burning in the fires of Hell," he repeated ruefully.

The anger smoldered inside Godfrey's heart like hot iron in a forge. It seized his body, entered every muscle and sinew, and made his hair stand up on end.

Godfrey's countenance reminded the angel of an arrogant Mongol general he had witnessed long ago, who had been completely defeated in battle. This general, standing on a hill surveying the carnage of his decimated army, had become so full of frustrated wrath his head had literally exploded. The angel considered Godfrey might share the same fate as the Mongol and scooted into the corner better to avoid the flying flesh.

But then something odd happened: Godfrey, in the midst of his fury, stopped and stared into space with a curious, blank expression. Out of the clear blue, he burst forth with a hearty, merry, thoroughly incongruous laugh.

"God," stated Godfrey, "certainly has a flair for the ironic, does He not?"

The old angel was stunned. "You are not angry anymore?"

"No. Actually, it is all rather amusing," replied Godfrey.

"You are not afraid?"

"Of death? Not really."

"Not afraid of Hell?"

"It cannot be that much worse than Carthusalem. Have you ever been in the camel stalls on a hot August afternoon?"

"Yes, but—"

"Have you ever had a really bad toothache?" queried Godfrey, quick to interrupt.

"In another lifetime, yes, but I don't—"

"Pain, Hell . . . whatever comes," said the brave Godfrey, cutting him off again, "I'm ready."

The old man cocked his head and stared at Godfrey in

awe. "Your courage is . . . praiseworthy."

"It is not courage," said Godfrey. "I have given up. I have stopped resisting. I am in His hands."

"After all of this, you still believe in Him?"

"Why not?" replied Godfrey. "What is the point in *not* believing? I have spent my whole life contemplating things, thinking and pondering and hoping and dreading and dreaming. Now I am just going to ride it out. I will see what happens. Have I any choice? And if there is one thing I *have* learned in my short life, it is this: one has absolutely no control over what happens to one. I could never have foreseen these twists in my life nor this strange finale. Despite all of this, I do have control over how I *react* to these events. I can at least choose how I *feel* about them."

The old angel seemed dazzled by Godfrey's words. He shook his head several times, as if trying to displace a confusing notion, as if his brain were a boot and Godfrey's declaration a vexatious pebble lodged therein.

"Hell is a terrible place," said the angel finally.

"We will see," said Godfrey.

"You will burn forever."

"It could not be much worse than being in love."

"Your skin will crackle like a chicken on a spit."

"Heigh-ho."

"Nasty bird-creatures will pick the eyes from your skull," put forth the angel.

"Then I will not have to look at the damned place anymore," replied Godfrey irately. He was becoming rather annoyed with this pessimistic angel.

"Err . . . but your eyes will grow back again, like the organs of Prometheus when he was chained upon the rock and the great Eagle came and devoured his liver—"

"And the next day it grew back again," snapped Godfrey. "I know. I've heard the story."

"Hell stinks!"

"Try living with Short Clog."

"Don't you understand? Eternal suffering."

"You are quite morbid for an angel."

The angel sat back against the wall and scratched his chin. "There is one more option left, Godfrey: I can sign you over to me and then we can contest the demon's contract."

At that moment a moth—a Gypsy moth—glided into the cell through the tiny window and landed on Godfrey's bent knee. It peered up at him and seemed to shake its head as if to say, "No."

"I have the papers right here in my pocket." The angel held a blank piece of papyrus to the dim light.

"There's no writing on this contract," said Godfrey.

"Invisible ink."

"Have you a quill?"

"All we need is a teeny prick."

"Say again?"

"You must sign it in blood."

"Blood?"

"Quickly, the day grows near."

Godfrey shook his head slowly, smiled wryly, peered at the angel and said, "Purvious."

The angel was confused. "Pardon?"

"I never told you about Purvious," said Godfrey. "But you knew all about him . . . knew that I had accidentally killed him." For the first time, Godfrey noticed that the angel's eyes were gleaming a dull crimson color. It reminded him of when he was a child: he would hold his finger up to a candle in a darkened room, and the flesh behind the fingernail would glow red—his father had called this trick 'making a devil's eye.' Now Godfrey felt all his nerves tingle with a sudden realization. "Fool me once, shame on you. Fool me twice, shame on me," he said triumphantly.

"Ohhh . . . filth and squalor!" cursed Azfall, and his eyes flamed to life like red-hot coals.

"I should have recognized your ancient foul breath the moment you opened your mouth," said Godfrey. "What game do you play with me, devil?"

"Demon," replied Azfall crossly.

"You had my signature once. What happened?"

"Nothing."

"Somehow, you lost it."

"No, I didn't," shot back the demon.

"You lost it," said Godfrey mirthfully.

"Didn't!" hissed Azfall. "Someone pinched it."

"Poor devil. Someone swiped the soul you stole from me." Godfrey sat back and let forth a great belly laugh.

Azfall stared up at the ceiling with a churlish expression on its demon face.

"So why the elaborate ruse?" asked Godfrey after his high-glee had subsided. "Why pretend to be my guardian angel?"

"I wanted to test your faith," replied Azfall. "I wanted to see you squirm. I wanted to hear your despair. I wanted you to denounce Him. It would have made me so excruciatingly happy."

"Well, you can go to Hell," said Godfrey. "I mean, go *back* to Hell. Like I said before, I am resigned to my fate."

"I can knock down this wall with a puff of my breath," offered the demon.

"I'll wager you could melt Saint Peter's holy prong with your rancid exhalations," growled Godfrey.

"I could transport you to any place on this globe . . . in the universe for that matter," tendered Azfall.

"It would mean nothing without Mamooshaka," stated Godfrey emphatically.

"Why did I have to be assigned you?" spat Azfall. "Talk about blasted luck!"

The door burst open and a cloaked figure carrying a lanthorn rushed into the cell.

"The Dim Avenger!" cried Godfrey.

"Come, Gypsy!" exclaimed the Dim Avenger lustily. "I've bought your freedom from the guard with the money I saved from thieving. We don't have much time." He slipped a key into Godfrey's manacles and the hateful fetters clanged to the ground.

"I could have done *that*," said Azfall with a little scoffing snort.

Before they left the cell, Godfrey took the Dim Avenger by the arm and stared into his eyes. "I will come with you only if you promise to make a list of all the people from whom you have stolen so that I may pay them back one day when I am able."

"Surely you crack a joke with me?" asked the thief with wonder.

"I have learned many things these strange days," replied Godfrey, "and one of them is indeed a touch of cynicism. Yes, I was cracking a joke." He turned to Azfall. "Farewell, foul-breathed devil. I hope you never get your horns or whatever it is they deem down there a sign of success."

After Godfrey and the Dim Avenger had fled the jail, Azfall changed back to the shape of the fair enchantress. The she-devil grimaced and grizzled and cussed and cursed. She was not amused.

Antonio suggests, merrily, that the demon burst into flames and turn into a little cone of ashes and bones, like a chicken's carcass that falls off a spit onto a pile of coals. I tell him that the demon's role is not quite finished.

27

THE
MASQUERADERS
(And an Ending)

G odfrey and the Dim Avenger ran hand in hand
through the forest in the direction of the Verrazanno
estate. The sun had not yet crested the mountains in
the east, but already its light had begun to spread across the
bottoms of the clouds; the earth was filled with that portentous, ethereal quality that comes with daybreak.

"Soon after you were taken to the prison," said the Dim
Avenger, "your good man, Short Clog, came running to me
with the news. We went in search of Thomas, the wandering
merchant. He told us to meet him in Mamooshka's garden for
we would see and hear something unexpected, unlooked for,
and most welcome."

"Thank you for saving me," replied Godfrey.

"I do it out of love for my friend Mamooshka. And you
and I have a friendship, do we not, *Godfrey?*"

They came to a stop outside the walls of the Verrazanno
garden. Godfrey squeezed the Dim Avenger's hand tightly.

"We do," said Godfrey. "The Gypsy and the Dim Avenger shall be friends forever."

The Dim Avenger smiled, reluctantly disengaged his hand from Godfrey's grasp, and nodded toward the door in the garden wall. The two crept into the shadows, peered into the garden, and waited. Soon after, they observed Thomas enter the place from the servants' quarters. He sat on a stone bench next to the bubbling fountain. A moment later, Egelbun waddled from the house and peered in the direction of Thomas.

"Who lurks there?" asked Egelbun with false bravado.

Thomas raised one hand slowly, enigmatically, mysteriously.

"Ah, you. The magician. So you're the one who sent me the message for this meeting?"

"Verily," whispered Thomas.

"I will no longer have need of your services," said Egelbun curtly. "Thank you and goodbye." Egelbun headed back toward the house, but Thomas' words made him stop dead in his tracks.

"I know everything," snarled Thomas. "I know what the sailors did to your brother."

Egelbun turned and took a couple of jerky steps in the direction of Thomas. His face, formerly the color of rancid lard, had turned a shade paler: the complexion could now be compared to the hue of the buttocks belonging to the day-old corpse of a Swedish albino.

"What nonsense do you speak?" asked Egelbun with a croak in his voice.

"Sharks!" barked Thomas.

Egelbun's jaw quivered. His tongue gibbered.

"I know what you did to Purvious," growled Thomas. "I know you switched the daggers."

Egelbun pulled a giant handkerchief from his sleeve and mopped his face. His flesh had become as moist and slimy as fermenting cheese. He walked slowly toward Thomas and hissed, "What do you want? Money?"

"I want to see you decorate a gallows."

"Get out of here!" Egelbun's voice came in a whispered shriek. "Before I have you arrested. Like dead-as-a-doornail Godfrey!"

"Godfrey isn't dead," replied Thomas with a devilish grin.

"What do you mean?" replied Egelbun, flabbergasted. "It's sunrise! His head should be in a basket."

Thomas stood up to his full height, towering over the cowering Egelbun. "Your brother is alive too," he said through clenched teeth.

"Liar!" squealed Egelbun. "He's been feeding the fishes at the bottom of the ocean for these past three years."

"You were the one who devised his *intended* death," said Thomas. Egelbun withered under his cold stare. "There was no shipwreck," he continued. Now he pitched his voice toward Mamooshka and Godfrey, so they would be sure to hear. "The crew mutinied and Zalman Verrazanno was thrown overboard on the high seas. He was marooned many thousands of miles from home. Captured by slavers and forced to row in a galley. He escaped from that hell and took on different vocations—a caravan leader, a desert bandit, a mercenary soldier, a fisherman, a petty merchant—merely to stay alive. All those years he dreamed of the day he would come back home and take revenge on his brother."

Whilst he had been speaking, Thomas' voice had changed: it was as if he had been disguising it all along and now his true accent and tone were revealed. The Dim Avenger recognized it at once and instantly felt a tingling sensation in the palms. Godfrey discerned it too, and the hairs on his neck stood to attention. Egelbun knew it as well, and his bowels went as slack as a sack full of wet manure.

"Nay! Nay! Nay!" screamed Egelbun.

Thomas threw off his hood and roared, "For I am Zalman Verrazanno, your very much alive half-brother!"

Egelbun fainted dead away. The Dim Avenger ran from the shadows straight at Zalman and leapt onto his body, embracing him and covering his face with kisses.

"Father!" cried the Dim Avenger and pulled off the thief's mask and hood to reveal a womanly face with long, curling hair.

Zalman let forth a shocked laugh. "Mamooshka? Thou art the Royal Scamp?"

Godfrey swooned and leaned against the rock wall. *Mamooshka? The Dim Avenger?* Memories of their meetings flashed in his mind's eye; he realized what a fool he had been not to guess the highwayman's identity.

"What happiness I feel!" thundered Zalman.

Egelbun opened one eye, stared at his brother, then shrieked hideously and convulsed like a man with the quaking-palsy.

Zalman cast a stern glance at Egelbun. "Not only will you pay for my attempted murder, but for the very real deaths of my ship's captain as well as the *podestà's* son."

As if on cue, Short Clog and Gurditta Singh scurried forth from the servants' quarters carrying the very stiff, wrapped-up body of Purvious. They dropped their rigid burden on the ground as if it were a piece of lumber.

Godfrey, who had been lurking in the shadows of the garden gate's alcove, lest he see Mamooshka and revert back to his old wretched self, let forth a surprised exclamation at the sight of identical Short Clogs.

"Two Short Clogs?!" he exclaimed.

"Twins, sir," replied Short Clog nonchalantly. "As it turns out, my father, in his youth, was a sailor. In a far and distant port he fell in love with a young woman. They were married, and soon after, we two were born identically. Twins as it were. During a great war which ravaged the land, our parents were separated from each other, one fleeing to the west, the other to the east, each with a child whom they raised to adulthood."

"And where is your mother?" asked Mamooshka.

The figure of an old woman breezed through the garden doorway, practically knocking Godfrey to the ground. She ran up to Short Clog and Gurditta Singh.

"Here! I am their mother!" she cried, and hugged and tweaked the two little brutes with feigned affection.

Godfrey instantly recognized that the "old woman" was Azfall. In her haste, she had been unable to metamorphose into a proper old crone, and had merely put on a theatrical witch-nose and gray wig (she kept these in her demon pouch in case of emergencies).

"Mother!" wept Short Clog and smiled like a puppy on the pap.

Godfrey ran up to the old woman and pulled off the false nozzle and thatch. "This woman is a demon," he cried. "She tried to steal my soul!"

Azfall shoved Short Clog and Gurditta Singh aside and glared at Godfrey who, in turn, made the mistake of glancing at Mamooshka and instantly regressed to his old, hump-backed, ill-favored self.

Egelbun chose this moment to pull off his own wig, beat his fists into the sod, and scream like a four-year-old urchin. "I did not kill Purvious!" he howled. "Godfrey did!"

Zalman rolled his eyes. "We all know about the plan, you polenta-brained ninny." He stepped aside to reveal Loutronio and Drapslod.

"Leviticus! Dicksocks!" squawked Egelbun.

"I told them everything!" said Loutronio and flicked his thumbnail against his front teeth at Egelbun in that charming Veronese gesture of discourtesy.

"And we know you switched the daggers, Egelbun!" said Zalman.

Drapslod walked to the prone Egelbun and stood over him holding the trick dagger.

"Dicksocks," wheezed Egelbun, struggling to his feet. "My faithful servant."

Drapslod could take it no longer. He stabbed Egelbun in the chest repeatedly with the trick dagger and screamed, "My name is Drapslod! Drapslod! Drapslod!" Once again, Egelbun shrieked and fell senseless.

Azfall had been eyeing Zalman's robe with a suspicious scowl. "That is my robe you are wearing! You hit me on the head and stole it from me!"

"I'm the one who struck you on the head," said Mamooshka, putting a hand on her sword. "And I'd do it again, wench!" She was still angry at the demoness for kissing the Gypsy in the meadow.

Zalman put a hand on Mamooshka's sword arm. "There, there, child. I will give the robe back to this creature if indeed it belongs to her." He handed the robe to Azfall who grabbed at it greedily.

She searched all of the pockets for the contract and when she couldn't find it, her eyes flamed to life like cones of incense. Everyone stared at her with dread.

"Where is it?" she croaked. "Where is the piece of parchment that was in my pocket?"

"I used it to write a letter and sent it to Godfrey," replied Zalman.

Azfall turned on Godfrey who shrugged and gibbered.

"He says, sir," jumped in Short Clog. "'That he never received—'"

"Shut your pie-hole," sneered Azfall. "You little twit! I can understand everything your master says. I always could!"

"Well, if you're going to be insulting," replied Short Clog with a hurt tone, "I won't tell you what happened to said article that you're so anxious to find." He picked his nose and thrust out his lower lip.

Azfall raised a single, looming finger and it turned as black as a charcoal stick. A dozen flies descended upon it and buzzed disgustingly.

"How would you like me to poke you with 'The Repulsive Finger of Pestilence'?" asked the demoness.

Short Clog eyed the finger apprehensively, then said rather quickly, "We two, that being my new-found brother and all, bumped into each other yesterday and unknowingly took the other's letter. Which I brought it to Mamooshka."

"Give it to me!" said Azfall, casting her wolfish eyes on Mamooshka.

"I don't have it," replied Mamooshka. "I wrote my own letter on it and gave it to Godfrey to send to the Gypsy. And," she added haughtily, "even if I did have it, I wouldn't give it to you, thou putrefied succubus!"

Azfall ignored her and leered at Godfrey. "The Gypsy," she said with contempt. "Then *you* had it all along."

Godfrey slowly put a hand to his pocket and felt the note from Mamooshka crinkle under the cloth.

Azfall waved a hand majestically and her rags disappeared to be replaced by a fetching black ensemble that showed off her immodest figure. All at once, she was beauteous again—as comely as a Houri in the Gardens of Euphoria. "Give it to me, Godfrey," she importuned in a musical, honeyed voice.

Godfrey stared at her with bedazzled eyes.

"It is rightfully mine," she said and pouted winsomely.

"Don't do it, Godfrey," cried Mamooshka. She would have attacked the demon, but her feet were rooted to the ground by some enchantment.

"You have no choice, Godfrey," Azfall stated matter-of-factly. "We made a deal."

Godfrey fought against her spell. Everything she said, however, seemed so reasonable.

But you cheated, he finally forced himself to say in his mind.

"That doesn't matter," replied Azfall, reading his thoughts, and Godfrey let forth a gasp. Azfall smiled scathingly. "Yes. I could always read your mind, you silly fool. Your entire life I've been watching over you. Listening to your pathetic deliberations on life, your meditations on philosophy, and those endlessly insipid poems of love for that brat Mamooshka." Azfall turned and looked at the others who were watching her in amazement. "Mamooshka," seethed Azfall, saying the name like a jealous, petulant child. "Mamooshka, Mamooshka, Mamooshka! Of all the torments in Hell, that name drives me insane."

She walked slowly, sensuously toward Godfrey. She stroked his hair with a graceful hand—touched his cheek with her palm. "Now. We made a deal," she said, smiling libidinously. "You had the opportunity to gain that Jezebel's love and you never could have done it without me. But through your misguided approach to life, because of the pathetic goodness that seeps from you like honey from a hive, you ruined any chance you might have had to possess her. So give me the contract. You have no choice."

Godfrey slowly took the parchment from his pocket, held it in his hand, and stared at it with desolation. Azfall's fingers were inches away from plucking it from his hand when Short Clog shouted:

"Wait! You don't have to do that, sir."

"Would you quit interrupting me, you little toad?!" screamed Azfall. In that instant, her voice was no longer dulcet and mellifluous. Instead, it sounded hideous and vulgar.

Short Clog and Gurditta Singh opened a burlap sack that they had brought into the garden and out rolled the pig-man.

"This is the evil demon's nasty servant," said Short Clog, giving Azfall his best piss-eye. "I caught him at the Happy Cock, drunk as a bishop and doting on a table leg. He only speaks a strange dialect of gibberish; but because of my uncanny ability to act as translator for my formerly unintelligible master, I was able to question this little demented thing and understand him fairly well. It seems that since Godfrey is in *possession* of the contract, which it is rightfully his. She cannot take it from him."

Everyone shouted "Huzzah!"

Azfall turned to the crowd and raised her hand. Instantaneously, they all froze like statues. A strange music appeared in the air: it sounded like an evil baboon scraping lurid, descending minor chords on an ill-tuned violin.

"You know, Godfrey," said Azfall cruelly, "if you keep the contract, you go back to your old self. That pathetic, lard-skinned, humped-back beast with the articulation of a tongue-tied goat."

A Gypsy moth settled onto Godfrey's nose and he stared at it, cross-eyed. Then it trembled and took flight. He followed the creature as it flapped over to Mamooshka and alighted on her brow.

"She'll never love you, Godfrey," taunted Azfall.

Mamooshka was staring at him with tears coursing down her cheeks. Her mouth moved slowly, as if in a dream . . . as if she were trying to speak, but the demon's spell had taken away her voice. He could see her lips forming a silent word, over and over again. It was a name. His name. Not the Gypsy. She was saying "Godfrey." It was then he remembered something: when they were entering the garden that morning, and she was still in the guise of the Dim Avenger, she had called him "Godfrey!" Not "Gypsy." So she had known, in the prison, when she came to rescue him that he was Godfrey. She loved him. *Him*!

Azfall, who had been studying Godfrey's mind, knew that the game was up. "O Hell," she said.

Godfrey stared directly into the demon's eyes and ripped up the contract.

And everyone broke from the spell.

Godfrey slowly straightened his back. He stood taller than ever the Gypsy did. He smiled at Azfall. "I'faith, I do not know whether to be flattered or just sickened."

They all gasped at the clear, strong voice which flowed from Godfrey's mouth.

"I don't know what you're talking about," grumbled Azfall.

"You are in love with me," said Godfrey.

"I am not." Azfall turned away and chewed on a nail.

"This was all an elaborate plot to entrap me. I guess my torment in Hell would have been to be your plaything, your fancy man for eternity."

"Actually, ten thousand years," said Azfall. "And it wouldn't have been all *that* tortuous." She turned away and sniffled a little.

Godfrey looked at the others and laughed. "It was all a trick. Mere devilshine. All along. I could always speak. She just deceived me into thinking that I could not. And I could always appear like this . . . this man you see before you. She simply robbed me of my confidence."

Mamooshka ran to Godfrey and they embraced. He covered her teary face with kisses, and she sobbed joyfully, burying her head in his chest.

"How did you know it was me?" he asked. "When you came to rescue me at the prison?"

"It was in the garden," she replied. "Yesterday. When we kissed. I came for both of you. Godfrey *and* the Gypsy. For both of them are you."

"I love you," he said. "I never wanted to possess you, like

that evil creature claimed. I only wanted to . . . to be in your sphere of light."

"You'll never try to change me?" she asked.

"Never."

"I love you too, Godfrey."

Zalman burst into tears and grabbed the nearest person to him (it happened to be Loutronio) and crushed him in a massive hug. Short Clog and Gurditta Singh leaned on one another and sighed. Drapslod smiled for the first time in his life.

But Azfall was not finished. She had one more card in her hand. "I can give anyone here anything they want right now," she proclaimed. "Anything on earth."

Egelbun, who had been playing dead for the past ten minutes, leapt to his feet, scampered over to Azfall, and kneeled in front of her, covering her razor-sharp onyx-colored toenails with kisses and drivel.

"I'll do it, your wickedness," he snorted. "Where do I sign?"

"Anybody else?" asked Azfall hopefully.

Gurditta Singh took a step forward, jutted out his lower jaw defiantly, then cursed in the language of the noble people of the Punjab.

Short Clog embraced his brother and shouted, "I do believe my brother said 'Sod off!' My brother spoke!"

Azfall pulled a scroll from her sleeve and pricked Egelbun's finger with her golden needle.

Egelbun signed his name frantically with his blood, then looked at the others and laughed hideously. "You're all dead," he gloated.

"What do you wish?" asked Azfall of her new client.

"I want you," said Egelbun hysterically, "to kill everyone here and chop them up into tiny bits! Then I want you to make me thin and never let me get fat no matter how much I eat."

Azfall glanced at the contract, then frowned. "This is your name: 'Egelbun Verrazanno'?" Egelbun nodded his head. She ripped the contract in half. "Sorry, Egelbun. You sold your soul three years ago during a sodden binge. You probably don't even remember. Your brother's death was the price of your soul."

"But he's standing right there!" complained Egelbun.

"I can't be responsible for every stray altruistic porpoise in the ocean," replied Azfall callously. She clapped her fingers against her thumbs and they made a clacking noise like castanets.

Without warning, the ground gave way beneath Egelbun and he disappeared into the earth, pulled by green, scaly hands; the dirt closed up around him, and all that was left was his yellow wig, dirty and desolate, like the lost hair of a disconsolate Dane.

"Come, my little traitor," said Azfall to the pig-goblin. "We'll fill our quota somewhere else." As she walked past Godfrey, she gave him a wink which made him shudder.

"Let us go inside," said Zalman after Azfall had passed through the garden gate. "We shall feast and talk and make insignificant the many years we have missed apart. And we have a wedding to plan!" He embraced Mamooshka and Godfrey, leading them into the house.

Loutronio and Drapslod picked up the corpse of Purvious and carried him back into the servants' quarters.

"You know, I have been thinking," said Loutronio. "The two of us might have a future together, now that we have both lost our masters."

"How, sir?" asked Drapslod.

"It's actually a brilliant plan." Loutronio smiled. "Dicksocks."

Drapslod sighed morosely. "My name is Drapslod, sir."

"No. We corner the market on dicksocks."

"Oh! Aha!" replied Drapslod.

After they were gone, Short Clog and Gurditta Singh stared at one another and smiled.

"I always wanted a brother," stated Short Clog. "And it's nice that we're the same size; though I'll wager I'm slightly taller. Shall we enter the house as we came into this world? Together that is? Wait! I've a better idea." He climbed on Gurditta Singh's back and urged him to walk into the house. "Now if I cry out as we pass under the lintel, remember, it is only out of pure joy."

Short Clog smacked his head onto the door frame, and cried out triumphantly "Wonderful!"

I left Antonio in the room. He was tucked into my bed with a contented smile on his face, staring at the stars through the window, reliving the happy end of the story over again in his mind. I, however, was drawn to another place. A tangible, visceral realm of stone and fire and flesh—*la cucina*.

On the way down the stairs, I heard muffled shouts and plaintive cries emanating from the kitchen. I flung open the door to witness the most astounding, offensive sight of my entire life: Sophia's back was up against a wall, and the Hungarian doctor, sporting his birthday suit, was on his knees in front of her, weeping and clawing at her thighs. His slobber had defiled her garment! Sophia's hands slapped at the top of his scraggly head as she cried out, "Leave me alone, you dirty old goat!"

"I do not bluff! Eef you vill not let me haff you," threatened the doctor, "I vill tell ze French gendarmes zat Herr Smythee iss *ein* shtinking shpie! *Und* zen he vill be taken to ze prizon, *und* tortured, *und* zen hiss scrawny neck vill be put on

ze guillotine block *und* . . . schlock!" The last word came out
as a hideous grunt in the back of his throat.

My skin went cold and my palms tingled with pins and
needles. My breath caught in my gorge. *Dear God, no!* I
thought. *Not smirking French gendarmes, cruel torture, and death
by that satanic machine!*

Sophia saw me in the doorway, pale with fright and cowering, and her lovely eyes beckoned me to flee.

"No!" she said to the doctor. Suddenly, her voice was as
brave and mighty as queen Boudicca of Briton, she who led
the glorious but doomed revolt against the Roman invaders.
"Do no harm to the *signore*. You may have me."

She began to undo the strings of her blouse and at the
same time beseeched me go with a wordless mouthing of her
quivering lips.

The doctor reached a greedy paw toward her slender ankle
and—

"Unhand her, foul fiend!" cried a fell and powerful voice.
The Hungarian doctor jerked to attention. His head snapped
back to regard the owner of the voice—to my own surprise,
me.

"You shtinking, afflicted Inglishman!" he wheezed as he
crawled a few feet toward my direction. I could see now that
he was heinously drunk, for his face was bright red and he had
to shake his head to bring his eyes into focus. "If it vasn't for
you, ziss *frau* vould be *mein!*" Then he rose to his full height,
staggered, caught his bearing, and grabbed a long knife from
the cutting board. In his haste he neglected to detach it from
the wooden scabbard, but he meant to use this sheathed
blade with deadly force nevertheless.

Sophia screamed. Instantly, I grabbed a rolling pin from
the kitchen rack, lunged forward, and caught the doctor in the
gut; he let forth a tremendous "*Au!*" My next blow, a savage
downward pate-wallop, sent him to the floor for a good

night's rest. I hit him so hard, however, that the shock sprained my wrist cruelly. Without thinking, I let go of the rolling pin and it landed directly on my naked big toe.

"O, my darling *signore!*" cried Sophia, as I hopped about on one foot, rubbing my wrist and making smarting sounds.

Dear Sophia picked me up in one graceful motion and carried me up the stairs. My heart leapt like a wild hare in springtime. Her right sleeve had fallen off her shoulder. Instinctively, I covered her bronze skin with kisses; she let forth a primitive grunt and quickened her pace. Kicking open the door to her bedchamber, she dropped me on the mattress, then moved away, shyly, with her back to me. I could see that she was breathing hard, almost gasping for air. Slowly, she turned her head in profile. Her dark, exotic eye peered as from an Egyptian hieroglyph, asking if I indeed wanted her.

I smiled like an idiot and tried to nod yes. My head, however, had lost all connection with my spine: it wobbled ludicrously, like a spinning plate on a balancing stick—a plate that has lost its momentum and is about to fall to the ground.

Sophia's luscious lips parted, then closed. She arched her back and her nightdress slid to the floor. I gazed at the taut skin of her thighs, the pear-shaped knolls of her fulsome buttocks, the perfect, smooth mound of one of her breasts, and the tresses of her black hair. In that moment, the glory of God's creation on earth was revealed to me in the body and being of that ideal woman. I moved toward her and she turned to face me. Coronation music surged from the heavens—sagbutts and cornets announcing a full measure of corporeal joy. I was about to learn what I'd been missing.

Epilogue

The next morning, when I entered my chamber, I found Antonio perched on the sill, staring out the window and weeping.

"Antonio. What is wrong?" I asked him, sitting gingerly upon my own bed—I could hardly move from my night of gladness.

"Err . . . I've got something in my eye," he replied.

"You should never be ashamed of crying," I said.

"I'm just so sad. About Godfrey and Mamooshka."

"But my dear boy, their tale had a happy ending."

"I know."

"And is not that how you wished it to end?"

"Yes . . . "

"The lovers united. The villain punished. The wanderer returned to his rightful place of honor. Evil vanquished. And some pleasant banter from the rubes and rustics. What could be more perfect?"

"Nothing," he replied with abject misery as he brushed away the hot dewdrops that dripped from his eyes.

"Then why the tears?"

"Because the story is over. Waaaaaah!" His wail was like a swaddling babe's.

"But there will be other stories," I stated earnestly.

"There will?" he asked hopefully.

"Yes. And other adventures."

"Adventures? Here?"

"You look around this room with the weary eyes of an inmate, bound to the service of a bedridden do-nothing."

"I didn't say that," he said apologetically, but he knew that his look had betrayed his thoughts.

"No. Do not deny it. It is quite all right. Because it is the truth!" I strode to the window and pulled back the curtain. "The sun comes up, the sun goes down. The dust settles like ancient soot in a pharaoh's tomb. You are tired of sticking that hose up my arse, and I am tired of getting it stuck there. As of this moment, no more enemas!"

"Thank you, Christ in Heaven!" exclaimed Antonio with relief.

"I think that you and I should see a bit of the world before it is too late. We must cross the Rubicon. Take the Appian Way."

"What do you mean, *signore*?"

"We need to get out of this house. We need some bracing sea air. We require the sun on our faces. I have just now realized how sick to death I am of this bed. My gluteus maximus feels like a mummy's fist."

"A journey?" he asked hesitantly.

"Yes," I replied. "A journey."

"Where?"

"The land of Ulysses, perhaps."

"Who's he?" inquired Antonio.

"Ulysses. The Greek traveler," I answered.

"Aha! The one who sells olives at the market?"

"The Aegean," I clarified. "Athens. Constantinople. Even Carthusalem. We will outrun that goblin Bonaparte. Flee to the ends of the earth. To India and the birthplace of the Gypsies. (For several German scholars with whom I have corresponded believe that the Gypsy race originated on the subcontinent, in the Deccan plane, to be exact.) Antonio, bring me my sword!" I commanded.

"Your sword?" he cringed.

"Yes. Bring me my saber! My trusty flatchet!" I insisted.

"It's broken," he replied timidly.

"How can this be? It was Toledo steel."

"We were using it to dig up weeds from the flagstones and it snapped in half."

"A-hey! Well, never mind, lad. We'll get one on the way. And a stiletto for you. We must be wary of bandits, huzzay, huzzah! Now let us pack. Hand me my britches!"

"But the Hungarian doctor is coming today," protested Antonio.

"He will not be coming anywhere for a spell," I replied cryptically. "And when he does, he will bring with him French gendarmes to arrest us. Ha! Ha! But we will have long since departed."

"*Signore*. You look flushed."

"My cheeks are burning. It is a lovely feeling."

"Maybe I should take your pulse."

"Damn the pulse and pass the small clothes!"

Antonio, finally realizing that I was ardent in my plans, clapped his hands with glee. "I'll get the trunks."

"No. The valises," I explained. "We are traveling light. Not a soul must see us leave. Saddle the horses."

"We've only got one: old Stinker, the sway-backed, one-eyed, grumpy gelding."

"Then saddle up the abhoreson bugger. Sophia will ride him whilst we walk alongside."

"Sophia is coming with us?" he asked in astonishment.

Bound For New Adventures

"Yes. For she is to be my wife."

Antonio shook his head absurdly and rolled his eyes as if I had banged him on the skull with a shovel.

"Does *she* know this?" he asked at length.

"Of course!" I said.

"When are we coming back?"

"Faith! I cannot tell."

"What about the book?"

"What about it?"

"The printing and binding of seven times seven copies, one sent to each of the finest universities in Europe."

"That does not matter anymore," I said and pointed to my heart. "It is all in here."

"In the left breast pocket of your lounging jerkin?" he asked with a baffled look.

"Antonio. It is in my *heart*; and in yours."

"Oh. Ah. Aha! I get it. In *there*," he said and beamed like a child who has been told a marvelous secret.

"I will leave the manuscript here, in this room," I said. "Perchance we will return to write another chapter in the story. If fate leads us in another direction, however, then let us hope that some kindred spirit will find Godfrey's tale and read it and gain from it the same pleasure that we did."

For those who wonder at our route, I have decided that our first destination must be Venice—that ancient gateway to the East. (Next we will hire passage to Dalmatia and thence to Carthusalem.) There is a painting in Venezia, at the church of San Giorgio Maggiore, that I long to see in person, having read about it for years, and studied engravings and other copies of the work. It is Tintoretto's final canvas, his master-piece: *The Descent from the Cross*. In this depiction, the body of Christ is supported by many hands as he is lowered from his place of torment. His face is waxen. His eyes closed in eternal sleep. His well-knit arms—spread wide in the attitude of the cross—are no longer stretched and taut but slack in death. His abdomen is caved and constricted, frozen in the sunken posture of his final exhalation. But, startlingly, his legs are portrayed in a living state . . . they are animate! They seem to have kicked the winding-sheet away so that they could move about unhindered; the toes are pointed in a dancer's posture.

It is as if he is dancing over death.

Finis

Here Follows A

GLOSSARY

Which May Prove Useful When Reading The Tale

STOLEN *from* GYPSIES

*In Which Certain Words, Notions, And Historical Personages
Known To Ambrogio Smythe, The Author Of That Work,
And Which May Now Seem Archaic Or Strange
To The Modern Ear, Are Clarified For
The Venerable Reader By Noble Smith,
A Modern Writer*

A

Abhoreson: Someone or something that is repugnant or loathsome in nature.

Acre, Siege of: Jerusalem fell to Saladin, Sultan of Egypt, in 1187. This spurred the Christian armies to gather for a Third Crusade to the Holy Land. Led by Guy de Lusignan of Poiteau, the Crusaders laid siege to the city of Acre, twenty miles north of Jerusalem. For over a year the city held out against the northern invaders, whilst malaria, starvation, and discord took their toll on the Christian army. Finally, King Richard of England arrived to join the forces. He brought with him a great pre-fabricated siege tower, **mangonels,** and massive boulders for ammunition. He then directed ceaseless attacks on the castle walls and towers. Relief efforts from Saladin were thwarted and the city finally gave up. One hundred and twenty thousand Crusaders gave their lives in this quest. Richard had taken two thousand Mohammedan prisoners during the siege. When their ransom was not instantly paid, the rash Englishman mercilessly executed all of them in sight of Saladin's army.

Twelve years later, during a siege in France, Richard was haughtily strolling around the outskirts of the castle surveying its weaknesses (sans armor), when he was wounded by a bolt shot from a crossbow. The superficial injury became infected and Richard died of blood poisoning. His brother John thus inherited the throne of England.

Akimbo: Hands on hips.

Alexander the Great: Born in 356 BC, Alexander was the son of the king of Macedonia, the land to the north of Greece. Alexander, tutored by **Aristotle**, was a brilliant military tactician and political leader who defended Greece against the Persian Empire. In his thirteen-year reign he subjugated most of the lands between Greece and India. His army was a multiracial force drawn from the nations he had conquered. He ordered his officers and encouraged his soldiers to intermarry with women from subjugated lands. He died suddenly at the age of thirty-three after a feast, quite possibly from malaria, perhaps from poison.

Amiens, Peace of: In March 1802, the British and French declared a truce in the long war between their two nations. The British surrendered several colonial conquests and, in turn, the French left Egypt. Many English tourists visited France during this lull between the conflict. It was short-lived, however, as war resumed three years later.

The Appian Way: Via Appia was the main highway of ancient

Italy. It was named for Appius Claudius who built the first section of the road in the fourth century BC.

Arbor Vitae: A penis, from two Latin words meaning "stem of life."

Argonaut: A Greek word meaning "sailors in the ship of Argo." The Argonauts were the followers of the Greek hero Jason. They sailed with him on many adventures, including a quest to Colchis to obtain the legendary Golden Fleece, a magical ram's skin protected by a dragon.

Aristotle: (384-322 BC) Ancient Greek philosopher who had a profound influence on Western thought. He tutored the teenage **Alexander the Great.** One ancient source claimed that Aristotle had spindly legs, beady eyes, and spoke with a lisp.

Atoms: A theory that objects are comprised of tiny particles was first argued by Democritus in the fifth century BC. The Greek word *atomos* means "invisible."

Attila the Hun: (434-453 AD) King of the Huns, a nomadic people who originated in north-central Asia. Their method of warfare utilized quick, mounted archers for hit and run cavalry attacks. In victory they were merciless. They ravaged much of eastern Europe for decades, exacting huge tributes from Poland, Russia, and Germany. Attila, called the Scourge of God, was condemned by contemporary Christian writers for his cruel practice of breaking up families of Christian captives and selling them into slavery. Attila and his horsemen were finally driven out of France to northern Italy. (Some of the terrified Italians took refuge in a desolate, marshy lagoon. These were the founders of Venice.) The Huns ravaged Italy for many years, but upon Attila's death they dispersed and were lost to history.

Austerlitz, Battle of: (Dec. 2, 1805) One of **Napoleon's** greatest victories. His force of 68,000 men routed 90,000 Russians and

Austrians at Austerlitz in Moravia. Napoleon's shrewd tactics involved luring his enemy into a trap and then launching a daring attack uphill to take a weakly defended but strategic plateau. After the battle, the Austrians made peace with France, and the downcast Russian Emperor took his wrecked army back to Russia.

⫷ B ⫸

Bachelor's Son: A bastard.

Back-door Usher: A sodomite.

The Bard: William Shakespeare.

Beau Sabreur: A skilled swordsman.

Becket, Saint Thomas: (1118-1170) Archbishop of Canterbury who was murdered by knights loyal to Henry II, King of England. Becket was a very spiritual man who, according to his contemporaries, led a celibate life. This was remarkable in an era when it was common for priests and popes to have mistresses, bastard children, and even secret wives. King Henry and Thomas were once best friends. After Thomas refused to support the King in his quarrels with Rome, Henry started to hate Thomas, especially after the Archbishop had him excommunicated for breaches of papal prohibition.

One day the King railed bitterly against the Archbishop, and four of his knights took his words to heart. They went to Canterbury and cut Thomas down with their swords inside the cathedral itself, desecrating the Holy Altar. When Becket's corpse was undressed by the monks, they found that he was wearing a hairshirt, a garment made of clipped horse hair. The wearing of hair shirts was an ascetic practice. The constant itching of the horse hair shirt reminded the wearer that the world is full of pain and suffering, and that our true home is with God. Henry II lamented the murder of the saintly Becket and walked barefoot from his Palace to Canterbury as a penance. He then allowed himself to be ritually (and painlessly) beaten by the monks of the abbey.

Bedlam: The nickname for the Hospital of St. Mary of Bethlehem, the first lunatic asylum established in London, England, in the year 1247. In the seventeenth and eighteenth centuries, it was open to spectators.

Beetleheaded: An intellectually blind person. Stupid.

Bitche Prison: The most feared prison in Napoleonic France, the Bitche was used to hold British prisoners of war. The gloomy fortress was located in the Province of Lorraine on a high, rocky plateau. The prisoners were kept in vaults underground, in appropriately named *souterrains*, and hardly ever saw the light of day.

Black Death: The Bubonic Plague, a devastating disease that spread through Europe in 1346-61, killing millions of people. The plague was spread by *Rattus rattus*, a sleek, black-haired rat that lived in human homes and barns. The rats were infested with fleas. The fleas contained the deadly bacteria in their digestive tracts, and when they bit humans, the plague would pass to them.

This simple concept of disease spreading from insects was unknown to the people of the time. They believed that the Black Death was caused by the wrath of God. A strange cult called the flagellants arose. Its members wandered about the barren villages beating themselves with whips as penance (at least until they too died of the plague). Some fanatical groups accused the Jews of poisoning wells and murdered thousands in retribution.

Before showing signs of the sickness, the victim became very depressed and apathetic. Then black buboes or pustules broke out under the armpits and groin. Victims usually died within three to five days of infection. England was hardest hit—over a third of the population was wiped out. Almost half the population of crowded London perished. In one country monastery, only ten of the fifty monks lived. The Scots took this opportunity to invade their old enemy to the south, but their army became infected and spread the plague to Scotland.

One beneficial result of the Black Death was that after its passing, peasant labor was in great demand, and the serf system died out in England as a result. In Europe, the poet **Petrarch** was a survivor of the pestilence. He wrote that no one who did not live through the plague would believe the stories about the absolute desolation, misery, and horror that afflicted the world during that evil time.

Blore: To cry out like an animal.

Boccherini, Luigi: (1743-1805) Italian cellist and composer, Boccherini was from a family of poets, musicians, and dancers. He helped develop the string quartet as a musical form, and wrote over 467 compositions. Much of his elegant work is instilled with a gentle melancholy. He died a poor man in a single, squalid room, leaving behind his three motherless children.

Bonaparte, Napoleon: (1769-1821) Napoleon was one of the most successful military and political leaders in the history of the Western world. Ironically, he graduated near the bottom of his class at the military academy. He was born on the island of Corsica, shortly after it was handed over to France by the Genoese Republic. His father, a lawyer of Tuscan descent, sent him to France at the age of nine to be educated. Short and frail, Napoleon rose to power through his superior intelligence and prowess as a political and military strategist. Curiously, he could not win at chess. At one point his Empire included all of Europe except Britain. He was thwarted from invading the detested English island by the English Channel and the heroics of **Nelson**.

Like all egomaniacal leaders in history, Napoleon overextended his domain. His disastrous foray into Russia weakened his army and his power. And then his forces were defeated once and for all by the British and Prussians at the Battle of Waterloo in Belgium. Napoleon was exiled to the tiny, desolate island of St. Helena where he died of stomach cancer or, so it has been rumored, poison. (See **Musée de Napoleon; Austerlitz**.)

The Book of the Courtier: *Il cortegiano* was written by a courtier named Baldassare Castiglione (1478-1529) and published in Venice in 1528. Castiglione used the chivalric court of Urbino, where he served for over ten years, as the setting for his treatise. His aim was to teach young courtiers how to become wise and accomplished counselors to better serve their employers. Charles V called Castiglione "one of the world's finest gentlemen." Castiglione's portrait by Raphael hangs in the Louvre Museum. (See **Sprezzatura**.)

Bosch, Hieronymous: Late Gothic Flemish painter. Known for his esoteric, disturbing, and haunting scenes illustrating man's vulnerability to the temptations of evil. The central panel of the triptych *Garden of Earthly Delights* (Prado, Madrid) is a chaotic masterpiece showing humans, animals, and fantastical creatures engaged in bizarre sensual activities with each other and massive fruits.

Botticelli, Sandro: (1445-1510) Botticelli was the son of a poor tanner. His name means "the Little Barrel." He was a sickly boy who grew up in the city of Florence near **Piazza di Santa Croce**. He was apprenticed to the workshop of the painter Filippo Lippi where his skills as a painter flourished under this kind, loving master. At one point in his youth, Botticelli painted in the same workshop as **Leonardo**. Botticelli's greatest works are his drawings for **Dante's** *Divine Comedy*, and his mythological pieces *The Birth of Venus* and *La Primavera* which hang in the **Uffizi** Museum in Florence.

Boudicca: (died AD 60) After suffering humiliation at the hands of the Romans, Queen Boudicca, a native Briton, raised a rebellion which nearly succeeded in driving the Italian invaders from her homeland.

Bouillon, Godfrey: (1060-1100) Duke of Lower Lorraine. Godfrey was a tall, handsome knight and a leader of the First Crusade. He became the first Latin ruler in Palestine after the city of Jerusalem was taken from the Muslims in 1099.

Brahe, Tycho: (1456-1601) One of the founders of modern astronomy. He lost his entire nose in a duel and, thereafter, wore a copper nose attached to his face with glue. The King of Denmark was so impressed by Brahe's skills as an astronomer that he gave him an island where Brahe built an observatory. Brahe discovered a new star (a supernova) with the naked eye. He was convinced that the solar system revolved around the Earth.

Brancacci Chapel: The chapel in Santa Maria del Carmine in Florence containing the frescoes of the *Lives of Saint Peter and Paul* by **Masaccio**.

Brueghel, Pieter: (1520-69) Netherlandish painter who depicted humorous scenes of peasant life. His work *The Peasant Dance* hangs in the Kunsthistorisches Museum, Vienna.

Brunelleschi: (1377-1446) Florentine architect who designed the **Duomo**. Brunelleschi was one of the first Renaissance artists to introduce geometrical principles in architecture and painting.

Bucintoro: Venetian **doge's** state barge, a magnificent, carved and gilded galley. It was scuttled on order of **Napoleon** as a symbol of his conquest of Venice and the removal of the doges from power. (See **Dandolo**.)

Buona Roba: Italian. Literally, "fine dress." A woman of easy virtue.

Byzantine Empire: The eastern province of the Roman Empire, which survived for a thousand years after the collapse of Rome. Constantinople, the capital city of the Byzantine Empire, was founded by Constantine the Great in 330. The secret knowledge of **Greek fire** and the manufacture of this weapon allowed the great fortified city to keep attackers at bay. Constantinople fell to the **Ottoman** Turks in 1453. The city is now called Istanbul.

≈ C ≈

Cacafuego: A bully or loudmouth. From two Spanish words meaning "shit fire."

Cachinnating: Loud and unrestrained laughter.

Calais: French seaport on the Strait of Dover. The army for **Napoleon's** intended invasion of England camped there until the Battle of Trafalgar destroyed this plan once and for all. (See **Nelson**.)

Caledonia: Roman name given to northern Britain or Scotland.

Carbuncle: An inflamation of the skin.

Cazzo: An Italian word meaning "penis."

Celerity: Quickness, speed.

Celtish Monks: During the so-called Dark Ages in Europe, Celtish art and learning flourished in Ireland and the Hebrides in isolated monestaries. The Book of Kells, one of the finest examples of illuminated manuscripts, was made around the year 800 A.D. It is a handwritten version of the Gospels with intricately designed pictures drawn and painted on vellum or animal skin. It is kept at Trinity College, Dublin.

Chariot-and-four: A light, four-wheeled carriage with two seats, drawn by four horses.

Chinker: A copper coin.

Churl: An upstart.

Circe's Pen: Circe, the daughter of the Greek sun-god Helios lived on the vowel-rich island of Aeaea. When **Odysseus** and his companions landed on the magical island, she turned all of his men into pigs. Her pigpens were notoriously evil-smelling.

Cloak Twitcher: A thief who lurked in alleys and snatched the cloaks from unfortunate passers-by.

Cockshut: Dusk. When poultry go to sleep.

Cocksman: A lecher; a rake.

Codpiece: From the fifteenth through seventeenth centuries, men wore close-fitting hose, or breeches on their legs. The codpiece was a bag-like appendage that fit over the hose, covering the bulge of the privates. They were made of leather or fabric, often eye-catching and sometimes even ornamented with precious stones.

Cods, The: The testicles.

Commedia dell' arte: A comedy technique characterized by improvisation with established roles played by actors who specialized in those parts. A quintessential skit involved a young couple thwarted in love by their quarrelsome parents. Some of the stock character types were old men, *zannies* (wacky servants), gruff soldiers, bawds, and maidservants. The Harlequin was often a capricious or cruel lover.

Corfu: An island in the Ionian Sea situated on the trade and invasion routes to and from Italy and the Balkans. For centuries it was controlled by Venice, until that great city state fell to **Napoleon** in 1797.

Cossack: A warlike Turkish people living on the Black Sea. They were famous for their horsemanship and physical, ecstatic dancing style.

Cove: A man, a guy; sometimes a rascal or rogue.

Croaker: Slang for a physician, as death so often came hard on their heels.

Cromnyomancer: A Roman form of magical fortune-telling. From two Greek words meaning "divination by onions."

Cunny-thumbed: An insult. To make a weak "girl's fist" with the fingers wrapped around the thumb.

Cupid's Itch: A venereal disease attributed to the love deity, most probably crabs.

⇗ D ⇖

Dandipratt: An insignificant little man. A pygmy.

Dandolo, Enrico: The blind **doge** of Venice who led the Venetian navy against **Constantinople** during the **Fourth Crusade**. During the assault on the city walls, the eighty-year-old man stood at the prow of the lead ship in full armor, and when his galley ran ashore, he leapt down and planted the banner of St. Mark (the symbol of Venice) into the ground. His men, who had been reluctant to storm the shore, were so inspired by their leader that they attacked with courage.

Danish Play: Shakespeare's play *Hamlet, Prince of Denmark*.

Dalmatia: A long, narrow, mountainous strip of land and nearby islands along the eastern coast of the Adriatic Sea. First settled by the ancient Greeks, Dalmatia has had a constant history of occupation by foreign powers including Rome, Byzantium, Venice, Croatia, the Normans of southern Italy (see **Robert de Hauteville**), France, Nazi Germany, and finally the Soviet Empire.

Dante, Alighieri: (1265-1321) Italian poet, writer, political thinker, and philosopher. He is best known for his epic poem *La divina commedia*, or *The Divine Comedy*. The poem is an allegorical journey through hell, purgatory, and paradise. He wrote the work in Italian, rather than Latin. Because of this, some vicious critics of the time called it "a poem fit for cobblers." His work, however, had a profound influence in western Europe, and Italian became the literary language for several hundred years. In Dante's vision of Hell, the underworld was a vast, funnel-shaped cavity with nine descending circles. Dante invented clever and horrific punishments for the sinners and villains that his hero meets there. For example, in the Seventh region are all of the souls who have wallowed in the blood of others. They are guarded over by the **Minotaur** and must squirm forever in a river of boiling blood.

Deadly Nevergreen: Slang for a wooden gallows: a lifeless tree which always bears fruit.

Demosthenes: Ancient Greek statesman and famous orator.

Descry: To see, observe.

Devilshine: Magic or demonic power.

Diabolo: A female of devilish nature.

Dilletto: An Italian word meaning "dildo."

Dog Buffer: One who steals pet dogs with nefarious intent.

Doge: The top magistrate in the Republic of Venice.

Duomo: Set in the heart of Florence, the Duomo, or Cathedral of Florence, is the tallest building in the city. Designed by **Brunelleschi** (completed in 1420), it was the largest dome of its time built without scaffolding.

⇜ E ⇝

Eyebitten: Bewitched by someone's eyes.

⇜ F ⇝

Fancy Man: A man kept by a woman for love-making; a gigolo.

Fart Catcher: A servant or footman, named for his habit of walking behind his master.

Fartleberries: Dung which clings to the hairs of the anus.

Fell: Fierce, terrible.

Firenze: The Italian name for the city of Florence.

Flatchet: An amazingly obscure name for a sword.

Fleak: A disparaging term for a woman of low standing.

Fleer: To laugh in a coarse or impertinent manner. To mock. From a Danish word meaning "to grin."

Flerk: To twitch.

Florins: The gold coins minted by the city of **Firenze**.

Flush: Plentifully supplied with an abundance of money.

Flux: Dysentery.

Foppa, Cristoforo Caradosso: (1452-1526) Famed designer of medals.

Fourth Crusade: (1202-1204) What started out as another quest to retake Jerusalem from the **infidel**, ended up with the dismantling of the **Byzantine Empire** by northern Europeans. At the start of the Crusade, Byzantium was in political turmoil. The emperor Isaac Angelus had been deposed and blinded by his own brother. Isaac's son, Alexius IV, fled to the west. He offered to give the Crusaders a vast sum of money and a large army for their effort in the Holy Land if they would seize Constantinople and put him and his father back on the royal seat. The Crusading army successfully took the magnificent city and installed Isaac and Alexius on the throne. The Crusaders, camped outside the city, soon became discontent with the father and son monarchs. They decided to win the place for themselves. Alexius and his father were murdered, and Constantinople was sacked and plundered. The Empire was then divided up among the Crusading forces. Thus weakened, it would eventually fall to the **Ottoman** Turks. (See **Dandolo**.)

Fugger: German banking family who dominated European business in the fifteenth and sixteenth centuries.

⮜ G ⮜

Gadje: A Gypsy term to describe a non-Gypsy. The word means "barbarian" or "hick."

Gibraltar: A tiny British colony on a narrow peninsula of Spain's Mediterranean coast. "The Rock," as it has been called by the British, is only 2.25 square miles. The military base that guards the entrance to the Mediterranean Sea has been held by the British since 1704. Although it came under siege for several years during the Napoleonic wars, it never fell.

Geheimtinte: A German word meaning "invisible ink."

Gehenna: From a word of Hebrew origin meaning "Hell."

Gezan: A medieval Arabian port.

Gingambobs: The testicles.

Golgotha: From a Hebrew word meaning "skull." Golgotha is the name given to the mount where Christ was crucified.

Gorgon: Female deity from Greek mythology. The Gorgon was a hideous creature whose hair was a mass of writhing snakes. The Gorgon's stare had the power to turn humans into stone.

Greek Fire: An incendiary device similar to modern napalm that was used in ancient and medieval warfare. Greek fire was invented by Callinicus, a Greek Jew born in Syria (AD 673) who fled the Arabs to Byzantium (See **Byzantine Empire**). Callinicus was granted a monopoly on the making and selling of the chemical, and the components were kept a strictly guarded state secret. Ready-made shipments of the concoction were sold to allies, but the ingredients were never revealed. Greek fire was a horrible weapon that could be launched in barrels from catapults or sprayed through siphons. It combusted upon contact, even on water, and was thus lethal against ships.

Gros: French painter whose *Bonaparte Visiting the Plague-Stricken at Jaffa* hangs in the Louvre. The painting was commissioned by the French state and completed in 1799.

Groundling: A theatre patron who stood in the cheap seats or "pit" of an Elizabethan theatre. A person of questionable taste.

Gull: A dupe, a sucker.

Gullion: A worthless wretch of a man.

Gypsies: The Gypsy people most likely originated in northern India. The various Gypsy languages have root word ties to Sanskrit, the ancient tongue of the Indian subcontinent. Over 1500 years ago, the ancestors of the Gypsies migrated to Persia, then into the Balkans, and finally into Europe. The traditional Gypsy way of life is a nomadic existence with an oral, rather than a written, tradition. They have unique codes of conduct and morality. For centuries, Gypsies have wandered Europe and gained a reputation as fortune-tellers, musicians, animal traders, tinkers and entertainers. Unfortunately, they have also been branded as thieves and a public nuisance. The stories of cruelties committed against this people are endless. In the fifteenth century, in the Slavic countries, many of the Gypsies were put into slavery. During World War II, the Nazis murdered an estimated 400,000 Gypsies. And even in post-war Europe, Gypsies were banned from certain pubs in England and from campgrounds in France. The most assimilated and settled Gypsies live in Spain and Wales.

⤚ H ⤚

Hand Sinister: The left hand. From the Latin word for "left."

Hannibal: (247-183 BC) General who commanded the forces of Carthage against the Romans. The city of Carthage was founded by the Phoenicians on the north coast of Africa in what is now the city of Tunis.

Happenny: A half-penny.

Hapsburg: An Austrian royal house that reached its zenith of power in the late sixteenth century through intermarriage with other European royal families. They are infamous for attempting to maintain control of Europe through inbreeding.

Harrison Chronometer: John Harrison, a self-taught clock maker, was born in Yorkshire in 1693. He built the first chronometer (watch) which kept perfect time, even on rough seas, thus enabling navigators to find longitude.

Hastings, Battle of: In the year 1066, William the Bastard, Duke of Normandy, led an invasion of England. The Saxon King Harold, having just come from a spectacular victory over Scandinavian intruders in the north, met William at Hastings (in East Sussex). Harold was struck in the eye by a chance arrow. Upon his sudden death, his dismayed army gave up and left the field. The Normans took over the country and, in short time, displaced almost all of the Saxon nobility.

Hauteville, Robert de: (1015-1085) A Norman (French) knight and adventurer. Robert was a handsome, physically powerful man with a genius for military strategy and politics. After taking over southern Italy, he succeeded in conquering Naples, Calabria, and Sicily. Many beautiful cathedrals and Benedictine abbeys were built in these lands under his direction. He died during a siege.

Herzschlags: A German word meaning "heartbeats."

Holy Sepulcher: The church built around the sight of Christ's supposed crucifixion and burial.

Homunculus: A tiny man. Also, the manmade, humanoid creature from Goethe's *Faust*.

Hookah: A Turkish water-pipe. As the smoke is sucked through a long tube, it passes through water, thus cooling and mellowing the taste.

Horesco Referens: A Latin phrase meaning "I shudder to recall it."

Horse-prickers: Slang for "spurs."

Houris: Beauteous, voluptuous nymphs who inhabit the Mohammedan Paradise.

⮞ I ⮜

Iberian Peninsula: Spain and Portugal.

Infidel: One who does not believe in Christ. From a Latin word meaning "unfaithful." This term came to be used by Crusaders to describe the Mohammedans.

☙ J ☙

Jericho: A walled town in the Holy Land that has been occupied for over 10,000 years.

☙ K ☙

Knights Templar: A league of knights who, during the first Crusades, protected pilgrims in the Holy Land. Over the years, their power and wealth grew immensely, allowing them to establish castles and estates throughout Europe and the Middle East. King Philip IV of France feared their influence and envied their wealth. He accused them of committing heresy and blasphemy during their secret rites of initiation. In 1307, Philip IV ordered the French Pope to arrest the Templars, and they were all brutally exterminated.

Krieg: German for "war."

☙ L ☙

Lackeyjackal: A toady. From an Old French word meaning "footman."

Lanthorn: A variant of "lantern."

Lazybones: A device resembling a set of interconnected scissors with tongs on the end, used for picking up objects from a distance.

Libertine: A man who ignores moral law, especially in his relations with the fairer sex. One who leads a loose, lewd life.

Lickspittle: A repulsive parasite.

Leonardo da Vinci: (1452-1519) Leonardo was a masterful painter, sculptor, musician, athlete, architect, engineer, geologist, anatomist, town planner, botanist, physiologist, philosopher, and astronomer. His studies of aviation, hydraulics, optics and weaponry were centuries ahead of his time. He was born to a prosperous Tuscan notary and his peasant mistress. He lived a happy childhood in the countryside. He was not forced to change his natural left-handedness, and developed a unique backwards writing style which he used for all of his compositions. He spent his early years in the cosmopolitan city of Florence in the workshop of the master artist and sculptor Verrocchio, where he led a wild, sensual life. Afterwards, he worked for the powerful **Medici** family. Later in life he would say that they "made and broke him." He spent his last years in France in the court at Amboise as a sort of resident genius. Some of Leonardo's greatest works are the *Mona Lisa* (Louvre), the *Last Supper* (Milan) and the *Virgin of the Rocks* (National Gallery, London). "Impatience, the mother of stupidity, praises brevity," wrote Leonardo. And no quote could be more suited to such a curt and cursory description of such a full life.

Lepanto, Battle of: (7 October 1571) The resounding defeat of the Turkish navy outside the Gulf of Corinth by the Holy League, an alliance between Venice, Phillip II of Spain, and Pope Pius V.

Looby: A dolt.

Lucubrations: To work diligently by artificial light, thus night study. From a Latin word meaning "lamp light."

Lully Prigger: A thief who filches wet linen from the clotheslines.

🐬 M 🐬

Magyar: The ancient tribe that ruled Hungary.

Malebolge: The eighth circle of Hell in **Dante's** fictionalized account of a journey into the underworld.

Mangonel: A catapult used to hurl projectiles at an enemy's fortifications. The mangonels of Richard The Lionheart's era (see **The Siege of Acre**) were capable of hurling a 50-pound rock 500 yards with great accuracy. The Romans called this machine the *onager*, or "wild ass," because of the way it bucked after throwing its load.

Marengo: Napoleon's beloved horse, or, rather, his pony. It was fourteen and a half hands high or four feet eight inches. The bones of this creature are on permanent display at the British War Museum in London.

Masaccio: (1401-1428) Along with **Brunelleschi** and Donatello, Masaccio established what is called the "Renaissance of the Arts" in Italy. *The Tribute Money*, a scene from the *Lives of Saints Peter and Paul*, in the **Brancacci Chapel**, is considered by many to be the starting point of the Renaissance style. His use of perspective and the mechanics of light combined with his ability to portray human emotion and reactions to great spiritual events were revolutionary for the time.

Medici: Florentine family that rose to power through international banking in the late Middle Ages. Their control over the city of Florence became tyrannical. They were lovers of the arts, however, and acted as patrons to many Renaissance artisans.

Medina Sidonia, Duke of: The reluctant Spanish Admiral who led the ill-fated Armada to invade England in 1588. One hundred and thirty ships and thirty thousand men made up the fleet. They were met by terrible weather and numerous disasters along the way. Less than half returned to Spain.

Minotaur: A monster with the torso of a bull and the legs of a man. It lived in the center of a labyrinth or maze built underground on the island of Crete. The Greek hero Theseus took on the task of slaying the beast and found his way back out of the maze by following a trail of golden thread he had laid.

Mercury Pills: Mercury was used in early medicine to treat any number of ills. Unfortunately, mercury is a deadly poison. The body instantly tries to flush it from the system by creating massive amounts of saliva, which doctors of the time saw as a sign that the "medicine" was driving out the ill humors. Extended doses of mercury leads to tooth, bone and hair loss, and ultimately death.

Monomachist: From two Greek words meaning "one who battles alone." A man who fights in single combat.

Morality Play: A type of drama from the Middle Ages in which characters portray moral qualities.

Mother's Loll: A mama's boy.

Murano: A small island near Venice famous for its glass blowers. Venice moved its glass furnaces to the island in 1291 as a precaution against fire.

Musée de Napoleon: In the year 1803, the public art museum in Paris, the Musée Central des Arts, was renamed for Napoleon. It soon became a repository for the thousands of paintings that were seized on his campaigns throughout Europe. Napoleon was described as having a great lust for the best things in every country, and he was anxious to send this war-booty back to his capital city. One of these paintings, the colossal *Marriage of Cana* (taken from the Refectory of San Giorgio Maggiore in Venice) remains there to this day. The museum is now called The Louvre.

☜ Π ☞

Nadirs: The buttocks.

Necromancy: The magical practice of conjuring spirits from the dead. From two Greek words meaning "prophecy by raising the dead."

Nelson, Horatio Nelson, Viscount: (1758-1805) Nelson is one of the most beloved national heroes in the history of England. Born to a parson in a remote village, Nelson went to sea at the tender age of twelve. He rose in the ranks due to his boldness and, often times, disobedience in battle. He was a kind, gentlemanly man, however, who had an uncanny ability to inspire deep devotion in his friends. **Napoleon** hated Nelson more than any other Englishman, for Nelson was the scourge of the French navy. (This is high irony because in his youth, Napoleon wrote to the British Government asking to be accepted into their navy.) Nelson's saying, "Never mind the maneuvers, just go straight at them," proved a success against the French, over and over again.

In Egypt, Nelson made an unexpected and seemingly suicidal dusk attack on the French fleet at anchor in Aboukir Bay. It led to a miraculous and stunning victory. At the Battle of Trafalgar (1805), off the coast of Spain, Nelson's brilliant command of the British fleet crushed the combined French and Spanish navies, and put an end once and for all to any plans Napoleon had for invading England.

Nelson was not an imposing man. He was five feet six inches tall, and rail thin. (His tiny shoes and bloody socks on display at the Maritime Museum in Greenwich attest to this fact.) By the time he was made admiral he had lost an eye and an arm in combat, and most of his teeth to scurvy, and was plagued by reoccurring symptoms of malaria. He died during the battle of Trafalgar after being shot on deck of his flagship *Victory* by a French sniper. His devoted men stood by his body and wept, and after he died they preserved his corpse in brandy for the journey home. Soon after, when Nelson's death effigy was put on display at St. Paul's Cathedral in London, Westminster Abbey lost much of the tourist trade.

Nénés: A woman's breasts.

Nest of Spicery: An English euphemism for a woman's pudenda and surrounding hair.

☌ ☉ ☍

Odysseus: Greek hero of Homer's epic poem *The Odyssey*. The story recounts his long and adventurous return home from war. He used his ample wits to escape monsters, cannibals, and rapacious women.

Ottoman Empire: The Empire created by Turkish tribes in the region of Anatolia. During the fifteenth and sixteenth centuries, it was one of the world's most powerful dominions. The Ottomans captured Constantinople, the capital of the Byzantine Empire, in 1453. It became their capital city. The Empire's army was made up of an elite class of men called *jannissaries*, Christian slaves taken from the Balkan countries and trained from childhood to be fierce and loyal warriors.

Ozkack pirates: Fell pirates who roamed the Adriatic sea.

☌ P ☍

Palazzo Vecchio: This imposing brick keep and bell tower was completed in 1322 to serve as **Firenze's** town hall.

Petrarch, Francesco: (1304-74) Poet Laureate, Latin scholar, and early humanist born in Florence. While studying in Avignon, Petrarch fell madly in love with a woman named Laura and wrote love sonnets about her. She died of the **Black Death** in 1348.

Phyz: The face.

Pict: The Picts were the pre-Celtic aborigines who inhabited northern Briton (Scotland) before the invasion of the Romans.

Prior to battle, they painted themselves with a blue dye made from the *woad* plant. Their name comes from the Latin *Picti*, "painted." They were killed off by the Scots.

Podestà: An official responsible for law and order in an Italian town.

Podgy: Fat, fleshy.

Poop-noddy: The pastime of love and flirtation.

Poplolly: A girlfriend or lover.

Portsmouth: A famous port in Hampshire, England. It has been the site of military dockyards since the fifteenth century. Lord **Nelson's** flagship Victory is anchored there.

Potato-finger: A euphemism for the penis.

Prognostication: Prophecy. From two Greek words meaning "to see beforehand."

Prometheus: In Greek mythology, the Titan Prometheus took pity on barbarous humans and brought to them the gift of fire. As a punishment, the god Zeus chained him to a rock where an eagle repeatedly ate his immortal liver.

Pushing School: A brothel.

Puffguts: An obese man.

⟜ R ⟜

Road-rattler: Slang for a horse-drawn carriage.

Royal Scamp: A highwayman who steals money only from rich travelers.

Rubicon: In 49 BC, Julius Caesar and his army crossed the Rubicon, a stream that separated Caesar's province of Gaul from Roman Italy. This act was a declaration of Civil War. "Crossing the Rubicon" means taking an irrevocable step.

🠾 S 🠾

Sagbutts and Cornetts: Medieval brass wind instruments used especially for coronation music.

Saint Vitus' Dance: The name given to a strange disease that spread throughout Europe in the Middle Ages. This epidemic caused mad contortions, convulsions, and hysterical dancing. The sickness was probably mental rather than physical.

Santa Croce: The gothic church of Santa Croce was built in 1294 and contains the tombs of Michelangelo and Galileo.

Samarkhand and Bhokhara: Ancient cities in central Asia which lay on the trade routes from China and India.

Saracens: Name given to the nomadic peoples of Syria and Arabia by the Greeks and Romans. In the Medieval era, a Saracen was any Mohammedan or **infidel**.

Scapegallows: One who has unjustly escaped a hanging; a rogue.

Scheherazade: Narrator of the Arabic epic *A Thousand And One Nights*. Scheherazade married King Shahryar, a woman-hating monarch who slayed his wives after the wedding night. To stay alive, Scheherazade spun him a yarn each evening, leaving the ending incomplete. The King became so enraptured by her entertaining stories that he put off her execution each day, and finally gave up his wicked marriage ritual altogether. Among the myriad of stories contained in the work are the tales of Sinbad, Ali Baba, and Alladin.

Schelmenstreich: A German word meaning a "joke" or "jest."

Schnippchen: A German word meaning "Pulling of a fast one."

Schwachsinnige: A German word meaning "moron."

Scofflaw: A villain; a lawbreaker.

Scottish Play: Double-speak used for Shakespeare's play *Macbeth*. It is a superstition in the theatre that uttering the name *Macbeth* aloud is very bad luck, especially when inside a theatre.

Scroggling Apple: An apple that has withered on the tree.

Seneca: (4 BC-AD 65) Roman statesman, orator, tragedian, and philosopher. His essays were concerned with a wide range of moral dilemmas. He was forced to commit suicide by his political enemies.

Shirt Lifter: A sodomite.

Sirrah: An insulting way to address somebody, implying that the speaker is superior in station.

Slack-bowels: Dysentery.

Slapstick Bladder: A sheep's bladder filled with dried peas and attached to a stick. Court jesters used them to comic effect by smacking people with the bladder on the head. The sound resembled a human fart with uncanny effect.

Slibber-sauce: Any slimy, foul-tasting medicine.

Small Clothes: The undergarments, underwear.

Smoke It: Slang meaning "To get it," to understand or have an inkling.

Snipples: An apostrophized curse for "God's Nipples." (See **Zounds**.)

Sotto Voce: Italian, literally, "under the voice." To speak in an undertone or an aside. A direction used frequently in music and upon the stage.

Spice Islands: Also called the Moluccas. Nine small islands at the lower end of Indonesia's Banda Sea.

Spinkies: An apostrophized curse for "God's Pinkies." (see **Zounds.**)

Sprezzatura: An unforced ease of accomplishment; a courtly, self-possessed bearing considered by Castiglione to be the hallmark of a gentleman. (See **The Book of the Courtier.**)

Stichomythia: Rapid fire repartee of single lines of dialogue. A device invented in ancient Greek drama.

Stronzo: Italian expletive for "shit."

Succubus: A demoness who comes to men in the night and takes carnal pleasure of them. The myth of this creature arose in Medieval times.

Swallow-fart: Daybreak.

🐟 T 🐟

Tachygraphy: Quick writing or shorthand. From two Greek words meaning "swift writing."

Terra Firma: Latin, means "solid ground." Originally the name given to the shore directly off the coast of Venice.

Thanatophobe: One who fears death.

Thunder Mug: A chamber pot. Also called "Thunder Pot." A vessel used as a portable repository for bowel movements.

Tintoretto, Jacopo Robusti: (1518-94) Born the son of a dyer, Tintoretto became one of the leading Venetian painters in the sixteenth century. He was a devoted family man who was joined in his workshop by three of his children. Tintoretto was a master of the human form. His technique of first quickly sketching the figures to be painted imparted a dynamism and fluidity to his works.

Tom Jones: Published in 1749, *The History of Tom Jones, a Foundling* has been called the "father of the English novel." The hero of this sweeping, comic, ribald, romantic tale overcame numerous obstacles to gain the hand of his beloved. It was written by Henry Fielding (1707-54), a playwright, novelist, and lawyer.

Tongue Scraper: A device used to scrape the scum from the surface of the tongue.

Treacle: Syrup made from uncrystallized sugar.

Tricorne: A hat worn by gentlemen and officers in the eighteenth and early nineteenth centuries. It had a low crown and broad brim that was "cocked" or turned up on three sides.

❧ U ❧

Uffizi: The world's most complete collection of Italian Renaissance painting is displayed at the Galleria Degli Uffizi in Florence. This former **Medici** government building was first opened to the public as an art gallery in the eighteenth century. The works of **Botticelli** are among the stunning highlights in this museum.

Ulysses: The Latin form of **Odysseus**.

❧ V ❧

Venezia: The Italian spelling of Venice.

❧ W ❧

Warwickshire: The county in the Midlands of England that is known as "The Heart of England." One of its towns, Stratford-upon-Avon, is the birthplace of William Shakespeare.

Z

Zounds: An abbreviation of the curse "God's Wounds." During the Elizabethan era, these forms of "minced oaths" appeared in response to Puritan dictates against profanity used in the theatre. The name of God and his body parts were truncated to such ludicrous words as: "God's Teeth" or 'Steeth, "God's Balls" or 'Sballs, "God's Nails" or 'Snails, "God's Tailbone" or 'Stailbone, etc.

Zwerg: The German word for "midget."

Acknowledgments

This book would have never been
published without the encouragement
of three excellent friends:
David Wheeler, Randal Prater
and Daniel Thompson.
Cheers!

Noble Smith is an award-winning playwright living in Vermont. This is his first novel.

Carol Ingram lives with her family in Ashland, Oregon. She works as a painter, art teacher and illustrator.

This book is also available in unabridged audio from:
Blackstone Audio Books
1-800-729-2665
www.blackstoneaudio.com

For more information about RiverWood Books, visit
www.riverwoodbooks.com